WILD MIND

A TYE CAINE WILDERNESS MYSTERY

DAVID BARBUR

COUGAR ROCK PRESS

PROLOGUE

Christopher ran west, toward the setting sun, until his lungs filled with blood.

When the bullet hit him, it felt like someone punched him in the back. He was surprised to find himself still on his feet, still charging pell mell down the old logging road. The tall Douglas firs on either side were blurred in his peripheral vision.

Another shot ricocheted off a rock in the middle of the road, showering his legs with fragments of stone and bullet jacket. He hooked left and charged through a tangle of salmonberry, breaking through to the open forest floor on the other side. The trees here were tall and straight. The interlocking canopy shaded the ground, so little grew underneath the trees.

It was darker here. He slowed, both because of the darkness, and because his legs felt like lead, but he didn't stop. He knew if he stopped, he'd never start again. The hope that somehow his injuries were minor went away when he coughed a fine spray of blood. More blood dripped from his fingertips.

Behind him, he heard the crunch of tires on gravel. Would they find his trail where he'd broke through the salmonberries?

Christopher tried to make himself run, but the best he could manage was a fast shuffle. At first there had been no pain, but now an iron band tightened around his chest, and each exhale felt like he was breathing out fire.

His first instinct had been to run toward his people in the hopes they could save him. But Christopher realized he was dying, and the only thing that would accomplish was to lead his pursuers to his friends.

To his right, he saw a small clearing full of huckleberry bushes. He detoured, pushing his way into the center, and shed his pack. The supplies inside were important. He didn't know if his people would find them, but he would give them a chance.

Free of the heavy pack, he picked up the pace. He felt like he was drowning with each breath. Just like the wounded deer he'd tracked, he instinctively headed down the hill into heavy cover, stumbling in the deepening gloom but somehow managing not to fall.

After a while, the pain went away. His vision narrowed to the ground in front of his feet. Over and over, he told himself he'd take four steps and then rest, only to take four more without stopping.

Finally, his legs buckled. He fell to his back and looked up at the stars overhead. He felt the brush of the evening breeze on his cheek. A raven settled onto a tree branch overhead.

His last thought was *I'm sorry.*

1

"So much evil has entered your life over the last couple of months," Hattie said.

Tye sat next to the old wood stove, letting the heat from the fire he'd just lit drive the chill out of his bones. The old two-room cabin smelled of woodsmoke and herbs hung from the rafters to dry.

"I don't know what to do," Tye said. Hattie was an old woman who lived up in the mountains. He'd come up here to help her get ready for the oncoming winter. Today he'd cleaned out the stovepipe and lit the first fire of the season.

Hattie took a sip of applejack from an old Ball canning jar. Tye couldn't guess how old she was. Sometimes he could believe she was sixty, sometimes he would have guessed eighty. Her long black hair didn't show a touch of gray. She was a little stooped, but surprisingly strong from living a life where she did for herself. Tye was unsure of the details, but at least some of her ancestors had been Native American, Cree, from the upper Midwest.

"Sometimes you see people who died," she said. It was a statement, not a question.

"Yes." It was getting easier to admit that, but he still had to choke the word out.

"And you try to help people," she said. "Lost people. Sometimes people who have been murdered."

"Yes."

"You have fought evil men."

"Yes."

"Why?"

He sat with that question for a moment. The wood in the old stove hissed and popped. He'd helped her move wood from the drying shed out back to the front porch and spent an hour splitting kindling.

"I guess I just feel like I'm supposed to. When I was a kid, we didn't have much, but my parents always tried to help people. If I'm able to help somebody, why wouldn't I?"

"But you've been hurt."

Tye shifted in his seat. Last month he'd nearly frozen to death in the cold water of Puget Sound. It seemed like he hadn't felt warm since. The month before that, he'd been knifed in the ribs. The cut was healed. The stitches were gone, but the scar was still tender. Sometimes he would move the wrong way and it felt like an electric shock traveled across his ribs.

"Yes," he said again.

"And you still have dreams and see people that shouldn't be there."

This time, all he could do was nod.

"You should find someone to help you with this."

He blinked.

"I was hoping you could help me."

She cocked her head back for a moment, then laughed.

"Why? Because I'm Native? I'm sorry, but I know nothing about this. I'm Native, yes. But my mother and father both had the Native beaten out of them at Indian School. They didn't speak the language, and neither do I. This isn't like those stories where the confused white boy goes and finds the mystical Indian woman living in the woods and she explains things to him."

"Oh," he said.

She took another sip of the applejack.

"This is getting better with every batch your friend makes. Tell him thank you."

"I will." Tye's friend Gary distilled the applejack at home. Tye still didn't care for it, but Hattie loved it.

Hattie fixed him with a stare for so long, Tye began to squirm in his seat.

"I can't help you. But I might know of some people who can. Relations of relations. People I haven't talked to in decades. But that isn't something you should count on, you understand? It might take a long time for me to hear back, and I might never hear back at all."

"I appreciate it."

Outside, he heard a chicken scratching in the dirt under a windowsill and the plaintive cry of a mourning dove from the tree line. The doves would be gone soon. They would fly south for the winter, ahead of the approaching cold.

Hattie nodded, staring at an empty chair. Tye had never seen her sit in it, and she'd always gestured for him to sit somewhere else when he visited.

"Yes. I do believe you're worth helping. I've met so few men that are. It's never ceased to amaze me how some men can be fifty years old, but still be boys. My Delbert wasn't like that. I don't think you are either."

She looked at him and fixed him with a gaze that made him feel like a bug on a pin.

"You keep doing what you're doing. You'll find your way through, I imagine. I appreciate the applejack and the help with the stove. I'm worn out from all this work and I need my nap."

He stood to go. "Thank you."

She nodded and saw him to the door. "Next time you come, you bring that girl of yours with you. The librarian. What's her name? Kaity."

Tye wasn't sure if Kaity counted as "his girl," but he nodded anyway.

"I'll bring her up."

She shut the door behind him. He flipped up the hood of his jacket before he stepped off the porch. It wasn't quite noon and the sun still hadn't burned through the morning mist. It hadn't rained, but the air was humid and cool. Hattie lived on the edge of the Gifford Pinchot National Forest, in a mist-shrouded valley. The nearest neighbor was a mile away. Tye walked down a well-worn path through tall Douglas fir trees to where his truck was parked on a rugged two-track that led to a paved road.

He stopped at the sight of tracks in the muddy path. They were oval-shaped, four toes, no nail impressions in the soft mud. They were clearly coyote tracks, and not a domestic dog.

"Better stay away from the chickens, song dog," he said quietly. "Old Hattie has a single-shot twenty gauge by the door with your name on it."

Somehow, seeing the tracks put him in a better mood. He opened the door to the truck, and a raven unfolded from a branch high above him. One second, there was a dark spot in his peripheral vision. The next the bird's four-foot wingspan was overhead. It circled once with a *quoark,* then flew off into the valley.

"And good morning to you too," Tye said.

He bounced down the rutted two-track, careful not to bust the truck's oil pan on a rock. As soon as the engine warmed up, Tye turned on the heater full blast.

By the time he turned on to the paved road, he felt a familiar pain behind his eyes. Migraine headaches had plagued since he was a child, and he knew the signs all too well. He gritted his teeth and drove. He knew he'd have enough time to make it home if he didn't dawdle.

Early November in the Pacific Northwest was quiet, wet, and still. It hadn't rained for a few days, but the vegetation still dripped with moisture from the overnight dew. Tye was originally from Appalachia. He had traveled all over the western United States, but when he set foot in these lush forests of Washington state, it had been like coming home to a place he'd never been. Despite the pain in his head, and the worries he carried from his conversation with

Hattie, he felt some peace as he drove among the giant Douglas fir trees.

Tye almost didn't see the man standing on the left side of the road. At first he thought it was just a shadow, then as he drove past, he realized a man was standing there in knee-deep ferns, clad in a torn and bloody t-shirt. He looked young, with shoulder-length blond hair. As Tye zoomed past, it seemed like the man's mouth was open, like he was trying to say something.

Tye hit the brakes hard, almost to the point of sliding on the slick road, but still went past the figure. He put the truck in reverse before it even came to a complete stop, causing a racket from the transmission. He looked in the side mirror as he backed up, looking for the man.

He was gone.

Tye was certain he had the right place. He backed the truck up until he was even with a distinctive fallen alder tree. There was a first-aid kit strapped to the back of the truck's passenger seat headrest. Tye pulled it free and hopped out, expecting to find the man lying in the tall ferns.

He wasn't there.

He never had been.

Tye was a tracker. He could follow faint sign, trailing small animals across rocky surfaces. He knew that for an adult man to have stood in the patch of ferns, there would have to be an unmistakable disturbance. There would be bent and broken vegetation, so obvious an untrained person would see it easily.

The ferns here were unbroken. Droplets of water hung on the fronds like little jewels, droplets that would have shaken free had even a raccoon brushed against them.

"Hello?" he called, but there was no sound other than the soft hiss of the wind in the trees and the burble of his truck's exhaust.

He walked back to the truck, pulled it safely off the road, and shut off the engine.

Then he spent the next forty-five minutes examining the side of the road, going far past where he'd seen the man in either direction. He found exactly what he knew he would find: nothing.

He wound up back at that spot by the fallen alder, looking at the undisturbed ferns. Part of him felt like he should drive to a high spot, where he could get enough reception to call 911 and report a possibly injured man lost in the woods, but he knew the sheriff's department would come and find exactly the same thing as him: nothing.

All the time he'd been searching, he'd felt the pressure building in the back of his head. His scalp felt too tight, and his mouth tasted like iron. He felt this way just before something was about to happen. It was like the pressure ahead of a building storm.

"I am too tired for this," he said. "I just need to rest. Can I please just rest?"

There was no reply from the silent forest.

After a few minutes, he got back in the truck and started the engine, debating what to do next. His phone was in the center console. He'd been trying to do a better job of not losing it and had even been keeping the battery charged lately. There was no signal here in this valley, but he knew some side roads that would take him to the top of the ridgeline where he could make a call.

"I'm just going to go home," he said, and put the truck in gear.

2

—————

Home was near the east fork of the Lewis River, eight miles or so outside of a little town called Yacolt. He had to pass through town on the way, and as he rolled past the combination trading post and gas station, his phone dinged from the center console. He pulled over into the parking lot to check his messages.

The text message was from Kaity, his part-time business partner and potential romantic partner of constantly undefined status.

You probably don't know where your phone is, as usual, but we have a case. Meeting with a potential client at one this afternoon. It would be great if you could be there. If I don't hear from you in 15 minutes, I'm going to drive all the way to your house and see if you are there.

Kaity was one of the few people Tye knew that used full sentences and proper grammar in text messages. The message was from two hours ago.

He laboriously typed a reply. The keyboard on the phone always seemed too small for his fingers.

Was at Hattie's. In Yacolt now. Be there soon.

The reply came in seconds.

You actually responded to a text? Who are you and what have you done with the real Tye Caine? Seriously, are you feeling alright?

He gave a bitter laugh at that last question. No. He really wasn't feeling all right. But a job was a job. Rather than take the time to peck out another reply, he just started driving.

Once he was out of town, he turned left and went east along the north bank of the river canyon. The longer he drove, the farther apart the houses became, until a mile before the national forest boundary, he turned onto a narrow track that disappeared into the trees.

The 20 acres were steep. Tye owned half the land, and his friends Gary and May owned the other half. They lived in a dilapidated mobile home; he lived in a yurt on his half. Most of the property was too sloped to be of much use, but here and there were flat spots where they had fruit trees, chickens, garden beds, and a pair of goats.

Normally, Kaity drove a little economy car, but today, parked behind Gary's old International Scout, sat a newish-looking Jeep. Kaity and Gary were both looking at it as Tye parked his truck.

In his rearview mirror, he saw May, Gary's wife, pulling up behind him in her car.

Gary was tall and bearded, with a long queue of dark hair down his back. He wore stained work pants, a cotton hoody, and work boots. Out past the trailer, Tye could see stakes and string lines marking where they would pour the foundation for the new house.

Kaity was middling height, with glasses. Her short, dark hair was hidden under a watch cap, and she was bundled up in a puffy jacket. Not for the first time, Tye was both glad to see her and a little troubled. He felt like the ambiguous nature of their relationship should have resolved by now, but they kept entering each other's orbits and retreating.

Gary gave him a nod, and Kaity sent a smile his way.

"Hey, you made it," she said. She kicked the tire of the Jeep. "What do you think?"

Tye looked at Gary. "Are you getting rid of the Scout? I thought you didn't like Jeeps."

Kaity rolled her eyes. "You are such a dork," she said, and looked past him where May was unloading some boxes from her car. "Here, let me help you with that."

Kaity walked past him. May was tall, with a mane of curly auburn hair that fell almost to her waist. She handed Kaity a couple of boxes and put her heavy medical bag over her shoulder. May was a midwife, and Tye had heard her pull out before dawn that morning, on her way to help another baby be born.

"Need help?" Gary asked.

"Nope, Kaity and I have it," May said. She kissed Gary's cheek on the move as she went by, and Kaity followed her into the trailer without a look at Tye.

Gary cocked an eyebrow at him.

"That's Kaity's Jeep, isn't it?" Tye asked.

"Yep. Traded that little car of hers for it. People do that sort of thing."

"I really messed up by assuming it was yours, didn't I?"

"Yep."

Tye started toward the door of the trailer.

Gary held up a finger.

"My advice? Give it a minute."

Gary looked at his watch. "Besides, you and Kaity need to leave here shortly for a meeting with a client. Since you've been cleaning out stove pipes, you should change."

Tye looked down. His Carhartts were covered with soot.

"Good point. Thanks."

"One more thing," Gary said. "She's got a Jeep off-road parts catalog and is talking about buying damn near everything and bolting it on. If she tells you that, just go along. I'll be the one to try to steer her in another direction."

"Okay."

"Because you remember what Jeep stands for?"

"Just empty every pocket," they said in unison.

There was a well-trod path through the trees to Tye's yurt. His home was small, only a couple hundred square feet, but it was open and airy. He didn't own much, so he didn't feel cramped. They'd just had a financial windfall, but instead of upgrading, Tye had decided to stick with the yurt.

He stripped off his work pants and sweatshirt and walked over to the thrift store armoire he'd hauled into the yurt. At Kaity's urging, he'd bought some decent clothes to wear when meeting clients. He pulled out a pair of khaki pants and draped them over his arm. He was debating which shirt to wear when the door banged open.

"There you are." Kaity paused. "There you are totally not dressed," she said. "Boxers. I wondered about that. I guess I should knock."

"Umm. That's okay," he said.

Kaity bit her lip, and they were both silent for a moment.

"Wear the blue one. It goes with your eyes."

She spun on her heel and bolted out the door.

With a shrug, Tye put on pants and the blue shirt. He finished getting ready and found her standing in front of the yurt, looking away from the door with her arms folded across her chest.

"What's up?" he asked.

She started walking away from him without looking back. "We are meeting a client in town at the brewpub. Her son is missing. I'd offer to let you ride in my new Jeep, but I have to work right after the meeting, so you'll need your own ride back home."

By "town," Kaity meant the larger city of Battle Ground, Washington, about a half-hour away. Kaity worked at the library across the street from the brewpub.

"It's a nice Jeep," Tye said. "I'm sorry. I didn't realize it was yours."

She waved a hand in the air. "Don't worry about it."

"I'm dressed now," he said. "You could, like, look at me."

She stopped and looked over her shoulder. "Yep. Totally dressed now."

Tye realized she was bright red. She turned and started walking again.

"You have a truck. Gary has the Scout, which is not quite a truck, but it's still a big vehicle," she said. "I thought one of us should have a smaller, more nimble vehicle with good off-road capability."

"Good call," he said. Apparently, they were changing the subject.

She stopped. "I think I'm still a little mad at myself because I got my car stuck when we were trying to rescue Natalie."

Two months ago, they had all but demolished Kaity's little car on the atrocious road that led up Silver Star Mountain. They'd been trying to rescue a little girl at the time.

He stood there, not knowing what to say. The realization hit him like a hammer that the things that were bothering him probably bothered Kaity, too. She'd been right there with him through many of the events of the last couple of months.

"I was glad you were there," he said. "We would have never saved her without you."

She didn't say anything, just wiped her eye. Tye realized she was trying not to cry.

"Well. Enough of that. Let's get going. I'll lead the way in the Jeep. Try to keep up."

He just stood there as she hopped in the Jeep and started the engine. Not for the first time, he tried to figure out what the hell had just happened between them.

As he drove, he couldn't keep himself from watching the side of the road for the man he'd seen earlier. His face was etched into Tye's mind. Early to mid-twenties, thin, blond hair, blue eyes, scraggly attempt at a beard. Tye tried to remember if it was someone he'd met before, but he came up blank.

He'd spent years living among outdoor guides, ski bums, river rats, rock climbers, long-distance Pacific Crest Trail backpackers and similar folks. The man could have been any one of them, but he couldn't call a name or specific memory to mind. He couldn't fathom why that particular face would appear to him on the side of the road and then vanish.

Thankfully, there were no more apparitions on the way to town, and not much traffic. The city of Battle Ground was only about 20,000 people, but still too big for Tye. All his life he'd preferred the solitude of the forest, and when he was surrounded by concrete, traffic, and people, he began to feel panicky and smothered.

The parking lot of the brewpub was mostly empty. He parked his truck next to Kaity's Jeep. She was holding a leather briefcase.

"Her son is missing. She was a little vague on the phone. She said she wanted to talk about it in person."

"Makes sense."

"I emailed her the questionnaire. Hopefully, she filled it out."

"Sounds good." Using the National Association for Search and Rescue template, they'd crafted a questionnaire for prospective clients.

"I'll pay for lunch on the company credit card."

"Right." He kept forgetting they had a company credit card.

She reached over and straightened his collar. "You look nice."

"Um... You do too."

She opened her mouth to reply but stopped as a car pulled up. It was a small electric vehicle. Tye noted that it was covered in dust and had damage to the front right plastic cladding.

A woman got out. Tye guessed she was in her fifties. She had long gray hair and wore a flowing cotton dress and sandals. Both arms were covered in bracelets and bangles, and she wore several rings on each hand, mostly turquoise.

"Miss Rollins? Mr. Caine?"

"That's us," Kaity said, and stuck out a hand. So did Tye.

"I'm Grace Tompkin. Thank you for meeting with me." She seemed nervous, wringing her hands as she stood there.

"Let's go inside and we'll see what we can do for you," Kaity said.

The restaurant was nearly empty, and they were seated quickly. From her shoulder bag, Grace produced a neatly-filled-out questionnaire. While the server took their drink order, Tye scanned her answers:

Christopher Tompkin, last seen a week ago.

Height: 6'2"

Weight: 170lbs.

Age: 26

Hair: blond

A suspicion was forming in the back of his mind, one he didn't want to accept. His mouth was dry, and the tight band around his temples cinched down a little tighter.

"I tried the police, but they said there wasn't anything they could do," Grace said. "For the last two years, my son has mostly been living in the woods. He says he wants to 'rewild' himself, to become like a modern-day hunter-gatherer."

She was wringing her hands as she said it. She paused and looked from Tye to Kaity.

"He isn't mentally ill or anything," she said. She had an accent that Tye associated with people from the northeast who had been to impressive schools.

Tye nodded. "I've done similar things myself, from time to time."

Grace nodded. "I saw your TV show, so when I needed help, I thought of you."

A couple of years before, Tye had been on a survival reality TV show. Just when he hoped everyone had forgotten it, someone would bring it up.

"He made friends with people who were all trying to do the same thing. They've traveled all over together. Colorado, California, Utah. Apparently, you can't live in the same spot in the national forest for too long or you get in trouble."

"Fourteen days, if I remember correctly," Tye said.

"That sounds right," Grace said. "For the last two months, his friends have been moving from spot to spot in the Gifford Pinchot National Forest, here in Washington. Every week or so, I'd drive up from Portland and meet with him. It's been so nice. We haven't always gotten along." She trailed off and stared out the window.

"I would imagine that wasn't the life you envisioned for him," Kaity said.

Grace shook her head. "No. We were estranged for years at a time. Finally, I realized he was happy. Last Wednesday, I was supposed to pick him up in a town near where you live. Yacolt?"

"I'm familiar," Tye said.

"He never showed. I waited around. Sometimes he would be late. But I sat in the parking lot of that little store for hours, until dark, and

he never came. He refuses to own a cell phone. I came back the next
two days. Nothing."

"He always showed before?"

"Yes. He always came eventually." She hesitated. "I wasn't going to
call the sheriff, but..." She acted like she was working herself up to
admit something painful. "I had a dream Christopher died. I
dreamed his shirt was soaked with blood and he couldn't breathe."

For a second, it was hard for Tye to breathe. The pain in his head
was almost unbearable.

"That must sound crazy," Grace said. To Tye, she sounded like she
was far away and underwater.

"Oh, we're sort of used to things like that when it comes to
missing people," Kaity said. "Aren't we, Tye?"

Tye's words seemed stuck in his throat for a second. "Yep," he
finally managed to say. "Do you have a picture of Christopher
handy?"

Grace pulled a phone from her handbag and swiped across the
screen a couple of times before she held it out to Tye.

He took it, even though he already knew what he would see.

3

The face in the photo was the man he'd seen standing by the side of the road.

This sort of thing had happened enough times that Tye wasn't exactly surprised anymore. Still, he felt like control of his life was being yanked away by some force he couldn't see.

Tye forced himself to study the face on the screen. In the picture, Christopher was wearing a backpack. He stood on top of a mountain peak with his arms flung wide. Judging by the terrain he could see in the background, Tye was pretty sure it was the summit of Mt. Hood.

He looked like his mother.

"That's my favorite picture of him," Grace said. "He talked me into climbing Mount Hood with him. I didn't want to do it, but once we did, I was glad I went."

Tye handed the phone back. "It sounds like we've traveled in the same circles, but I don't recognize him," he said.

For a moment, he wanted to make some excuse, get up, and leave. Since mid-summer, he'd twice been involved in ordeals that nearly killed him. They all started very much like this: trying to help someone.

Instead, he took some deep breaths and tried to quiet his mind.

Tye had been a failure at every job he'd tried. He'd been fired from most of them. He grew bored and chafed under any kind of structure. Most jobs seemed meaningless.

Maybe finding lost people was what he was supposed to do.

"Tell me about Christopher," Tye said.

For a second, Tye thought she was going to cry. She pointed at the questionnaire on the table in front of Kaity. "I filled it out," Grace said.

"I appreciate that," Tye said. "And I'll look over that later. It'll be helpful, but right now, just tell me what kind of person he is."

Tye stumbled over that last sentence. He almost said, "what kind of person he was," because in his gut he knew Christopher was probably dead. He had learned to trust his visions. After years of denying them, he'd finally accepted that they usually showed him the truth.

Grace took a deep breath. "He was a difficult child. School was a struggle. He had all the diagnoses: ADD, dysgraphia, at one point even oppositional defiance disorder. But he was so smart. He could devour books in a matter of hours. If a subject interested him, he would dive into it until he'd read all the books in the library."

All of that sounded familiar to Tye. His own childhood had followed a similar path.

"When he was thirteen, I put him in an outdoor skills program. It was the only thing left. That's where he really blossomed. He would disappear into the woods for hours. When he was sixteen, I started letting him stay out for days at a time. He was going to do it anyway, so I gave him my blessing."

Their food came, and Tye picked at his salad. He wasn't very hungry, even though he hadn't eaten yet today.

"He became involved in environmental causes, protesting logging, pipelines, probably some stuff I don't know about. He managed to graduate high school. College was out of the question. I paid for him to go to a bunch of primitive-skills camps and tracking classes. He would work for one outfit or another for a while, guiding hunters, teaching classes, that sort of thing, but inevitably there would be some sort of falling-out and he would quit or get fired."

Kaity shot him a glance. Gary had nicknamed Tye "Ace" because he'd managed to get fired from five jobs in a row.

"I have to confess, I watched all this in horror. My family values education. The idea that he barely graduated high school and wouldn't go to college seemed terrible to me. We argued for years. We would fall out and not talk for up to a year at a time. Finally, I realized he was happy."

Grace hadn't touched her food the whole time. She had dark circles under her eyes and there was a slight tremor in her hands. Tye realized he was looking at a woman who was struggling to look poised, but she was falling apart inside.

"I just accepted who he was," she said. "It was one of the hardest things I've ever had to do. When he was a baby, I envisioned him being a doctor, or an artist, something like that. His father was never in the picture. I don't have much family. He is all I have."

She stopped and visibly fought for control. Tye felt embarrassed for her and made a mental note that in the future, they wouldn't meet with clients in such a public place.

"I can look for him," Tye said. "But I need a place to start. The Gifford Pinchot National Forest is a big place. Is there anybody else that might know where he was staying?"

"I never met his friends, the ones he's been living with. I feel like we were leading up to that, like I had to earn his trust back. I felt like there was something big he wanted to tell me but wasn't quite ready yet."

She moved her salad around on her plate with her fork.

"I realize that isn't much to go on," she said. "I'd hoped to get some information out of people at his old job, but they won't even talk to me."

"Where did he work?" Kaity asked.

"Nature's Way Outdoor School in Portland. He worked there for a little less than a year. I'd hoped it would last, but apparently there was some kind of falling-out."

"Nature's Way?" Tye asked. "Let me guess. Holly answers the phone and blows you off every time you call."

"Yes. You know them?" Grace asked.

"I worked for them part-time before I went on the TV show."

"Did you quit so you could go on the show?" Kaity asked.

"Something like that," Tye said. He turned back to Grace. "I think I could get them to talk to me. I still know some people down there. The easiest way would be just to drive down there and ask."

"I want to go with you," Grace said. "I guess I should mention that. If I'm to hire you, I want to accompany you. I want to be there when you find him."

Tye drummed his fingers on the table, trying to think of what to say next. "Can we play that by ear?"

"I'm afraid I must insist," she said. Something about her tone made him think she was used to getting what she wanted from people, especially if she was paying the bill.

"Here's the thing," Tye said slowly. "Often when I'm on a track, I go into the woods, and I have no idea when I'm coming out. I might wind up spending several nights in the field. I might walk twenty miles in a day, carrying a twenty-pound pack. So if you want to come, you need to decide if you're up for that. If you're not, you're going to jeopardize my ability to find Christopher."

He watched her chew on that for a moment before she nodded.

"That's reasonable. And acceptable. I would like to accompany you to the Nature's Way school, however."

Tye looked at his watch. "The best time to get there will be in a couple of hours. The after-school program will be running, and all the staff will be there."

"What shall we do in the meantime?" Grace asked.

Kaity had been scanning the questionnaire as they'd been talking. "It says here Christopher had some of his things stored at your house," Kaity said. "Tye, would it be helpful for you to look at them?"

"What kind of stuff?" he asked Grace.

"Books. Outdoor gear. Things he's collected over the years."

Her mouth was a hard line, and he could tell this wasn't a train of thought she was particularly interested in pursuing.

"Up to you," Tye said.

She moved the salad around some more, not looking up. Tye took an opportunity to eat a little of his meal. He still didn't feel hungry, but often, once one of these adventures started, time to eat would be in short supply.

"We could stop by the house on the way to Nature's Way," she said finally.

"Well," Kaity said. "I guess the last thing we need to do is have you sign our standard fee agreement." She produced a manila folder from her briefcase and handed Grace a stack of papers and a pen. "I've put sticky notes at all the places you need to sign or initial."

Tye ate some more while Grace signed the form. She didn't seem to bother reading it before she shoved it across the table at Kaity, who stowed it back in the briefcase.

Last month, Tye had done some work for a bunch of billionaires who owned a tech firm. By the end of it, his property was paid off, and he had some money left over, which he and Kaity had used to make their search-and-rescue consulting business a little more legitimate by having a lawyer draw up a boilerplate contract. Kaity had done all the work, and Tye just nodded at what he hoped were the appropriate times and hoped he looked like he knew what he was doing.

"Perhaps we could leave soon?" Grace asked Tye with a raised eyebrow.

"Sure." He wiped his mouth with a napkin while Kaity flagged down the server and handed her the credit card.

The sky had clouded up by the time they stepped outside. It was sure to rain soon. Pacific Northwest winters were dark and wet, and this year he was contemplating taking a trip somewhere sunny for a break.

"I suppose you could follow me to my home in Portland, and we could share my car from there. I can't imagine that gets very good gas mileage," Grace said with a jerk of her chin toward Tye's truck.

"Sure," Tye said.

"I have to go to work," Kaity said. She grabbed Tye's arm. "I need to talk to my associate for just a moment."

He followed her over to the Jeep.

"Something is going on," Kaity said. "I could tell by the look on your face when you looked at his picture."

He stared at her for a moment, not sure how to answer.

"Is it one of your visions?" she asked. "A dream?"

"Kind of. I can explain later."

The visions were no longer a secret between them, but that didn't make it easy to talk about.

"Take care." She reached over and touched his cheek for a second, then it seemed like she realized what she was doing and jerked her hand back.

"Bye."

She turned and walked toward the library.

4

Tye followed Grace into Portland. The deeper they drove into the city, the more he felt like he was trapped.

Town was too busy, with too much traffic all around him. The expanses of concrete and pavement seemed like a maze. He'd known this was coming. That made it a little easier, but he still had to force himself to take deep breaths and not panic.

Grace pulled into the parking lot of an upscale grocery store. Tye pulled in beside her and rolled down his window.

"Parking is very tight on my street," she said. "I thought we could leave your truck here."

Tye was used to leaving his truck at remote trailheads, so everything valuable was locked up inside the camper shell covering the bed. He grabbed a light jacket and a shoulder bag with some odds and ends and squeezed into her car.

Grace's house was in an older neighborhood in Portland. The houses were immaculate. The yards were full of drought-resistant native plants and most of the roofs were covered with solar panels.

As neighborhoods went, this wasn't bad.

There was also plenty of parking. Tye had suspected Grace's real motivation was that his twenty-year-old full-size pickup would stick out among the hybrid and electric vehicles parked along the street.

He followed her onto the front porch, which was covered with potted plants. As she opened the front door, he heard a crash and the sound of running feet. Over her shoulder, he got the briefest glimpse of a figure running toward the back of the house. He saw a bunch of papers scattered on the living room floor. The back door slammed.

Without thinking, he pushed past her. He had a vague impression of a sparsely but tastefully decorated living room as he charged into the kitchen. It was empty, but he heard feet crunching on the gravel outside. Then a dog started barking furiously.

His hand was on the knob of the back door when he came to his senses. Instead of charging out, he took a minute to look out the window over the sink. There was a small backyard. The gate in the fence was still swinging on its hinges. This was the older part of town, so there was a gravel alley between the backyards.

Reasonably sure he wasn't about to get ambushed, Tye charged out the back door. He saw a footprint in a bare patch of ground halfway to the gate and steered around it. He heard an engine rev and tires squeal.

Whoever he was chasing was out of sight but had kicked up enough gravel to leave a visible trail. He turned right out the gate and jogged down the alley. There was nobody in the backyards he passed. Everyone was probably either at work or school, although he provided some excitement for a shaggy dog of indeterminate breed.

He stopped at the cross street. Dust from a lugged boot sole had left a partial print on the blacktop. There was another print, just a smudge of dirt, right next to a pair of marks on the asphalt where someone had peeled out and smoked their tires on a jackrabbit start. The smell of burnt rubber was still in the air. Tye touched the tire marks. They were still slightly warmer than the surrounding pavement.

The vehicle was probably rear-wheel drive, judging by the way the tires spun when the driver mashed down on the accelerator. The marks were a confused mess, but Tye was sure they were a heavy, off-road tire, but the vehicle had a narrow track, so it was more likely an SUV than a big truck.

He looked at the boot print again. Probably about a men's size ten, which suggested an average-sized male. The distance between the marks in the gravel was consistent with a man about 5'10" who was running. He followed the trail back to the house, keeping an eye out for anything that might have been dropped, or any other evidence. He saw nothing but the dog standing there with his nose pressed up against the fence. The mutt seemed torn between wagging its tail and barking at him.

Tye stopped and looked at the dog, taking a moment to get his breath.

"Too bad you can't talk and give me a description of the guy."

The dog ran back toward his house and returned a second later with a ball. It sat there, wagged its tail, and looked at him expectantly. The fence was too high to reach over, so Tye shook his head.

"Sorry, buddy."

The dog sighed and sprawled out on the ground in a sunbeam. Tye retraced his steps back to Grace's house, pausing at the print in the patch of dirt to make a quick pencil sketch in his notebook.

Grace was sitting at the kitchen table when he walked in the back door, staring at her cell phone.

"I've been sitting here trying to decide whether to call the police. Did you see him?"

"Nope."

He told her about the footprints and the tire marks.

"Did they take anything?" he asked.

She stirred at that question and walked to the living room. "That's a good question. I'm not sure."

As they walked through the living room, Tye made note of what wasn't taken. There was a guitar case in the corner by the couch and an Apple laptop sitting on the coffee table. He followed her into a bedroom. It was tidy, except for a DSLR camera on the floor. The lens was broken and the door to the slot that held the memory card was open.

"Christopher's room is down here," she said.

The house was small. The second bedroom was only a few steps down a hallway, with a bathroom in between.

This room had been trashed. The mattress was tipped up against the wall. Drawers had been dumped out and clothes strewn around the floor.

"Oh no," Grace said. She put her hand over her mouth.

"Is anything missing from in here?" Tye asked.

"I have no idea. He mostly left outdoors equipment in here. When he was younger, he bought lots of expensive gear, but the more time he spent in the woods, the less he carried. He said he wanted to live as much like a pre-contact hunter-gatherer as he could."

As she spoke, she reflexively started picking stuff up and putting it away. Tye joined her. It didn't seem to matter to her if things were put in a particular place, just that the clutter was put away. Tye noticed an expensive knife and plenty of other outdoor gear left untouched in favor of dumping out drawers.

After things were mostly picked up, she sat on the bed, picking at a loose thread on the comforter. "Do you suppose this was just a coincidence? Just a random burglary?" she asked.

"No. They left all sorts of stuff your average burglar would have been happy to grab. I think they were looking for something."

Tye started a systematic search of the room. Many of the things he found were identical to stuff he owned. Apparently, both he and Christopher were both partial to the same brand of broadheads for their big-game hunting arrows, and preferred wool hunting clothes over synthetic. Probably 75% of the books on Christopher's book-shelves overlapped with his own. Most of the field guides to plants and animals were the same, but Christopher's tastes also ran heavily toward books about conservation and political action. Tye fingered the spine of a book called *Coyotes and Town Dogs* he remembered Gary reading, but he'd never read it himself.

There were no pictures, notes, papers or anything. There were also no electronic devices in which they might have been stored.

He found a deer hide that had been carefully rolled up and stored in a cloth bag. He took it out and spread it out on the floor. Tye's practiced eye could tell it was brain-tanned, instead of preserved using the harsher chemical method. It was well done, soft and flexible, and none of the hair had slipped. The wound was invisible from the hair side, but when he flipped it over, he could see where the long slits from an arrow had been sewn up. One entrance, one exit.

"He was proud of that. He asked me to bring it to him, but I forgot about it the last time I met with him. He was upset with me but tried not to show it. I carried it around in the car with me when I went up to look for him but put it back in here because I didn't want it to get stolen. I never thought I'd have to worry about somebody taking it from my house."

Grace's hands were shaking. Her phone sat on the bed next to her.

Tye nodded toward the phone. "You going to call the cops?"

She looked away from him. "For what? So they can do nothing, like when I told them Christopher was missing?"

He busied himself for a minute, flipping through the pages of some of the field guides, looking for anything that might be hidden inside. He found her reticence about calling the police odd. Tye tried to avoid police involvement whenever he could, but until recently, he'd been an itinerant woodsman living out of the back of his pickup truck. Cops tended not to like people like him. Grace, on the other hand, lived in an expensive home in a nice neighborhood. Normally, people like that would be screaming at the 911 call taker by now.

"That's your decision. I'm not seeing anything here that tells me why somebody might want to break in. Is anything missing?"

She shook her head. "Not that I can find. Can we just get in the car and drive over to that school?"

"Sure. I'd like to take one last look around before we leave."

She walked out of the room, and Tye stood there for a minute. It was jarring to see so many objects that were familiar to him in a space he'd never been. He wasn't sure what he hoped to find. He could spend hours in here, probing every nook and cranny, but it wouldn't help if he didn't even know what he was looking for.

He ran his finger along the spines of the books, stopping at the copy of *Coyotes and Town Dogs*. He'd always meant to read it, but never got around to it. He plucked it off the shelf and opened it to a random page.

A business card fluttered out of the pages and landed face up on the floor between his feet. Even before he bent over to pick it up, he knew what it would say:

Latrans and Corbis, Attorneys at Law: *Compromissum pro defensione matris terre.*

Tye slid the card in his pocket and put the book back on the shelf. He already knew what the Latin phrase meant: "No compromise in defense of Mother Earth." Tye and Kaity had had a run-in with the two lawyers a couple months ago, during the case of the missing little girl. Tye felt a shudder crawl down his back. It wasn't that he was scared of the pair, it was that when he was around them, he felt like he was standing too close to a secret he didn't understand.

He didn't mention the card to Grace. He wanted a little while to think about the implications. Before they left, he fixed the back door as best he could. The trim around the doorjamb was splintered from being kicked in, so he nailed it back together with some finishing nails Grace found and the back of a tomahawk from Christopher's room. A hard shove would probably make it all break loose again, but it was the best he could do.

He noticed the deerskin in the back seat when he climbed in the car.

"It makes me feel close to him," she said as she started the engine.

5

Grace followed the navigation prompts on her phone and pulled into the parking lot of Nature's Way. It was based in an old building that had formerly housed a printing company, and the parking lot was filling up as parents arrived to pick their kids up from summer camp activities.

Just inside the lobby doors, Tye stopped to look at a giant poster board that read "Coming Soon! The New Nature's Way Learning Center!" There was a drawing beneath of a wooded property with round buildings with solar panels on top. The poster was dusty and faded from the sun.

A young woman with spiky black hair and facial piercings at the front desk greeted them. She looked at Grace first and didn't quite roll her eyes, then saw Tye. She smirked at him.

"What can I help you with?"

"Hello, Holly. I was hoping to talk to Isaac."

"He stepped out for a few minutes to run an errand," she said, and stared straight ahead.

"Oh well, in that case, I'll just drop in on Dylan and say hello."

She opened her mouth to say something, but Tye just walked down the hallway to her right.

"What's her problem?" Grace asked after she caught up.

"Holly was born with the unbearable burden of being cooler than everybody else on the planet," Tye said. He was counting doors in the long hallway. He hadn't been here in a while.

He hooked a right into an office. Wooden bows, arrows, spears, and tribal masks covered the walls. A long, black rifle case leaned in one corner. A tall man with a couple days of beard and an unruly mass of dark hair sat behind a computer, typing and muttering under his breath. He looked over his reading glasses when Tye appeared in the doorway.

"Huh," he said. "You spend all the money you made on that TV show and need a job?"

"Nope. But I could use your help with something, if you've got a minute?"

The other man stood and stuck out a hand. "It's been a while, Tye."

Tye shook briefly. He gestured at Grace. "This is Grace Tompkin. Grace, this is Dylan Hart. He owns the school."

"Pleased to meet you," Hart said, and shook her hand too. At the name "Tompkin," Tye thought he saw a flicker pass across Dylan's face. He kept glancing back and forth from Tye to Grace, clearly trying to figure out their relationship and why they were here.

"You bought that land over in Washington you were talking about?" Tye asked. "When will you start teaching there?"

Dylan broke eye contact. "Oh. It'll be a while. Zoning. Permits. All that." He waved a hand dismissively. "It's great to see you, Tye, but I have to run out for a meeting in a few minutes. What can I help you with?"

"Grace's son, Chris, used to work for you. He's gone missing, and I'm helping her find him. We were wondering if we could ask you a few questions."

At the mention of Chris's name, Hart took half a step back from Tye and Grace and folded his arms across his chest.

"We let Chris go over a month ago," Hart said.

"Why?" Grace asked.

"He wasn't meeting our expectations as an employee." Hart's tone was flat and measured. To Tye's ear, he sounded like one of those corporate spokesmen you saw on the news when their company was caught doing something they shouldn't. Tye thought of a wet, cold night in a debris shelter, almost ten years ago now, when he and Hart had talked about what it meant to live a truly free life.

"What happened?" Tye asked.

Hart shook his head. "That was an internal personnel matter, and I can't discuss it because of privacy concerns."

That answer sounded rehearsed as well. Tye had another flash of memory, this one of Hart talking ninety miles a minute about his grand idea to save the world by educating children about nature.

"Can you at least tell us if you have any idea where he might be?" Grace pleaded.

"I don't know. We gave him his last check and parted ways."

Hart looked pointedly at the door. "I really need to get back to work. I'm due to fly out in a couple of hours."

Tye nodded toward the rifle case in the corner. "Hunting trip?"

"Montana. I drew an early-season tag."

"Did you hire a guide?"

A pained expression crossed Hart's face. "Yeah," he mumbled. "I haven't had time to scout his year." He didn't quite meet Tye's eyes.

"Well, hopefully, your guide will have some luck. Thanks, Dylan."

Tye turned and walked out of the office. Grace caught up to him in the hallway and grabbed his arm.

"It would be really nice if you could clue me in on what's going on. I'm not going to just follow you around."

He stopped and looked at her. "I'm sorry," he said. "I'm not doing a good job of explaining things. I'm used to doing this by myself. Can you wait until we get in the car?"

"I guess."

He ignored the smirk he got from Holly and walked out into the sunshine. While they had been in Hart's office, buses had pulled into the parking lot, discharging dozens of muddy, tired children who clutched handmade bows and arrows, woven baskets, and various leaves and rocks they'd collected.

A Jeep pulled up behind the vans and a burly guy in his early thirties got out and started talking to a parent and child when Tye caught his eye. Tye waved, then jerked his head out toward the road. The other man nodded and held up five fingers.

"You know that guy?" Grace asked as they climbed back into her car.

"That's Isaac. He doesn't want Dylan to see him talking to me, so we'll meet him down the road in five minutes."

"That was a lot of communication for a few hand gestures."

"We've hunted together."

She rolled her eyes but started the car and pulled out into traffic. Tye watched over his shoulder to make sure Isaac was watching them and would see which direction they had turned.

"Okay. Spill it," Grace said.

"Dylan and I have known each other for almost ten years," Tye said. "Gary and I spent some time at the Forest Drum Nature School. Dylan and Isaac were there too."

"That's the one in Wisconsin?" Grace asked. "Christopher talked about going there, but he never went."

"He was probably better off. When that school went out of business, Dylan started Nature's Way. I've done some part-time work for him."

"I detected some tension between you two."

"Many people feel like Dylan stopped prioritizing teaching kids about nature and started prioritizing separating the kids' parents from their money."

"Are you one of them?"

"He's done very well for himself. Let's pull into this parking lot up here. Can you pick a spot where Isaac will be able to see us from the street?"

She pulled into a drugstore parking lot and chose a spot visible from the street.

"I bet that's why Chris got fired. He hated compromises."

Tye nodded. "Dylan has developed a reputation for expecting his staff to toe a party line."

The streets were filling up with mid-afternoon traffic, and Tye grew increasingly edgy. There were too many cars, too many people, too much fast movement, and too much noise.

Isaac rolled up in his battered old Jeep and parked next to them. Tye got out and shook hands with him.

Isaac was about Tye's age and almost exactly the same height. He was brawny and wore the survival-skills instructor uniform of cargo pants, t-shirt, and boots. They'd camped and hunted together a few times, and Tye found Isaac didn't go too deep with people. Tye wasn't sure what was beneath the friendly, cheerful exterior because Isaac never showed anybody.

"What's up, dude?" Isaac affected a kind of California-surfer persona that could be a little irritating. Another thing Tye had noticed was that Isaac had a habit of staring at women's breasts, and as Grace walked around the bumper of the car, Isaac's eyes dipped down, probably without realizing it, and Grace crossed her arms over her chest. He wondered if she was even conscious of the gesture.

"Isaac, this is Grace. She's Chris Tompkin's mother. She's a little worried about him, and we're hoping you can help us find him."

Isaac looked at Grace again, this time without looking at her chest. "Oh, wow, Chris's mom? Okay. Let's see. I gave him a ride up to Indian Heaven. What was it, two weeks ago?"

Indian Heaven was a wilderness area in Washington state, inside the Gifford Pinchot National Forest.

"What's up there?" Tye asked.

Isaac looked back and forth from Tye to Grace. "His tribe. Don't you guys know? Chris hooked up with a group of honest-to-goodness rewilders. He started hanging out with them a year ago, then when he quit the school, he started full-time. I'd meet him from time to time and drive him back up there when he picked up supplies."

"Who is he with?"

"Nobody you'd know. I only met them once."

Isaac looked from Grace to Tye again, and for the briefest second, a smirk crossed his face. It was gone almost before Tye noticed it. Tye had seen that smirk before, and it was one of the things that made him wonder what was really under that affable exterior.

"How big is the group?" Tye asked.

"About a dozen. The head person is a woman named Penny. She seems pretty squared away. So far, none of the usual bullshit has happened."

Over the years, Tye had watched several groups try to start a communal, wilderness-living group. They all seemed eventually to collapse into power struggles, factionalism, love triangles, or some combination of all the above.

"Why did my son get fired from Nature's Way?" Grace asked.

Isaac looked at Tye. "Inner tracking," he said.

"What is that?" Grace asked.

Tye looked across the street, where a homeless guy was asking for spare change from people as they walked out of a coffee shop with five-dollar cups of coffee. Most of them just gave the guy an irritated look and shook their heads.

Tye answered Grace slowly, choosing his words carefully. "When you spend a bunch of time out in the wilderness, particularly tracking animals, you change. Cities become unbearable. It's too loud, too fast, too much going on. You also start not wanting to take part in some regular social stuff. Sports aren't terribly interesting. Small talk bores you. You ask fundamental questions about how people live and whether it's healthy."

Grace nodded as he talked. "That sounds like Chris."

"Some of the older teens really got attached to Chris," Isaac said. "They started questioning everything. They wanted to drop out of school, live in the bush, reject consumerism, start a commune, stuff like that. People here love to be all environmentalist and alternative, right up to where their kid declares that instead of going to a nice private college, they want to go live in the bush so they can hunt deer and eat berries."

"The parents got mad," Tye said.

"Worse," Isaac said. "One kid got yanked out of the school by his parents. He killed himself. The parents are both attorneys and they are suing the ever-loving shit out of Dylan."

"That poor kid," Tye said. "And I bet Dylan was pissed at Chris."

"Epically," Isaac said. "I could hear the screaming all the way in the parking lot. I guess a couple of instructors were debating whether they should call the police when Chris came walking out with all his stuff in his pack. He flipped Dylan the bird on his way out and never came back."

Grace sighed. "That's my son."

"Reminded me of a younger version of you, Tye," Isaac said.

"Yep. Can you show me on a map where you dropped him off?"

Isaac pulled a well-worn Washington State Gazetteer out of his truck and flipped through the pages.

"Right here," he said and tapped a fingernail on a road junction.

"Thanks," Tye said. "We'll check it out."

"You'll probably find him up there living fat off the land with his new buddies. He probably is having such a good time up there he forgot to call you," Isaac said with a last look at Grace's chest.

She put her arms across her chest again, and this time, from the scowl, Tye could tell it wasn't subconscious.

"Thanks for the help," she said flatly, and walked back around the car to get in.

"Now what?" Grace asked as she pulled out into traffic.

Tye looked at the clock on the dash and tapped a finger against his front teeth, something he often did when he was thinking.

"By the time I get back to my truck and drive up to Indian Heaven, there won't be much light left. I guess I could drive up tonight and camp and get started at first light."

"I'm coming with you," she said.

He opened his mouth to offer objections, but she cut him off. "I'm not asking you, I'm telling you. I can either go with you or go by myself. I can get to Indian Heaven."

"In this?" Tye asked, patting the dash. "The road is pretty rough."

"I'll rent an SUV if I have to." There was a line across her forehead as she spoke.

"Do you have gear? Hiking boots, synthetic base layers, rain gear, backpack, stuff to spend the night in the woods in an emergency?"

"I'll have everything I need." That wasn't exactly an answer to his question.

"In that case, maybe it would be best to just meet early in the morning and go up together. We can take my truck."

She looked across the car at him, then looked back just in time to avoid rear-ending a school bus in front of them.

She drove through traffic for a while in silence. Tye tried to tune out all the noise and commotion.

"Thank you," she said after a while.

6

That night, Tye dreamed Kaity was pregnant with their baby. They were happy, living in Tye's yurt, but then the scene shifted. He dreamed he was running down a forest road, when somebody shot him in the back.

Tye sat up in bed and put his hand to his chest. His other hand scrabbled for the flashlight on the nightstand and switched it on.

He'd expected to find the hand bloody, but it wasn't.

He sat there for a long while, waiting for his heart to calm down and listening to the breeze in the trees.

In the late summer, he'd stopped Bodhi, a man who'd kidnapped a little girl and May, Gary's wife. They'd fought on the summit of Silver Star Mountain. Tye had emerged bloodied and victorious. Bodhi was dead, mauled by a bear.

Unclaimed in death, Bodhi's remains had been cremated and were stored at the Clark County Medical Examiner's office. But a few times a week, Tye saw him in his dreams. He never saw Bodhi's face. There was just a dark figure that stalked him through the woods. Tye could never quite get away. The figure in his dreams was Bodhi, but somehow it was more than Bodhi.

Bodhi had tapped into some dark power Tye couldn't even begin to understand. In his madness, Bodhi had imagined that power would heal him of an incurable disease, make him all powerful. He'd drawn the silhouette of a dark figure everywhere, and it was that figure Tye saw in his dreams. He'd privately dubbed him the Dark Man, but he didn't ever say it out loud, because it reminded him too much of some horror movie villain.

Before he'd even healed from the fight with Bodhi, Tye had found himself doing battle again, this time on an island in Puget Sound and in the high desert of Eastern Oregon with a man named Owen Gaunt. Tye still wasn't entirely sure what the tech billionaire had been searching for, but the man had been obsessed with ancient artifacts and long-lost knowledge. He'd left Tye and Kaity for dead before disappearing.

Now Gaunt haunted his dreams too.

As he had all too often, Tye turned on the light next to his bed and read a book. He was re-reading *The Lord of the Rings,* as he'd done for more times than he could count. Somehow escaping into the world of Sam and Frodo, where simple, kind people triumphed over evil, gave him great comfort.

Finally, he was able to sleep again.

In the morning, Tye sat in the parking lot of the Yacolt Trading Post, sipping coffee, listening to John Prine, and watching the clock. He halfway hoped Grace wouldn't show. He was wondering how long he should give her when the lights of her little car swept across the parking lot two minutes early.

He reached across and unlocked the passenger door of the truck. She hopped in, pushing a backpack in ahead of her. In the glare of the dome light, he could see she was decked out in synthetic hiking clothing that all looked brand-new. The backpack still had a tag attached to the grab handle.

"Morning." She took a couple of minutes to arrange her gear. She put a travel mug in the cupholder and waved a paper bag at him. "Want a scone? They're vegan."

He took one out of politeness. It tasted less like sawdust than he expected.

Tye was not a morning person by nature. As he drove down the twisty road, he would have preferred to drink his coffee, listen to music, and watch out for deer as the sun came up. But Grace was clearly nervous and tried to make small talk about the surrounding landscape. She shifted in her seat, fidgeted with her gear, and almost dropped her coffee as Tye swerved to avoid a doe in the road.

After a set of hairpin turns, he turned onto Highway 503, and the ride smoothed out as they drove up the Chelatchie Valley. The surrounding land opened up into farm fields that were still shrouded in mist this early in the mornings. Ahead of them, the foothills of the Cascade Mountains disappeared into the clouds.

The road paralleled the north fork of the Lewis River for miles. They passed lakes and reservoirs and climbed into the foothills. Soon they were in the national forest, and the trees closed in around them. The tall Douglas firs here grew close and thick, with very little light making it through the canopy. Tye knew the route by heart. This was one of the areas that had made him fall in love with the Pacific Northwest. He'd camped, tracked, and hunted elk up here. All the other concerns of the day aside, he was looking forward to spending time in the area.

Grace pulled a topographical map out of her pack and turned it to keep it oriented correctly as they followed the road. The map was old. It had been folded and refolded, and the edges were curled.

They went from pavement to well-graded gravel to a road so rough Tye had to slow down and pick his route. The truck had plenty of ground clearance, but slamming the tires into the ruts would needlessly accelerate the wear on his suspension, and there was always a chance he could blow a tire or pop a ball joint.

"I need to pee," Grace said. "Can you pull off up there?"

She pointed at a pullout on the outside of a corner in the road. Tye obliged by parking the truck, and she hopped out. "I won't be long," she said, and walked off into the woods.

Tye got out and stretched. The sun was fully up, and the day was starting to warm.

Out of habit, he looked in the dirt of the pullout. He could make out the tracks of a couple trucks wearing heavy, lugged off-road tires. Superimposed over them was the narrower tread of a small passenger car. He saw a scrape mark on the rock where the smaller vehicle had bottomed out going over a rock as it pulled back onto the road.

Grace was back in a few minutes, rubbing her hands with sanitizer as she walked up.

"Find what you were looking for?" Tye asked.

She frowned at him. "I guess," she said.

About a mile past the pullout, Tye came to a fork in the road. The main route continued to the left, and while rutted in spots, was in decent repair. The fork to the right was a potholed mess.

"That way, right?" Grace said and pointed to the right.

"Yep," Tye said. They slowed to barely a walking pace as he picked his way around deep ruts and a partial washout.

"This is terrible," Grace said as she grabbed the handle attached to the roof. Gary liked to call it the "oh shit handle," and in this case, the description was apt.

"It is," Tye said. "We're not the first ones to come this way lately, though."

Grace craned her neck to look over the hood. "Tracks?" she asked.

"A set going out, then a set backing up, like they didn't have space to turn around. If I find a spot to get the truck off the road, we're walking the rest of the way."

She nodded and clutched her backpack.

Tye slammed on the brakes, put the truck in park, and hopped out.

He'd noticed the dark red splotches in his peripheral vision fifty feet or so back, but they hadn't registered in his mind until they reached a clear section of the road.

They were half the size of the palm of his hand and a dull rusty color. Now that he wasn't in a moving truck, he saw smaller, fainter splatters, too.

"What is it?" Grace asked as she walked around the front of the truck.

"Blood."

"From a person? Or an animal? Like a deer?"

"Not unless the deer was wearing shoes."

The footprints were faint, but they were there. The stride was long, probably from a fairly tall man running. The prints went in the direction Tye and Grace were traveling.

Some of the footprints were more distinct than others. He found one clear print of a right foot in a pool of dust. He pulled a notebook out of his cargo pocket and started sketching. The shoe pattern was distinctive, a series of lines and oblongs, with a definite heel. It was probably a heavier shoe than a tennis shoe or sneaker, but not quite a full hiking boot with a lugged sole. Most likely it was a hiking shoe or trail runner.

"Why are you drawing it?" Grace asked. "Can't you just take a picture?"

"Drawing helps lock it in my mind. It's rare to get a full, clear track like this one. From now on, what I'll be looking for is a partial track, sometimes just a few square inches of impression."

They got back in the truck and followed the blood trail slowly until he found a spot where he could squeeze the truck off the side of the road with enough room for someone to get by. It was unlikely anyone would come this way, but it was bad form to block a forest road. Some people would express their displeasure by slashing tires or emptying a magazine from their AK-47 into the offending vehicle.

He parked the truck, climbed out, and donned his small day pack. He had a sick feeling in his stomach. Tye had been a hunter his whole life. He'd followed blood trails more times than he could count, but up until recently, the trails had always been animal, not human. Since he and Kaity had started their business, death seemed to be all around him.

Dust had settled over the spots of dried blood, so the trail was old, more than a day, but Tye wouldn't speculate beyond that. No one had driven down the road since the trail had been laid, he was sure of that.

It wasn't hard to follow. He moved at a normal pace. He could hear Grace behind him but didn't want to turn and look at her. Bringing her along had been a mistake. He'd searched for dead family members plenty of times, and more than once, had to break the news that someone was gone. He'd never found the body with the dead person's loved one following along.

"Do you think the tracks could be somebody following a blood trail that was already there? Maybe the blood from an animal?" Grace asked from behind him.

It was a perceptive question. Tye had considered the possibility but rejected it. There were actually two distinct trails of blood. One, made of the big spots that ranged from the size of a quarter to almost the size of his hand, ran right by the left shoe prints. In some places, he could tell the blood had hit the shoe first, then dripped onto the ground.

The second line was harder to see. They were fine droplets flung off to the left side of the line of tracks. Tye figured they were from blood dripping off someone's fingers.

"I'm not sure," Tye lied. "Let's see what we find."

The trail led to the right side of the road, then disappeared into a salmonberry thicket. The plants were nearly head high and thick. They grew along the roads, encroaching into the right of way despite the Forest Service's efforts to wipe them out with herbicides.

"Why don't you stay here?" Tye asked.

Grace was pale and her mouth was set in a thin line. She shook her head. "I'm coming."

He was tempted to argue but realized he wouldn't get anywhere. Instead, he pushed through the salmonberries. The patch was dense but only lasted for a few feet. They grew well in the sunlight along the road, but the tall Douglas firs choked out all the light.

Smears of blood covered the leaves. On the other side, he had to slow down. The forest floor here was dirt and duff, covered in brown fallen needles, and the dark blood all but disappeared. The scuffs in the forest floor from running footsteps would stay until there was a good, soaking rain, though, and he was still able to follow the trail. The sun filtered through the trees over his left shoulder, and occasionally he would have to squat to bring his eyes closer to the ground. Then the prints would show against the forest floor.

The tracks were getting closer together. Whoever made the tracks had slowed from a run to a walk. Tye could pick out places where clumps of fir needles were glued together by sticky, dried blood.

It was easy when tracking to get fixated on the ground immediately at his feet and not look ahead. Behind him, he heard Grace give a little gasp.

There was a sun-dappled clearing ahead, with a vague lump in the middle. Tye realized he was looking at the bottoms of a pair of hiking shoes, then the lump resolved into a body.

He jogged forward, wanting to get there before Grace. He looked back and realized he shouldn't have worried. She was standing with one hand over her mouth and the other holding a tree.

The height and build looked right for Christopher. He was wearing canvas work pants and a t-shirt. There was an entrance wound in his back, near his right shoulder blade. It hadn't bled much, just a spot the size of a quarter. Tye noticed pieces of blue nylon fabric around the perimeter of the wound.

Knowing he shouldn't, Tye rolled him over. The body was still stiff with rigor, but Tye didn't see any blotchy post-mortem lividity on his face. The bullet had clearly been fired from behind, but at an angle. The exit wound was the size of a fist on the side of his left chest. From there, the bullet had smashed into the inside of his elbow, before exiting out the arm. Tye noted that blood had dried on his arm and fingers, and that the wounds matched his guesses exactly. The clinically detached part of his brain took some pride in that.

He knew the rigor mortis and lack of lividity could be used to figure out how long Christopher had been dead, but he didn't know how. Tye was surprised animals hadn't been at the body yet.

He heard the scuff of a foot behind him, and Grace sat down heavily.

"It's him," she said.

"I'm sorry."

She just sat there, cross-legged with her hands on her knees. "I've never seen a dead person before, except at funerals."

Tye tried to think of something to say that would make her feel better, but everything that came to mind sounded stupid and trite in his head.

"Can you just let me sit here with him for a minute?"

He was ashamed that he felt relieved. "Yes," he said. "We're going to have to go somewhere with cell service soon."

She nodded, not taking her eyes off her son. "Just a few minutes."

His search-and-rescue training told him they should have left the clearing by now, retracing their steps. But Christopher had clearly been out here at least a day, probably more. Letting Grace sit with him for a few minutes wasn't going to make that big of a difference. Tye knew from experience that in a few hours the clearing would be full of cops measuring and photographing.

Right now, there was peace. The forest was quiet, except for a pair of kinglets chittering back and forth to each other in the crown of the trees. The late-morning sun was warm, but the breeze still held the coolness of the evening. It wasn't, Tye thought, a bad place to die.

"I don't suppose this could've been an accident." She was almost whispering.

Tye kept his voice low as well. That seemed to match the mood of the place. "I don't know," he said.

She took a deep breath. She reached out her hand like she was going to touch her son, then drew back.

"Let's go find the cops," Tye said.

7

G race was quiet on the ride out. She sat in the seat with her legs drawn up and her arms around her knees, checking her phone periodically for a signal.

After about half an hour, they came over a rise and she looked at the phone.

"I have two bars," she said, and he pulled off the road. Her finger hovered over the button for a long moment.

"I don't even know what to say to them," she said.

He held out his hand, and she dropped the phone into it. The phone call was shorter than might be expected. He'd written down the GPS coordinates of the body and had anticipated most of the dispatcher's questions. He was told to wait where he was and stay by the phone in case they needed to call back.

"It's going to be a while," he said as he handed the phone back. "I'm really sorry about your son. I want to help you, but I don't know how."

She surprised him by reaching over and squeezing his hand. "Thank you. Right now, I'd really just like to be by myself."

Feeling like he was doing something wrong, he left her there in the cab of his truck and walked around to sit on the tailgate. It was shaping up to be a warm, beautiful day. As he sat there eating, he watched a redtail hawk catch a thermal and soar over the valley below. Not for the first time, Tye contemplated the fact that he was alive and somebody else was dead. Tye was barely into his thirties, had dealt with far more than his fair share of life and death, but so far, he hadn't figured out any rhyme or reason for it. He'd searched for people who had gone into the woods almost comically unprepared, and found them alive, but found experienced, well-equipped outdoors people dead. He'd tracked a couple of people that he firmly suspected had walked into the woods with the intention of dying, even though no note had been found.

He was quite certain that someone had shot Christopher in the back with a rifle. Tye had killed animals for food more times than he could count. Each time he felt a mixture of satisfaction for a job well done, sadness at the passing of a life, and the feeling that he'd done something wrong. Tye had a temper, but he couldn't imagine being angry enough to shoot somebody in the back with a rifle.

He heard the sound of an engine, and in the distance, he could see a white SUV with a police-style light bar coming up the road.

"Looks like the police are here," he said.

After a minute, the door of the truck opened, and Grace walked back to stand with him. She wiped her eyes with a tissue.

Jurisdiction out here was a funny thing. The land belonged to the US government, and was managed by the Forest Service, who had their own police, but they primarily investigated things related to resource protection. Tye had used a map to figure out they were in Skamania County. It was a rural county, sparsely populated, and the Sheriff's Office was responsible for crimes committed on hundreds of square miles of US-government-owned land, despite the fact that it didn't receive a dime of tax money from the land.

The deputy was young. He was polite but distant, and after getting a look at Tye and Grace's identification, followed them to Christopher's body. After that, he directed them to wait about half a mile up the road. After another hour, Tye lost count of the number of SUVs that had shown up at the scene.

An unmarked SUV pulled in behind Tye's truck and a woman in her mid-thirties got out. She had shoulder-length brown hair and wore khakis and a polo shirt with "Clark County Sheriff Office" embroidered on the chest. She wore a gun and a badge clipped to her belt.

"You," she said to Tye as she walked up. Earlier in the year, Tye had been involved in a case of a kidnapped child. Evans had been the lead detective.

"Hello, Detective Evans. Aren't we in Skamania County?"

"We have a multi-county major crimes task force." She looked at Grace. "Mrs. Tompkin? I'm sorry for your loss. I know this is a difficult time for you, but I'm going to need to interview you so we can figure out what happened to your son. First, I'd like to speak to Mr. Caine privately."

The detective turned and walked back toward her SUV without waiting to see if Tye was following. He considered staying put out of spite, then thought better of it and followed her to the back hatch of her SUV.

"This is the second time in a couple of months you've been associated with a recently found dead body. I heard there were some shenanigans up on an island in Puget Sound, and over on the Oregon side of the border, too."

Cops made Tye nervous. He wondered if he should ask for an attorney. "It's been a strange year," was all he could think of to say.

"Want to explain how you came to find this particular dead body?"

He explained most of it. When he mentioned the burglary at Grace's house, she raised an eyebrow. When he mentioned talking to Dylan and Isaac at Nature's Way school, she seemed interested.

"So the owner was pretty pissed at him," she said.

"Yeah."

"You sit tight while I talk to your client. You might want to look into whether you are acting as a private investigator without a license."

He swallowed hard. Their attorney had assured Tye and Kaity

they weren't breaking the law, but that sounded ominous. He stood there shuffling his feet while Evans talked to Grace.

After what seemed like forever but was only fifteen minutes, Evans walked back to him. She was slipping her notebook into a back pocket as she walked up. "So, she told you she called the police and reported her son missing?"

"Yep."

"Well, she didn't. She denies doing it, and there's no record that he's been reported missing in Oregon or Washington."

"Huh," Tye said.

"Sounds like you need to have a talk with your client. Can you see that Mrs. Tompkin makes it home safely?"

Tye nodded. Evans climbed into her SUV and headed toward the crime scene.

"I get the feeling she didn't believe us," Grace said.

Tye took a swig from his water bottle. "Look at it from her perspective. You knew your son was missing somewhere in the Gifford Pinchot National Forest, and you and I come up here and just happen to find his body?" Tye climbed into the driver's seat and started the engine.

"But isn't that what you do?" Grace asked as she climbed into the passenger seat.

"Yeah, but they don't understand tracking. They figure there has to be something I'm hiding."

He felt a headache starting behind his eyes and took a swig of water, though he realized it probably had little to do with dehydration.

"Thank you," Grace said as they bounced down the road. She said it so quietly, Tye almost didn't hear her.

"You're welcome. I'm sorry we had to find him like that."

"He was shot in the back, wasn't he?"

"Yeah. With a rifle."

"You can tell from the damage?"

"The exit wound was pretty big. I'm certain it was from a rifle."

"It was awful."

He nodded. He knew he'd see it in his sleep tonight. He also knew eventually it would fade. Tye had known people who had recovered bodies that never worked search and rescue again. He didn't hold it against them. It was gruesome, troubling work sometimes, but so far, he'd managed to keep his equilibrium. He'd take it easy for a couple of days, try to relax, and soon he'd be ready to go out again.

"I was wondering if you would keep helping me," Grace asked.

"With what?"

"I want to know who killed my son. I don't think those people are going to find out."

He chewed on that for a moment. What he wanted to do was drive her back to her car, offer his condolences one last time, and go home. But there was that pain behind his eyes starting up, and he knew that would probably make it worse.

"Why don't you think the cops will figure out who killed Christopher?" he asked.

She shrugged. "It's like she didn't believe me."

"Did you tell her everything?"

She shot him a look. "Yes," she said, but he could hear the hesitation in her voice.

She was holding something back from both him and Evans.

"We didn't find his backpack," she said. "He always carried a big blue backpack when he went out in the woods."

Tye thought about the pieces of blue nylon fabric around the wound. "Did you tell Evans that?"

"No. I just thought of it." She was lying. He was sure.

"What do you want me to do?"

"I want to find his backpack. I want to find those people. His tribe."

"I think Evans pretty clearly wanted us to leave the area."

"We can come back tomorrow. I'm coming back one way or another. Just like I said before, I can rent an SUV if I have to."

He drove for a while in silence, steering around the ruts in the road.

"I can pay you more," she said.

"It's not that," he said.

"What, then?"

"I feel like you haven't told me everything," he said.

"I have." But she didn't look at him, just looked out the window.

The timing was good — or bad, depending on how you looked at it. Up ahead, Tye saw the spot where they'd stopped earlier so she could walk into the woods.

He parked the truck and hopped out.

"Where are you going?" she asked.

"Bathroom."

He walked into the trees, retracing her path from earlier with ease. He found the plastic tube stuck in between the roots of a tree, where it wouldn't be seen by a casual passerby. A rubber gasket around the screw-off lid made it reasonably watertight. He upended it, and a rolled-up piece of paper fell out.

Where are you? I'm worried about you. I have a guy helping me. I'll try to check this every day, but it's hard on my car.

He walked back to the truck and climbed in. He put the message tube and the note on the dash.

"If you want me to help you, you need to tell me everything."

She took a deep breath when she saw the tube. She reached out and took the note, smoothing the paper with her fingers.

8

He made tea. It was something to do with his hands. He'd backed the truck under some trees and pulled two folding chairs out of the back. Grace sat in one and rolled the message tube over in her hands.

"He was working with an environmental law firm, gathering information on a timber company up here. When I would meet him in town, I'd courier information for him. Usually, it was an SD card from a digital camera."

Tye handed her a cup of tea, and she nodded her thanks.

She gestured behind her at the woods. "This place was our fail-safe. If he couldn't reach me any other way, he was supposed to leave a message here."

"It's like something out of a spy movie," Tye said.

She blushed. "It's called a dead drop. I read a bunch of spy novels when I was a kid."

He sat in a chair next to her and started to eat his lunch. "What was the timber company doing wrong?" Tye asked.

"I don't know. Christopher hasn't... hadn't told me the whole story about anything for years. It was like I slowly had to earn his trust back. All I know is he had pictures he wanted to go to some environmental lawyers in Portland."

"Did you look at the pictures?"

She shook her head. "He asked me not to, and I honored that."

"Do you think he was shot because of the work he was doing for these lawyers?" Tye asked.

"Maybe? But I can't tell the cops about all this."

"Why not?"

"Christopher had some... radical beliefs. Do you remember the housing development construction project that was burned a couple of years back?"

"The one in Oregon?" Tye asked. "Where they were going to cut down some old-growth forest and put up McMansions?"

"That one." She nodded. "Two days after that story appeared on the news, he showed up at my place with his hands bandaged and burned. Most of his hair was singed off. He gave me some story about an accident with a camp stove and knew I was pretending to believe him."

"But that doesn't matter now."

"But his friends. Maybe it matters to them."

"What do you want me to do?" he asked after a while.

"Help me figure out who killed my son, and why."

"But what then? You've already said you're afraid of cooperating with the police. What are you going to do if we find who killed Christopher?"

"I don't know what I'm going to do. I'll figure it out then. Right now, I just want to know."

He rolled the tea around in his mouth. Off in the distance, he heard the whine of an engine.

"I'll do it, but I have two conditions."

The look of relief on her face was almost painful. "What are they?"

"I'm not going to do anything illegal. I'm not going to prison for you."

"That seems fair. What else?"

"You tell me everything. If you lie to me or hold anything back, I'm out of here."

"There's more I need to tell you."

"I figured."

"The company Chris was spying on is owned by his father, Wade Tompkin. We split when Chris was a toddler. They were never close."

His tea had cooled off enough to be drinkable. "Is his dad crooked?"

"Wade is rich and never satisfied with what he has. It's his mother, Anna Lee, that really runs the show. Wade's father died when he was a child. Anna Lee always seemed to think I was after Wade's money. We would have split up no matter what, but she certainly hastened things along."

"Well, that's complicated."

"That's what I've lived with for the last twenty-five years. When we split, I refused to take any money out of spite. I didn't want her to be right about me. It was hard for me and Christopher at times. My degree is in art history, not exactly a marketable skill. But I started getting gallery work and eventually opened my own place."

She stopped and stared at a robin flitting from branch to branch. "I was glad when Christopher came back. I thought we'd be happy."

She fought back tears, and he stared into his teacup.

"Tomorrow we can meet at the same place and go try to find Christopher's gear and his friends," Tye said. "If you're up for it. If not, I can go by myself."

He looked across the road at the top of the ridge. It occurred to him that there hadn't really been any question in his mind about helping Grace. Sometimes Tye made deliberate, well-considered decisions. Other times he went with his gut, particularly at times when his dreams and his headaches were involved. He realized he couldn't very well tell her that he'd had a vision of her dead son and would've suffered from an excruciating migraine until he decided to help her. Gary and Kaity were the only ones who knew about those things, and Tye often didn't tell even them the whole story.

"Thank you," she said. "I wish Chris could have met you. I think you two would have gotten along really well.

He wondered what would happen if he told her about the dreams and the headaches.

She stood and folded her chair. "How did you know I'd been here before?" she asked as they were stowing their gear in the back of the truck. She pointed at the message container on the dash.

"The paint on the scrape mark on that rock over there matches the ding on your car's body panel. That and the tracks are a perfect match for your tires."

"I guess I should have read more spy novels."

"Maybe so," he said.

9

Instead of going home after he dropped Grace at her car, Tye headed for the interstate. He made it across the river into Portland just before the afternoon traffic started to get out of control. Most of it was going the other direction, cars full of people fleeing the city to their homes across the river in Washington state, but it was still a jarring change from the forests and hills of his home.

The office of Corbis and Latrans, Attorneys at Law, was in an old house just south of Hawthorne Avenue in southwest Portland. A familiar candy-apple-red truck was parked out front. It was festooned with dozens of bumper stickers. The "There Is No Planet B" sticker looked new. As Tye passed the bed of the truck, he saw a box of long metal spikes and a three-pound engineer hammer lying in the back.

The sign read: Latrans and Corbis, Attorneys at Law: *Compromissum pro defensione matris terre.*

The sign smelled of fresh paint. Someone had painted over the old wording with a coat of white, but the old letters still faintly showed through in spots.

The door to the office popped open, and a tall, lean man stepped out. He had a beard and graying hair in a long ponytail down his back. He was dressed in a western snap-front shirt, bolo tie, black vest, faded blue jeans, and scuffed cowboy boots. Under the vest, Tye saw a bulge he knew was an old Colt Single Action Army revolver.

"You changed your sign," Tye said.

"My partner's Latin translations are always horrible." Willie Latrans took a bite off the chicken leg he was holding in his left hand. "What brings you here, Mr. Caine?"

Tye produced the business card from his shirt pocket. "I found this in Christopher's Tompkin's things."

"So?"

"He's dead. Somebody shot him in the back and left him to bleed out up in the Gifford Pinchot National Forest."

Tye wasn't the best at reading nonverbal cues, but he could tell from the way Latrans blinked and his head jerked upright that this was news to him. Latrans stared over Tye's shoulder for a moment, then swallowed hard. "That is... unfortunate. What can you tell me about what happened?"

Tye shook his head. "Nope. Every time I'm mixed up in something that involves you, I feel like I'm blundering around in the dark. So let's change things up a little. Why don't you tell me what happened?"

Latrans's lip curled up in a snarl, and he fixed Tye with a stare that made the pit of his stomach go cold. Tye stood his ground and resisted the urge to take a step back.

"I don't think you know what you're dealing with, Caine."

"Nope. I don't. And I'm getting damn sick and tired of it. In the last few months, I've been stabbed, shot at, and generally run around like a rented mule. At least some of the time, you've been involved in that. You know more than you're telling. Now I know more than you, and if you want information, we're going to have a reciprocal exchange."

The look on Latrans's face passed, replaced with an impenetrable facade. "I'm afraid certain relationships between attorneys and clients are privileged."

"Chris Tompkin didn't even own a car, but you're telling me he could afford an attorney? Besides, he's dead."

Latrans tossed the chicken bone into the bushes by the porch.

"I'm afraid that's all I can say right now. I'll need to consult with my colleague before we issue any more statements. Good day, Mr. Caine." Latrans spun on his heel, walked inside, and shut the door.

Tye let out a breath. He'd been worried this would be a waste of time.

As he tried to put the key in the ignition in the truck, he realized his hands were shaking, courtesy of an adrenaline dump he hadn't seen coming. He drove slowly through the side streets and breathed deeply until it passed.

Instead of going home, he decided to stop and see a friend. Doyle lived in a retirement community in the town of Vancouver, Washington, right across the river from Portland. Tye supposed it wasn't too bad. Doyle had his own apartment, and access to common rooms and outside areas. It seemed less like a prison than other places Tye had seen.

Tye knocked softly and waited patiently, listening to the rustling from behind the door. One of his biggest fears was that he'd come out here and find Doyle dead in his easy chair, with his glasses perched on his forehead and one of his favorite mystery books open in his lap.

Not this time. Finally, the door popped open and there was Doyle. Tye was a little uncertain of his exact age, but he thought it was about eighty. He was slender and stooped, with a wiry halo of white hair. He moved slowly, pulling a little tank of oxygen behind him, but his eyes were bright behind his glasses.

When Doyle saw the mason jar of applejack in Tye's hand, his eyes lit up. "Sit down and I'll get some glasses," he wheezed and shuffled toward the kitchenette. Tye felt like he should offer to get the glasses for him but knew Doyle would refuse the help.

Tye felt beholden to Doyle. The old man was a retired detective. Tye and Kaity had asked him for help in a case a few months back, and Doyle had nearly been killed. His old condominium had burned to the ground, and Doyle would have burned with it if Tye hadn't dragged him out of the flames. Doyle had lost everything. He'd already been sick before the fire, but now he needed constant oxygen, and it was painful to watch him move around.

Instead of offering to help, Tye sat on the couch and started unloading books from the bag Kaity had sent. "I've got the new William Kent Krueger, and Kaity said she threw in a couple of surprises," Tye said.

"I thought I was way down the list for the William Kent Krueger," Doyle said as he came into the living room and sat down in his easy chair. He sounded out of breath.

"I guess it pays to know the librarian," Tye said. He poured a little applejack in each glass. Doyle wasn't a heavy drinker, but he enjoyed Gary's homemade beer, wine, cider, and applejack. Tye thought it was as much about having something made for him as it was about drinking alcohol.

"What's the latest?" Doyle asked between sips.

Tye opened his mouth to say something, then stopped.

"You're among friends here," Doyle said, his voice gentle.

Tye was self-aware enough to realize he sought out the company of older men sometimes. His father had drowned when Tye was still quite young, leaving a hole that had never been filled. The fact that Doyle was a former police officer was also fascinating. Most of his life, Tye had had a rocky relationship with authority figures, first as a long-haired woods bum growing up in West Virginia, then as he wandered the western United States, living out of the back of his truck and taking whatever odd jobs he could find. He'd found himself in conflict with various sheriffs, constables, and other law officers that seemed to have nothing better to do than to mess with a young man that just wanted to be left alone.

There had never been any kind of judgment from Doyle. Unlike any other cop he'd met, Doyle had an honest, open curiosity about other people. He seemed genuinely fascinated by people who were different from him. Tye was willing to bet that was what had made him a good investigator.

"You were a cop a long time," Tye finally said. "You saw a lot of bad things, I would imagine. Dead people, things like that. Did it ever bother you?"

"Still does," Doyle said, and took a sip of applejack. "About once a week I get a real humdinger of a nightmare. How about you?"

"Yeah. About once a week."

"You've had a hell of a year, my friend. First, you rescued that kidnapped little girl from that crazy guy. What was his name?"

"Bodhi."

"That was it. You're lucky all you needed was stitches in your ribs. He could have gutted you with that knife. Then you had that little adventure up there on that private island in Puget Sound where you almost got eaten by a lion, then almost burned alive."

"It was a tiger, but yeah."

Doyle took another sip of applejack. Then he held the glass up to the light for a moment, turning it this way and that, as if admiring the clarity. Finally, he set the glass down on the table in front of him.

"Dead people are one thing. People die. Car crashes, falls, heart attacks. That's one thing. It was the evil that got to me. People hurting other people for no damn good reason, other than greed or just because."

Tye found himself nodding. "I still see him in my dreams. Bodhi." *The Dark Man,* Tye almost added, but he knew it would get him a strange look from Doyle.

"It's one of the dirty little secrets of police work," Doyle said. "The nightmares. The drinking. The divorces. The suicides."

He fixed Tye with a look that made him feel like a butterfly on a pin, and Tye was once again reminded that Doyle wasn't just a doddering old man.

"Nothing that bad for me," Tye said.

"Keep it that way," Doyle said. "I lost a marriage over this. Not because of the things I saw but because I didn't talk about it. Didn't live my life. I just sat in a chair with a beer in one hand and a TV remote in the other, communicating by grunts. Took me a while to notice she'd even left. You're doing good work, but don't let this eat up your life."

Tye sat there nodding his head, not sure what to say. "Thank you," he said after a while.

"I'm just doing what I wish somebody had done for me all those years ago."

Tye stood. He had one more errand to run, and an early start to his day tomorrow. "Kaity says she'll snag that new Craig Johnson book for you as soon as your number comes up. Then one of us will run it over to you."

"I appreciate it. You don't need to come bearing books or apple-jack either. Drop by any time."

Doyle was maybe a little too old-fashioned to be a hugger, but it seemed like his handshake was a little firmer and lasted a little longer than usual.

10

G ary was sitting in the lotus position on a tree stump when Tye pulled up the driveway. He unfolded himself with an uncommon grace as Tye got out of the truck.

"Find him?" Gary asked as Tye walked up.

"Yep."

"Dead?"

"Yep."

"You look like a man that could use a drink."

"Or two."

Tye sat down on the porch and leaned his head against the aluminum wall of the trailer, while Gary rustled around in the kitchen. A moment later he appeared with a mason jar full of a dark liquid, and a pair of jelly jars.

"That's not applejack," Tye said as Gary poured.

"Nope. Blackberry brandy. I put it up last summer and forgot about it, so it should be well aged."

Tye took a tentative sip. Unlike Gary's attempts at making applejack, this brew didn't make his nose hairs feel like they were singed. It was smooth.

"We have a winner," Tye said.

"Yep. The alcohol content is low, but it does sip easy. Want to tell me about your day?"

Before Tye could respond, his phone started buzzing from his pocket. It was Kaity.

"This is convenient," he said. "Can I put you on speaker so I can tell you and Gary both what happened at the same time?"

"Sure," she said. "Make it quick. I'm on a break from work."

Tye described the events of the day as succinctly as he could.

"Wow. That's sad," Kaity said. "So, you're going to keep going?"

"I'll help her find her son's stuff and his friends. I'm a little worried about what Evans said about a PI license, though." Private Investigator licenses were difficult to get in Washington. In order to get a license, a person had to first be employed by an established agency.

"Our lawyer said we're not breaking any rules," Kaity said. "I can ask around a little, if that will help."

"It would ease my mind," Tye said. Listening to her voice made him remember the dream he'd had, and that made it hard to focus on the conversation.

"You want me to dig into the Tompkin family business?" Kaity asked. "It seems like they have a motive."

Tye thought about that for a minute. "Maybe. Remember, I'm just helping Grace find Christopher's stuff and his friends. We're not investigating the murder."

"I'll make a few inquiries. Maybe we can talk again tonight?"

"I'd like that," he said, before he considered his words.

"Sounds good. I have to get back to work. Catch you tonight," she said and clicked off.

"Yep. You'd like that," Gary said and grinned. "This has gone on long enough. The unresolved tension between you two is getting old."

"I've been resolving it all by myself lately."

"That's a temporary, unsatisfactory solution," Gary said. "If it wasn't for Kaity, I'd suggest you just find yourself a nice rowdy roll in the hay, but that's never been your style. Your dalliances have been infrequent, but intense. It's never casual to you."

"It's been a while."

"Company," Gary said and nodded toward the driveway.

A white Mercedes G-class SUV was pulling up the driveway. Tye noted the aftermarket off-road tires and wondered if they would match the tire tracks he'd found down the block from Grace's house.

The Mercedes stopped behind Tye's truck and a man in his fifties got out. He was almost exactly Tye's height, so his stride length would be a match for the tracks of Grace's burglar as well. Automatically Tye's eyes traveled downward. The man was wearing slip-on shoes, not boots.

He also wore a pair of jeans and an untucked shirt that seemed designed to hide the hint of a middle-aged paunch. There was something about the guy's face that looked plastic and unreal.

At first glance, Tye didn't like him. Those first impressions were something he had to be careful of, but more often than not, he was right.

A woman in her seventies got out of the passenger side. She was tall. Tye reckoned they would be eye-to-eye. She wore outdoor clothing and had gray hair pulled back in a severe ponytail.

The man strode toward Tye and Gary, cocksure and confident. He stopped right in front of Tye. "You looked taller on TV," he said.

That wasn't making Tye like him more. "I get that a lot. Can we help you with something?"

"I guess you don't recognize me. I'm Wade Tompkin. I'm here to offer you a job." He stuck out his hand.

"I'm sorry for your loss," Tye said, then realized he was assuming Wade knew about Christopher's death.

Wade shrugged. "It's a horrible thing, but I've been preparing myself for something like this for a long time." His expression didn't change.

He gestured as the woman walked up behind him. "This is my mother, Anna Lee."

"Pleased to meet you," she said, but didn't offer a hand. She had a

small, pinched face, and Tye detected the hint of an accent he recognized in her voice. Maybe West Virginia, his home state. Maybe Penn-
sylvania or Maryland.

"Is there a place we can talk?" Tompkin asked.

Gary cocked an eyebrow at Tye. "I'll go tend to the goats."

Tye led the way past the trailer and down the path to his yurt. It
was sparse inside, but still crowded with the three of them. Tye
owned one chair, and a stool made of alder he'd cut down off the
property. He moved the stool in front of his workbench, sat it next to
the chair, and sat down on the bed.

"You two have a seat. I'd like to hear what you have to say."

Anna Lee didn't sit, she just stood by the door with her arms
folded.

Wade wandered over to Tye's workbench. The parts to a
battered old Winchester Model 1886 rifle were strewn all over the
bench. Tye had stripped the stock down to bare wood and was
slowly removing all the surface rust with steel wool, oil, and elbow
grease.

At first, Tye thought Wade was going to pick up a part of the rifle,
which disturbed him. But Tompkin merely leaned over, studying it.

"Looks like it's time for a new rifle," Tompkin said.

"That one has sentimental value. A guy left it to me when he
died." The truth was far more complicated, but Tye didn't want to tell
that story right now.

Tompkin smirked. "I'm a hunter too. I've got more rifles than I
know what to do with. My favorite is a Blaser straight-pull bolt action.
Ever hear of it?"

Tye had. A Blaser rifle probably cost more than all of Tye's guns,
his truck, and everything else he owned was worth.

"I've got some stuff I need to do today," Tye said. "I don't want to
be rude, but if you can tell me why you are here, I'd really appreciate
it."

Tompkin's right eye twitched at that. A woman had once told Tye
that every time he started a sentence with "I don't want to be rude,
but...," the next thing that came out of his mouth was usually rude.

Tompkin looked around the yurt. "I can see you are a busy man. I'll cut to the chase."

Tye couldn't tell if Tompkin was being snide or not. He hated that feeling.

"My understanding is my ex-wife, Grace, has hired you. She gets many strange notions. I'd make it worth your while to tell me what she's up to."

"I'm sorry. I can't comment on my clients."

From the door, Anna Lee smirked. "If you're looking for a piece of the pie, what you need to understand is that Christopher had no legal entitlement to anything from any of the Tompkin family funds. Neither does Grace."

"Somebody shot him. Don't you want to know who did it?" Tye realized he'd just tipped his hand, but clearly, they'd already known about his relationship with Grace.

Wade shrugged. "I'm sure Christopher's death is the result of his own bad choices. The police will either figure out who shot him, or they won't."

"He was your son, don't you care?"

Wade blinked when Tye asked that. He started to speak, stumbled, and started gain. It didn't last long, and he recovered like a pro, but Tye knew he'd struck a nerve.

"Christopher began working actively against our interests when he went to work for that environmental law firm. They're a bunch of radicals that can't compromise on anything. He never really fit into this family, but when he went to work for them, I couldn't see it as anything other than a betrayal."

Tye had no idea what to say to that.

"We've gotten off track here," Wade said. "I'm willing to pay handsomely for information about what Grace is doing. It could save me lots of money in litigation in the long run."

"How much money do you have?" Tye asked.

Tompkin gave a little grin that made Tye want to punch him. "It's hard to say. It varies from day to day."

"Are you willing to give me all of it?"

Tompkin stood. He turned red, and he clenched his fists. Over by the door, Anna Lee laughed.

"That's a ridiculous question," Wade said.

Tye took a coffee can off a shelf over the workbench and dumped it out. He sorted through the pile of bills and loose change, then took the money out of his pocket and laid it on top.

"I've got seventy-three dollars and eighteen cents here. If I give it all to you, will you leave?"

Tompkin turned red. "What the hell kind of question is that?"

"It's worth all the money I have to get you to leave. But it's not worth everything you have for me to work for you. So I guess my convictions are a little stronger."

Tompkin turned to leave. "We're leaving." He stomped to the door. Before he left, he turned and looked at Tye. "I should have known better than to work with a high school dropout."

Tye laughed. At one time, that would have hurt. Without telling him beforehand, the TV network had made a big deal about him dropping out of school. For a while, it had made him angry, but now he just didn't care.

Tye gave the Tompkins some space but followed them to the car. Gary was sitting on the trailer's porch, his feet propped up on the railing. He was reading a book of Chinese poems translated into English and sipping iced tea. He watched Tompkin stomp by without comment.

Tye stopped and stood there with his hands in his pockets.

"What did he want?" Gary asked.

"He wanted to hire me to spy on Grace."

Gary and Tye stood there and watched as the SUV did a thirty-two-point turn to get out of the driveway.

"You say something rude?" Gary asked.

A raven flew off its perch, circled the SUV twice, then let go a massive load of bird dung that splatted on the back window.

"I don't care."

11

A s they drove into the national forest the next morning, Tye told Grace about Wade's visit.

"I don't want his money," she said. "I just want to know what happened to my son. Wade assumes everyone wants the same things he wants."

Tye was quiet as he watched oncoming traffic before turning onto Highway 503. He pulled over to let a log truck pass so it wouldn't tailgate him, then pulled back out onto the road.

"I guess I'm wondering if Wade killed Christopher," he said.

"I've wondered that same thing," Grace said. "All night. I just don't see it. Wade's a coward. I just can't see him killing anybody. Besides, Christopher wasn't that big of a threat. So what if they get fined by the state for improper logging practices? Wade has millions, and those fines are usually a pittance, anyway."

They rode in silence for a while, and he realized she was asleep with her head against the window. He left her in peace, predicting correctly she'd wake up once the road got rough. He tried to take the ruts and potholes as easily as he could, but still she jolted awake.

"Sorry," he said. "We're almost there."

He parked close to where they'd found the blood trail leading to

Christopher's body. Tye unlocked the back of the truck and pulled out his backpack and gun belt.

"A gun?" Grace asked as he checked the load on his .357 revolver.

"I guess that's my third non-negotiable condition," he said. "I just had a little adventure where everybody but me had a gun, and I'm not keen to repeat it. Since somebody around here is slinging lead, I'd like to be able to return the favor."

"You sound like a cowboy."

"I think most cowboys have an aversion to getting shot, but for the record, I've never been terribly good with livestock."

She seemed content to accept that he was carrying the gun. He settled the backpack on his shoulders and found the blood trail again. Much of it had been wiped away by vehicle traffic, but it was still detectable.

The sky was leaden, and he figured it would be a matter of hours before the clouds opened up. Rain would wash away the blood, and much of the other sign he hoped to find today.

He started following the trail in the opposite direction, toward where Christopher had come from, instead of toward where they'd found his body.

Christopher had pushed through the salmonberry thicket that left Tye wishing he had a machete. Behind him, he could hear Grace struggling.

"I don't understand how he did all this after he was wounded."

Tye had seen this sort of thing before. He'd watched more than one wounded elk or deer make a last-ditch, desperate sprint with a bullet through the lungs before finally collapsing. Christopher's effort had been Herculean, though.

Tye followed the trail through the forest duff, a small clearing, and then back to another road.

Tye guessed they were about a quarter of a mile from where Christopher had finally fallen. He trailed the blood across the road, through another salmonberry thicket, and toward a small clearing.

"You think we'll find his friends back over by where we found his body?" Grace asked. "I wonder if the police found them. I left a message for that detective, but she hasn't called me back."

"Christopher would have led the people that shot him away from his friends," Tye said.

Up ahead, he saw what he'd been looking for. The blue nylon backpack stuck out against the muted greens and browns of the forest floor. The color matched the fabric fragments Tye had seen embedded in Christopher's wound.

"That's his bag," Grace said and pointed. "The cops didn't find it?"

"Don't think they knew how to look," Tye said.

They stood over the bag. There was a clean, neat hole in the back side, centered perfectly in the logo. The padding on the front was soaked in blood.

"We've got a decision to make," Tye said. "This is evidence. We need to decide if we're truly on our own or whether we're going to leave this and call the cops back in."

Grace shrugged. "They didn't find it. I want to open it."

Inside the top zippered compartment, Tye found an envelope full of cash and receipts, a notebook, and a digital camera. He handed the camera to Grace and opened the main compartment of the pack, careful not to get any of the dried blood on his hands.

A bunch of rice spilled out. He pulled out a plastic bag, leaking grains through the bullet hole. Next came a bag of beans.

"He used to go into town to buy supplies. Lots of beans and rice," she said.

Next came several cardboard cartons of salt. He reached deep into the pack and pulled out some clothes, none too clean. After that, his fingers brushed a plastic bag. Inside was a box of .30-06 rifle cartridges. The end flaps were still sealed. There were also a dozen steel broadheads for hunting arrows, still in the package. The bag bore the logo of a popular sporting goods store.

"Anything else?" Grace asked.

He pulled his little flashlight out of his pocket and shone it inside. There was a round bottle rolling around on the bottom.

"Prenatal vitamins," he said, reading the label.

"Huh?" He handed her the bottle, and she stared at the label with a blank expression on her face. "Why would he have these?"

"Dunno."

Tye stood. Something was tickling the edges of his awareness, some sound or other stimuli that he'd only barely perceived while his consciousness was focused on other things.

They were quiet, and they were good at using the shadows and light to mask their movement. They came within fifty feet before Tye realized they were there.

The man on the right was stocky and held a rifle. The woman on the left was taller and had a wood longbow.

"I think that's our stuff," the woman with the bow said.

12

They were both young, probably in their mid-twenties. They were dressed in a motley assortment of wool and cast-off camouflage hunting clothes.

They didn't look hostile, but they didn't look all that friendly either. The rifle was slung over the guy's shoulder, and the woman with the bow didn't have an arrow on the string. They were all in a quiver on her back. Tye didn't put his hand on his gun, but he didn't let it get all that far away, either.

"This stuff belonged to my son," Grace said. She clutched the bottle of vitamins to her chest.

"Your son?" The guy with the rifle asked as he took a step forward. "You're Christopher's mother?"

She nodded, looking back and forth between the two of them. Tye couldn't tell if she was mad, scared, or some mixture of both.

"Where is he?" the woman with the bow asked.

"He's dead," Grace said.

The woman's eyes widened, and her mouth dropped open. "Oh no," she said. The guy just stood there impassively.

Another man walked up. He looked older, maybe thirty, and was taller than the other two, with long hair and a full beard. He wasn't visibly armed, save for a belt knife.

"I think we're getting off to a bad start. My name is Alex. This is Penny and Weasel," he said. "Did you say Christopher was dead?"

Grace took a deep breath. To Tye, it seemed like every time she said it, it got a little easier. He guessed that was a good thing.

"We found him dead. Shot in the back," Grace said.

Alex looked off into the distance for a moment, blinking back tears, then he walked up and took Grace's hand. "I'm so sorry. We really loved your son."

"Are you the people he's been living with?"

Alex nodded. "Yes. For almost a year now."

As far as Tye could tell, the surprise and sadness were genuine. He wished Gary were here. Gary was better at stuff like this.

"I need help figuring out who killed him," Grace said.

"We're camped a couple miles away. Will you come with us?"

She nodded, agreeing without consulting Tye, which irritated him a little, but he didn't blame her.

A look passed between Penny and Alex that he didn't know how to read.

"There's somebody else you should meet," Alex said. "Are you up for the walk?"

Grace nodded, and they set out. Thankfully, Weasel went first, staying about fifty yards ahead. Tye really didn't want anyone he didn't know behind him with a rifle.

They didn't talk as they walked. Alex, Penny, and Weasel were almost silent as they moved through the woods. They paralleled the road, following the occasional game trail, and picking the quietest route through the underbrush, which was usually the most efficient. Weasel was in the lead, with Alex behind and to his right, and Penny to his left. Tye and Grace hung back behind all three.

Penny slid an arrow out of her quiver and put it on the string. It was a blunt. Instead of a sharp broadhead, the arrowhead was a flat-faced hexagonal piece of metal. It was designed to kill small game.

Tye saw the grouse. It froze on a branch just ahead of Penny. He knew if he spoke, he'd spook it, so he held his tongue. Alex and Weasel were doing a good job of keeping track of her in their peripheral vision, because they froze, too. Grace took another couple of steps and the grouse almost bolted. Tye could see it tense, ready to take flight. Grace stopped and opened her mouth to say something, but Tye held a finger to his lips.

In one fluid motion, Penny drew, aimed, and loosed the arrow. It struck the bird at the base of its neck with a meaty thwack, and it dropped out of the tree. Weasel pounced on it, ready to grab it in case it fluttered off, but it was already dead. Alex started poking around in the ferns, looking for the arrow.

Penny took the grouse from Weasel and handed him her bow. She put a foot on either wing and pulled up on the bird's feet, pulling the guts out along with the legs. Tossing the innards aside, she drew a small sharp knife from a sheath on her belt and, with a couple of swipes of her knife, had two palm-sized pieces of breast meat cut off the bone. She wrapped them up in a clean cloth and deposited them in her shoulder bag.

Weasel handed her the bow, and Alex gave her the arrow. They both gave her a thumbs-up and they continued on their way.

The whole thing had taken maybe two minutes. The bird wouldn't yield that many calories, but it was something. One thing Tye had learned from his studies of Indigenous people was they didn't "go hunting" so much as they were always on the lookout for targets of opportunity like the grouse.

At a break in the heavy salmonberry that grew along the road, they paused and listened before crossing. The spot was at a bend. If they'd crossed in a straight stretch of road, they would have been visible for several hundred yards in either direction. Here at the bend, the line of sight was maybe half that.

They were on the outskirts of the Indian Heaven Wilderness Area where there were no vehicles or machinery allowed. The road was the boundary between the national forest and the wilderness area. The terrain was unusually flat for the Cascade Mountains. Tye had hunted elk up here and was managing to stay roughly oriented without having to pull out his map.

Grace leaned over next to him and whispered in his ear. "I am totally lost."

"It's okay. There should be a little spur road up ahead."

He could see a break in the vegetation up ahead. Alex, Penny, and Weasel started moving slowly, and stopped just inside the tree line. The road was rutted and clearly hadn't been maintained in years. If the map in Tye's head was correct, they were at least half a mile from the main road, and if he remembered correctly, a dirt berm had been constructed to keep vehicle traffic out of here.

It took him a minute to realize he was looking at two vehicles hidden under camouflage net and some native vegetation. There was a passenger van and a one-ton truck under there. They'd both been painted a flat, greenish gray, and the windows had been covered with burlap. The side-view mirrors were folded in to keep reflections down.

Apparently satisfied that no one had tampered with the vehicles, the three set out again, keeping a quick, ground-eating pace for just over half an hour. Tye guessed they'd gone a mile, maybe a mile and a quarter, when he started seeing snares hidden in the woods. They were simple loop snares placed in gaps in the underbrush where brush rabbits and similar animals were likely to travel. Penny clearly had the locations memorized. She went from snare to snare, checking for game. None of them held an animal.

The wind shifted. Tye smelled woodsmoke and food cooking. They came out in a clearing into a neatly organized camp.

There were several large backpacking tents and one canvas teepee. A couple of tables had been fashioned from timbers bound together with cordage, and there were coolers and boxes stacked underneath. A large cast-iron pot bubbled over a big firepit. A young man clad in a buckskin shirt stirred the contents with a long wooden spoon. He saw Tye and Grace with the others and did a double take.

"Nick, this is Grace," Alex said. "She's Christopher's mother. This is her friend Tye."

He smiled at Grace, then when he saw that Tye was carrying Christopher's blue backpack, his face fell.

Tye heard a rustle in the bushes behind him and to the left. He turned to see a young woman standing there. She had long blond hair and wore a woven hat. A bucket full of Oregon grape root dangled from each hand. She was bundled up in an old military field jacket.

She was also very obviously pregnant.

"What are you doing with Christopher's backpack," she said, staring at Tye. "Is that a bullet hole? Is that blood?"

Alex stepped around Tye and put a hand on each of her shoulders.

"I'm sorry, Robin."

She dropped the buckets and began to cry.

13

The same scene was reported several times again over the next few minutes as another half-dozen people walked into camp, singly or in pairs. Tye sat back and watched, unsure of what else to do. The members of the group seemed about evenly split between men and women. They were all in their early to mid-twenties, with long hair, plenty of tattoos, and the occasional piercing. Clothing was a mixture of thrift store castoffs. Tye had been around more than enough people who wore old clothes as some kind of statement about how thrifty they were, or to show how they were rejecting consumerism. These people just looked like they needed clothes while they got down to the business of trying to feed themselves.

Everyone seemed to be going out of their way to comfort Robin, who was still weeping inconsolably. Alex broke away and spoke softly in Grace's ear. He caught Tye's eye and looked at the large teepee. They all ducked inside. In the dimness, Tye saw food and gear stacked in boxes and crates. As they were getting settled, Penny slipped in after them. She was carrying a kettle of water that had been sitting over the fire.

"We really should have told you about that before we brought you into camp," Penny said with a look at Alex.

"Is that my son's baby?" Grace asked.

"It's really not our place to say," Alex said.

"Yes," Penny said an instant later. "It's Christopher's baby."

Alex shot her an annoyed look.

"He didn't tell me," Grace all but whispered. "Why didn't he tell me?"

"This is quite a bit to take in," Alex said. He pulled some mugs from a box. "Tea?" he asked.

Grace nodded.

Alex poured tea. It was some kind of herbal mixture. Gary probably could have made an educated guess at what plants were in it, but all Tye could tell for sure was it had some mint and didn't taste too terrible.

"Who are you people?" Grace blurted out after a sip of the tea.

Penny and Alex looked at each other, and by some unspoken agreement, Alex answered.

"Have you heard of rewilding?" Alex asked.

"Yes. Chris talked about it. Living out in the woods and stuff."

"There's a little more to it than that. We're trying to revive the hunter-gatherer way of life, live as close to the land as we can."

"Hunter-gatherer? Nobody can live like that anymore."

"I'd argue that seven billion people can't keep burning up fossil fuels and living on fast food for very long, either. Sooner or later, everybody might be a hunter-gatherer again. We're just ahead of the curve," Alex said.

"But you've got grocery store food. Christopher was bringing you beans and rice. You've got a van and a truck hidden out there in the woods."

Alex shrugged. "We can't go from depending on industrial economy to living the way we want to live overnight. Every day, we become less dependent. Right now, we have to supplement our nutrition with outside food, and use vehicles to move from one national forest to another. We can't stay in the same place for too long without breaking some kind of law."

Grace was staring into her tea. "Do you know who killed my son?"

"We don't," Alex said. "He set out into town a few days back to buy some supplies. At first, we didn't worry too much. Sometimes it's hard to get a ride back. We started looking for him yesterday."

"Why was he working with an environmental law firm?" Tye asked.

Alex and Penny looked at each other.

"Shit," Alex said under his breath. "He raised the issue of getting involved with fighting a nearby timber operation, but there isn't consensus within the group about how much we should get involved in environmental activism."

"That's because we need to stay below the radar and set up a long-term alternative to industrial society, not try to fight battles in a losing war," Penny said.

"But we have to make sure there's some wild lands left for us to go to," Alex shot back. Tye had the feeling he was watching a family argument that had been acted out dozens of times with no resolution.

They both took a deep breath and stopped talking.

"Anyway," Penny said. "The guy from that law firm tried to get us to keep an eye on that logging site, but we turned him down. Some of us suspected Christopher was meeting with them on the sly, though."

"The guy from the law firm?" Tye asked. "Old guy? Red pickup? Name's Willie?"

"That's him," Penny said. She gave a slight shudder when she said it.

"Can you tell us more about finding Christopher?" Alex asked, with a glance toward Grace.

She told him the story of why she'd hired Tye and how they'd found Christopher's body.

While he listened, Tye thought about the camp. The vehicles parked under the camouflage nets hadn't been moved in quite some time, so unless they had access to another vehicle, they probably weren't the people that broke into Grace's house. He really wanted to get his hands on the rifle that Weasel had been carrying, though.

Penny and Alex listened intently while Grace explained.

"None of this makes any sense," Alex said.

Penny was shaking her head. "I agree. I really don't know why anyone would want to kill Christopher. He was a nice guy. He got along with everyone. Some of the people that are drawn to this kind of life are difficult, but Christopher seemed like he would have been happy even if he lived in the city. He just seemed happier out here."

"What if the motive wasn't personal?" Tye asked. "What would somebody have to gain by killing Christopher?"

"That doesn't make any sense either," Alex said. "What is there to gain? He didn't really own anything. If he had two shirts, he'd give one away to somebody who needed one. He sold his truck not long after he met us, to help fund the purchase of our van."

There was almost a minute of one of those uncomfortable silences that Tye always debated whether to attempt to fill, then they heard the sound of a flute playing the same three notes over and over.

"That's dinner," Alex said. "Will you eat with us?"

Tye looked at Grace and she nodded. They rose and walked outside.

Dinner was communal. Everybody got a bowl full of the soup from the kettle. It was heavy on beans and rice, with some seasoning and strips of dried meat that had been allowed to reconstitute. Leif, the cook, had sliced up the grouse meat, cooked it a little over the fire, and then added it as well. It was bland, but substantial fare. Robin grabbed Grace as soon as she filled her bowl, and soon the two of them were in deep conversation. Tye found an open seat on the other side of the circle, next to Weasel. The rifle was nowhere to be seen.

"So, what were you hunting today with the rifle?" Tye asked.

"Bear. It's the only thing open," Weasel answered around a mouthful of soup.

Tye nodded. Deer-hunting season had just ended, and elk season wouldn't open for a few more days. One of the many open questions in Tye's mind was how well this group obeyed the fish and game laws.

On the one hand, getting caught poaching could be ruinously expensive, with fines, seized equipment, and lost privileges, but on the other hand, the odds of getting caught this far from a paved road were almost too small to calculate.

"Seen anything?" Tye asked.

"I took a shot at a big boar bear a couple of days ago, but I missed. It was only a hundred yards, so I think the scope might be off. I need to check the zero, but we've only got two rounds left. I thought I'd just not pull the trigger unless I saw something super close."

Scopes on rifles could get knocked out of adjustment, causing the bullet to strike inches or even feet from the intended point of impact. The only real way to check that it was in proper alignment was to go shoot the gun. Re-zeroing the scope could easily consume half a box of ammo if it was grossly out of alignment. Tye didn't mention the box of ammunition in his backpack. For right now, he thought he'd keep it to himself.

"Is that the only firearm you guys use?" Tye asked.

Weasel nodded and chewed. "It's a shared rifle. Everybody in the group buys licenses and tags. Some of us buy archery tags, some modern firearm. It spreads our chances around."

Weasel was distracted as they talked. He kept looking over at Grace and Robin. Tye wasn't sure which one held his attention until Robin got up and walked into the woods for a few minutes. Weasel kept staring at the spot where she'd disappeared, caught himself staring and looked away, then went back to it.

When she came back into view, Tye recognized the look on his face. It was the face of a man who wanted a woman he knew didn't want him. He'd been in that spot himself a time or two, and it had been the drive behind more than one of his bad decisions.

Dessert was huckleberries and some nicely roasted native beaked hazelnuts. Tye wasn't close to full, but he didn't go back for seconds. These people were living pretty close to the bone, and he had some food stashed in his backpack.

When the meal was finished, Robin and Grace were still talking. Tye helped clean up, pitching in wherever he saw a need.

Penny grabbed a bucket and handed another to Tye. "You mind helping me fetch water?"

Tye followed him down to a creek. Penny checked snares as they went.

"Was there ammo in Christopher's backpack?" Penny asked without preamble as she filled a bucket.

"Yep," Tye said as he filled his own.

"You have it?"

"Yep." As far as Tye was concerned, that was the way he wanted things to stay. There were apparently two guns in the camp, and Tye had one of them, and most of the ammo for the second.

"Are you two spending the night?" Penny asked.

"I suspect we will if you're offering. I don't think Grace is keeping track of time. The straight-line hike would take us through some thick woods in the dark, and going by road would be even longer."

"I'm wondering if you'd be willing to bring that ammo and go with me tomorrow and check the zero on that rifle."

"I could do that. Weasel tells me he took a pretty easy shot at a bear, but he missed."

"Yeah. That's what he said."

They both hefted the buckets and started back. Forty pounds of water wasn't an easy load to hang off the end of an arm. It would have almost been easier with the second bucket to balance things out.

"He wants her, doesn't he?" Tye asked.

Penny was silent for a while, navigating the twists in the trail carefully to spill as little of the water as possible.

"He went after Robin for a while. Weasel sucks at taking hints. Finally, she let him down as easy as she could, but she had to be pretty direct. That was right around the time Chris joined us. He and Robin took up pretty quick."

Penny put her bucket down next to a clump of rosehips neither of them had seen on the walk out. It was amazing how different a trail could look when you walked it in the other direction. She pulled a mesh bag out of a pocket, unfolded it, and started picking rosehips. Tye eased his own bucket down and joined her.

"That cause friction between Weasel and Christopher?"

"Not exactly. I think at first Weasel wanted to dislike him but couldn't. Everybody liked Christopher. I'm not even sure it's that he still wants Robin. I think he likes the idea of Robin, somebody like her."

That sounded awful familiar to Tye.

"It must get complicated in a group like this," Tye said.

Penny picked a particularly fat rosehip, and apparently unable to resist temptation, popped it in her mouth.

"It does," she said as he chewed. "Relationships form and end. Not everybody here had the most healthy childhoods. At least a couple of our folks got kicked out of the house for being gay. Most of us are pretty young. It's like a college dorm out in the middle of the woods, but we all get through."

"How did you wind up as a leader?"

She laughed. "Technically, we're leaderless, but it sure doesn't feel that way most of the time. Alex and I have just been at this longer than anyone else." She spit out the pulp and seeds from the rosehip. There were tiny hairs inside that could irritate a person's throat and gut if swallowed.

Penny stopped picking when they'd taken about two thirds of the rosehips, which was right when Tye would have quit. You always left enough for the birds and bears, and for the plant to reproduce. They both grabbed their buckets again.

"Anybody ever leave the group?"

"Plenty," she said. "We'd go to a primitive-skills gathering and come away with half a dozen people who wanted to live like us but would quit after the first month when they realized they couldn't order a pizza on a cell phone. I hate to say it, but we've learned to be a little more insular, and less inviting. People who don't stick are just a drain."

That made sense to Tye.

"Anybody ever get asked to leave?"

"Not yet. I've felt like we were getting close a couple of times, but the person always left of their own accord."

"The food part is hard, but the people part is harder."

Penny shot a glance over his shoulder. "Any more TV shows in your future?"

Tye had wondered if he'd been recognized. The primitive-skills community was small, and there weren't many degrees of separation between people.

"Maybe I'll drag a camera crew out and find you guys again."

Penny blinked and a look of almost horror crossed her face, then she realized Tye was joking.

"Funny, not funny," she said with a laugh.

"You don't know that half of it."

They deposited their buckets back at camp. A shy young woman named Meadow was showing several other people how to make reverse wrap cordage with nettle fiber. She was good at it but stuttered whenever anyone looked directly at her. The other students were kind and patient, and Tye got the idea that several of them knew perfectly well how to do it. He picked up some strands of fiber and followed along, careful not to get ahead of the lesson.

It was simple meditative work. Cordage was essential in the woods. Nettle fibers could be made into bow strings, twine for lashings, and even heavy rope. It would take hours to make a substantial length. It was prone to breakage due to abrasion and had a finite life. For a few dollars, a person could buy a roll of parachute cord, but there was a deep satisfaction that came from making as many of the things that you needed yourself.

This was a kind of calculation that Tye constantly engaged in. He could trade his time to an employer in return for money to buy the things he needed, or he could just use the time to do it himself. He'd concentrated on needing as little as possible, and doing as much for himself as he could, but these folks were taking it to another level.

The time passed quicker than he would have expected, and he was surprised how comfortable he was among strangers. Slowly people drifted away to bed, singly and in couples, until Tye was left alone by the fire. Grace finally walked up from wherever she'd disappeared, followed by Penny.

"I guess we're spending the night," she said. "I sort of lost track of time."

"We can do that," Tye said as he stood and dusted little pieces of nettle fiber off his pants.

"We'll put you two in the teepee?" Penny asked, looking from Tye to Grace.

"That's fine," Grace said.

Tye had a lightweight sleeping bag in his pack, so he left the stack of blankets in the tepee to Grace. She kept glancing at the door as she fiddled with the blankets.

"Uh, are you okay with me being in here tonight?" Tye asked. "Because if you're not, I can sleep outside by the fire."

She stopped fidgeting and gave one last look toward the door "Strangely, I am. I figure I've been stuck out in the woods with you for long enough that you must not be a secret serial killer or something."

"Uh... thanks."

Her headlamp was sitting on a bag of rice, and in the dim light he saw her smile. She leaned over and whispered in his ear, "I want to look at the camera and notebook."

He nodded and pulled the camera out of his bag. Grace made herself a nest of a couple of blankets to sleep on and pulled the rest over herself. Outside, the sounds of camp diminished until finally there was silence.

He fumbled with the camera before she finally lost patience and pulled it from his hands. She pressed the right combination of buttons and the contents of the camera's memory card displayed on the screen.

"This is a crap camera," she said as she scrolled through.

The pictures were grainy, and clearly had been taken from quite a distance, at the limit of the little camera's zoom. They showed logging equipment, cutting down trees, then stacking the logs on trucks. The final two shots were of a backhoe digging in the dirt beside the logging road. They had been shot at dusk, just before the light fell to the point that the camera would be useless.

"I don't understand what's so important about these," Grace said. "Everybody knows they are cutting down trees."

"I don't know. Maybe we'll see something different on a bigger screen?"

Someone stirred outside, and she shut the camera off and hid it under her blanket. They listened to footsteps fading away toward the area that had been designated as the latrine.

"Do you think my son died over those pictures? The ones that don't seem to show anything?"

"I don't know," he said. He thumbed the buttons to look back through the pictures. "Let's look at the notebook."

There was no writing, just pencil sketches. Christopher had been a fair artist, and Tye found himself admiring his work. Tye had always struggled with drawing. The first two thirds of the notebook was full of nature studies, mostly plants with the common and Latin name underneath. The longer he flipped through the book, the more sketches of Robin he saw. Christopher had been a surprisingly good portrait artist as well, at least when it came to drawing Robin's face.

Then the tone of the drawings changed. There were pictures of fallen trees and pits in the ground. Next came a hand-drawn map, with a dotted line of a path leading from an unnamed road to a spot labeled "cave."

The next page was a detailed drawing of a cave entrance, then drawings of dozens of pictographs. There were stylized animals, suns, moons, and people with bows and arrows.

Tye flipped the page and his mouth went dry. The whole page was taken up with a sketch of the Dark Man. Tye knew it was the same figure as the one in his nightmares, not just another random drawing of a silhouetted figure. There was something about the proportions, and the tilt of the head, that made Tye believe he and Christopher had been seeing the same thing.

"None of this makes any sense to me," Grace said.

Tye shut the book and set it aside like it was hot. "Me neither. What did you learn from talking to Robin?"

Grace was quiet for so long he didn't think she was going to answer. He heard footsteps coming back into the camp, and the sound of someone settling back into bed.

"At first, I didn't want to like her. I have this kind of knee-jerk reaction to pretty blond girls that really isn't fair. Do you think she's pretty?"

"Uh... I guess."

"Of course you do. Tall. Blond. Anyway. She's actually a really nice person. She's very thoughtful and kind. Talking to her is like talking to a female version of Christopher. It's all anarcho-primitivism this, rewilding that. It's no wonder they got together. I also think she's crazy."

Her voice was rising a bit. Tye almost tried to shush her, but he didn't want to sound condescending.

"Crazy? How?"

"She wants to have the baby out here in the forest and raise it as some kind of hunter-gatherer. She's not even going to get it a birth certificate or a social security number or anything."

It seemed weird to refer to the baby as an "it," but Tye realized Robin probably hadn't had an X-ray, or CAT scan, or whatever they used to tell whether it was a boy or girl. Ultrasound. That was it.

"What's wrong with that?" he asked.

Her voice rose some more. "How will this kid ever get a job? Or go to college? Or even go to the doctor? It's like he won't even exist."

He took a breath and chose his words carefully. "People lived for thousands of years without any of those things and did just fine."

She didn't answer that for a while, and Tye wondered if he'd done something to make her angry enough to quit talking.

"This is all so weird. No offense, but I thought you were weird. You track animals for a living and live in a teepee."

"Yurt."

"Whatever. And then I meet these people and it's like a whole order of magnitude weirder. But they're nice. And earnest. And all that is left of my son is in that woman's belly."

He didn't know what to say to that, so he just stayed there beside her, listening to her breathe until finally she fell asleep.

14

"Hey, Tye?" It was Penny. "Can we talk?"

"Yeah," Tye's voice was thick with sleep. He managed to extricate himself and slid out of his sleeping bag. Despite the noise, Grace didn't stir from her pile of blankets. He pulled on his jacket and boots before unlacing the door of the teepee. The air outside was cold and damp. A mist hung over the ground and a weak, milky morning light was filtering through the trees to the east.

Alex, Leif, and a couple of other people were warming up with some Tai Chi on the other side of the fire. Penny was standing there with the rifle slung over her shoulder. There was a small knapsack at her feet.

"I was hoping to go check the scope on this rifle and was wondering if you would come along and bring that box of cartridges," Penny said. There was a look of appeal in her eyes. Tye wondered how well Penny had slept, if she'd been awake all night, wondering what had really happened between Weasel and Christopher.

"Coffee," Tye croaked.

She pointed at a kettle on the fire grate. "We only do tea. There is hot water in the kettle."

Tye nodded and reached back inside the teepee to grab his gun belt and backpack. He kept his stuff packed, never let it get strewn out all over the place. He buckled the gun belt around his hip and unzipped the backpack.

Tye's thirty-liter Hill People Gear backpack was his constant companion. It was rarely all the way full, but he always had enough stuff to sustain him for a night or two. Hikers and backpackers had their list of ten essentials, the ten things they considered vital to survival in the wilderness. Tye considered some means of consuming coffee to be one of them. He pulled out a titanium cup and a packet of freeze-dried coffee. Within minutes, he was inhaling the steam coming out of the cup and feeling much better about life in general. He ate a quick breakfast of dried fruit and nuts and felt like a new man.

"Lead on," Tye said.

They walked across the clearing into the tree line. Penny carried the rifle slung muzzle-up with the bolt open, and Tye could look down into the magazine and see that it was unloaded.

"There's a spot about a mile away with a good backstop, so I thought we might shoot the rifle there." Penny patted the butt of the rifle. "Most of us don't really know much about guns. We've debated getting rid of this thing, but to be honest with you, we still get a bunch more animals with this rifle than we do with our bows."

"Bow hunting is hard," Tye said.

Most people thought hunting was as simple as going out and blasting the first animal you saw. In some places back east, that was true. Here in the thick forests of western Washington, far more hunters went home empty-handed than not, at least the ones that were following the rules.

After about a half-hour of walking, they came out into a clearing that Tye guessed was just shy of one hundred yards across. Penny handed Tye the rifle and fixed an eight-inch square of white cardboard to a tree stump with a nail she drove in with a rock. There was a steep bank behind the stump, a more than adequate backstop for rifle practice.

They both put in ear plugs, and Penny fed a couple of cartridges into the magazine of the rifle. Tye could tell she'd done it enough times to understand it, but her movements didn't have the fluidity that came with long practice. She kept the muzzle pointed in a safe direction, which was the most important thing.

Penny dropped into a prone position, and Tye winced. The .30-06 wasn't the most powerful rifle a person could buy, but it still had a healthy thump. Lying prone to shoot gave the best stability, but it would also give the recoil nowhere to go but right into her shoulder. She squirmed around, trying to find the right position. She started out with her eye way too close to the scope, and Tye opened his mouth to say something, but she repositioned her head.

Penny chambered a round, took a deep breath, and pulled the trigger. Even with the plugs, the rifle was loud here in the narrow draw. Tye managed not to flinch and blink, so he saw the bullet impact on the berm. It was even with the target elevation wise, but hit to the left, way off by several feet.

"Way left," Tye said. "Try another one."

She let another round fly. This one was still left by about half as much, but this time, it also hit a couple of feet high.

"Still left," Tye said. "Let's see it."

Penny handed him the rifle. After making sure it was unloaded, Tye unscrewed the caps that covered the scope's adjustment turrets. He stuck the rim of a fired cartridge in the adjustment slot. The dial spun freely, with no resistance. It should have had some friction resistance, or even a series of clicks.

"This might be our problem," Tye said. He pulled the ear plugs out of his ears and motioned for Penny to do the same.

He held the rifle up to his ear and shook it. He could faintly hear something inside rattling around.

"Scope's busted," Tye said. "We should have checked that first and saved your teeth from being rearranged from the recoil."

Penny nodded and rubbed her shoulder. "What do you think happened to it?"

Tye turned the rifle over in his hands and shrugged. "There are no marks on it. My guess? It's a cheap scope, and it just broke. It happens."

"So, Weasel was probably telling the truth when he said he shot at the bear and missed."

As she said it, Penny turned her head and blinked. Tye realized she was trying to hold back a tear and was trying to hide it. Tye turned his attention to the rifle and looked at the broken scope some more, even though there was nothing new to see.

"Sounds like you were worried," Tye said, his eyes still on the rifle.

Penny took a breath. "Most communities like ours fall apart after a while, not because of any practical concern, like getting enough food, but because people fight and argue. I really didn't think Weasel would kill Christopher, but I couldn't get the idea out of my head."

Tye pulled a multi-tool out of his backpack and used it to remove the scope from the rifle. There was a set of metal sights mounted on the barrel. They were less precise at long range but would still work fine here in the dense forests. A hunter would be lucky to see an animal farther away than the length of a football field, much less shoot at it.

Penny offered no objections when Tye dropped prone and fired a few shots to confirm the metal sights were adjusted correctly.

"Works pretty well as long as you keep the range short," he said.

Penny slung it over her shoulder, and they started walking back toward camp.

"Sounds like you've had some concerns about Weasel in particular," Tye said.

"People bring their baggage with them," Penny said. "Most people don't wind up trying to go live like a modern hunter-gatherer because they are completely happy with the way things are going in their life. We've got orphans, abused children, runaways, people who grew up in the foster system. Weasel's history is his own to tell, but he didn't have the best upbringing."

They were following a little brook, and Penny paused at a stand of nettle to gather some leaves for her foraging pouch. Tye pulled a mesh bag from his backpack and joined her, staying mindful not to get stung.

"We all have to cut each other some slack," Penny said. Everybody has their neuroses and hang-ups and ways they are not skillful. The big open questions are always 'how bad does it have to be before somebody can't be part of the group anymore?'"

"Has Weasel been close to that?"

"Yeah. A couple of times. But I don't think he'd kill anybody."

The broken scope seemed to have put Penny at ease, but Tye wasn't so sure. The scope could have been broken after Weasel shot Christopher. He might have even broken it himself, as cover. Not for the first time, Tye felt out of his element. Animals were easy to figure out. Human behavior kept him guessing.

They were quiet the rest of the way back, each busy with their own thoughts. Tye was inclined to like Penny, but someone had killed Christopher not too far from here. Tye was walking around halfway expecting a shot in the back at any moment, and that wasn't helping him feel real social.

When they could hear the sounds of the camp, Penny stopped and held the rifle out to Tye.

"Would you mind carrying this the rest of the way? It's a little heavy."

It seemed odd she wouldn't want to carry it the last few hundred feet to camp, but he didn't argue. He just took the rifle and slung it over his shoulder.

When they returned to camp, Grace had her gear packed at her feet and was sitting and talking with Robin. Their heads were so close they almost touched. Grace hopped to her feet when she saw Tye come out of the trees.

"I told Robin about your friend May," she said without preamble.

"She said she'd be willing to be treated by a midwife, as long as she doesn't use any modern drugs."

"I think she uses mostly herbs," Tye said.

Robin nodded. "That sounds great."

They made quick goodbyes. Tye shook Alex's and Penny's hands. Weasel just stared at them from across camp, his eyes barely leaving Robin.

Robin gave Grace a quick, tight hug, then put Grace's hand on her belly. "Soon I think you'll be a grandma."

Grace swallowed and hugged her again.

"You okay?" Tye asked after they were a hundred yards or so from the camp. "We've got a long walk ahead."

"I have no idea what 'okay' means right now," she said. "I just want to go see if your friend will help Robin. I think she's going to have that baby soon."

"I'm sure she will. It'll just be a matter of finding a time when May can get out here. She's pretty busy."

"There's something I want to do first. I went off into the woods to look at those pictures again. I still can't see anything on them. But there has to be something going on up there at that logging site. Why else would Christopher go up there and take pictures? I want to go check it out."

Tye had been thinking similar thoughts, although he'd been hoping to take Grace back to town and come back by himself. He didn't even bother trying to convince her to agree to that.

The truck was where they'd left it and wasn't sporting any new bullet holes, something you couldn't take for granted up here.

"This ridge right here," Tye said, tapping the map. "It should overlook the logging site. In fact, I'm pretty sure that is where Christopher took those pictures."

"We'll be retracing his steps?" she asked. He couldn't tell if she liked that idea or if it spooked her.

He drove about a mile and a half to another old landing where they could leave the truck. After refilling water bottles from the jugs in the back, and a final map check, they set out. The day was still and clear. The woods were silent. The birds and other animals had been busy in the couple of hours after sunrise, but now they had all gone quiet.

Tye had excellent map and compass skills, but to save time and effort, he turned on the small GPS attached to the strap of his pack. That way, he could keep his awareness focused on not being seen.

The walking was easy. The top of the ridge was flat and wide, with big Western Hemlock trees widely spaced. After about twenty minutes, they heard the far-off clank of machinery and the roar of a big diesel engine. Tye slowed down and started checking the GPS more frequently. He steered them over to the right side of the ridge and stopped short of breaking out into the open.

There below them was the logging site. It was a small operation, mostly confined to the bottom of the narrow valley. Tye focused his binoculars and saw most of the equipment was sitting idle, unusual for a job site like this. A panel truck bounced slowly away from the work site. The road was temporary and would be decommissioned once the job was over. The truck really wasn't suited to the rough surface.

An operator climbed into a harvester that looked like a robot from a science-fiction movie. It had treads and a long, articulated arm. It grasped a tree and ran a cutter head up and down the length of the trunk, stripping off the protruding limbs. Then a saw severed it from the base, and the cutter head grasped the middle of the tree and turned it ninety degrees. The operator drove the harvester over to a trailer and stacked it on top of the other logs.

They sat there for about fifteen minutes, watching. Four trees were turned into timber stacked on the log trailer. Tye realized there were only two people at the job site now that the truck had left. He wondered if that was some kind of safety violation.

Tye was not inherently against logging. He came from a long line of hard-scrabble, blue-collar people that made their living doing things like digging coal and cutting down trees. He would take an item made of wood over something made of plastic any day. But there was something about watching a single man in a giant machine, mowing down in minutes trees that had taken hundreds of years to grow, that was sickening. He felt like he was watching a mugging in progress.

He realized Grace had been busy taking pictures with her cell phone. He scooted over next to her. "Can you really get any detail from this distance?"

"Some," she said. "I can look at it on a bigger screen and maybe we'll see something."

She was grasping at straws, but he didn't want to tell her that. All that was happening here was some guys were cutting down trees. He busied himself with his map, compass, and GPS for a few minutes, estimating the limits of the cut. He could check that against the authorized timber sale later but doubted he would find a serious discrepancy. The Forest Service was pretty friendly with the timber companies, but they wouldn't let a logging operation go too far outside the boundaries of the sale.

The harvester operator stacked another log on the truck. Tye checked his watch. There were still hours to go until sunset, and this scene was liable to repeat until then, with little variation. He was tired and hungry and wanted a chance to sit down and talk with Gary. His head wasn't hurting, but he felt that tingle on the back of his scalp and the sharp metallic taste that warned him a migraine was imminent. He might be able to stave it off by being still in a dark room for a while, but most likely he was just going to have to ride it out.

"I'm not sure we're going to see anything different up here," he said. "I was thinking we could head back and ask May to come check out Robin tomorrow."

15

——————

"Well, at least I don't see any new bullet holes," Tye said. He squatted behind a patch of ferns about a hundred yards from his truck. They were on a slope maybe a hundred feet above it, and he could just see it through the trees. Out of long habit, Tye checked the area around the truck before walking down. Twice at remote trailheads, he'd found his windows smashed and stuff stolen from the cab, and one of those times he'd walked up on the perpetrator digging through his glove box and was nearly stabbed with a screwdriver.

This time he'd noticed the truck looked oddly tilted and pulled out his monocular. Both tires on the side facing him were flat, and he was willing to bet the ones on the other side were as well.

"Did we run over something on the way in?" Grace asked from beside him.

"Doubt it. They were fine a couple of hours ago."

He didn't see anyone around the truck, but his hand still brushed the grip of his revolver as he stood. Tye picked his way carefully down the slope to survey the damage.

All four tires were flat. The valve stems had been cut from each tire. Thankfully, the vandal hadn't slashed the sidewalls, but the truck still wasn't going anywhere under its own power.

"I don't suppose you can fix that."

"Nope. I'm all out of valve stems." He sighed. He'd been looking forward to going home.

Tye circled the truck. The gravel was too coarse to hold a track. There were a few pieces of overturned gravel. They might have been from the person who slashed the tires, or maybe not. He walked bent over up the road.

"Do you think the person who shot Christopher did this?"

"Probably not," he said. "Since they are the shooting kind, they could have just hidden up on the ridge and picked us off as we walked back to the truck."

Her foot scuffed on the gravel as she came to an abrupt halt. "What are we going to do? We are miles from anywhere and the truck is disabled."

For the first time, he noticed the note of panic in her voice that had been there for the last minute or so.

"Hey," he said. "I'm sorry. We're gonna be fine. I have plenty of gear in the truck."

He abandoned the track of the person who had slashed the tires. It probably wouldn't tell him much anyway. Instead, he unlocked the camper shell that covered the bed of his pickup.

"Gear is fine, but how are we going to get out of here?"

"I've got a gadget in here that should help us out."

First, he pulled out a folding camp chair and set it up for Grace. She settled into it gratefully. Her hands were shaking, and he realized, not for the first time, how different he was from most people. Being stranded out in the wilderness with a disabled vehicle was a catastrophe for her, a mild inconvenience for him.

He'd built a wood sleeping platform on one side of the pickup bed, wide enough for an inflatable mat and sleeping bag. From one of the locking storage compartments underneath the platform, he pulled a Garmin InReach satellite communicator.

Kaity had insisted they buy the device with profits from their business. He'd been resistant at first but had to admit it was about to come in handy.

He laboriously typed out a message to Gary.

Truck tires slashed. Could use a pick-up. The InReach had a handy feature that let him automatically send his location along with the message, so he didn't have to type in all the digits.

"Now what?" Grace asked. She sounded a little calmer.

"Might be a while before Gary thinks to look at his computer screen," Tye said. He busied himself with making coffee. It was rare that he indulged himself with anything fancy, but on occasion he treated himself to a pound of coffee beans from Pull Caffé, an outfit that used a woodfired coffee roaster. They were located only a few miles from Tye's property. He'd been amazed one day when he'd been out scouting for deer sign to find the heavenly smell of roasting coffee beans wafting through the forest.

He used a hand-cranked grinder while his little backpacking stove heated the water. He'd just poured the beans and water into his French press when the InReach beeped.

The rear end on the Scout is out again. I'm afraid we'd bend May's car getting to you. Kaity is working tonight but could come up in her Jeep after. I'm wondering if she should wait until morning.

Tye sighed. Gary's International Scout had been an excellent backcountry vehicle when it had been built almost fifty years ago. Nowadays, it spent almost as much time broken down as it did running.

The morning works, Tye typed. *We'll either camp in the truck or at this location.* He painstakingly typed in the coordinates of Penny's camp. Then added, *Can May come? There's a pregnant woman living in the woods up here.*

There was a long pause, and Tye imagined Gary looking for May on the property or calling her.

The InReach dinged again. *Sounds like there have been some interesting developments. May can come. See you in the morning.*

"So, we could camp here, or go back to where Robin is?" Grace asked.

"Up to you," Tye said. "Are you up to the walk back to their camp? It's a couple miles. You can sleep in the truck. I have a tent I can use to sleep out here."

Grace stood with her hands on her hips. "I feel like I should spend as much time with Robin as I can," she said. "I still can't believe I'm going to be a grandmother."

"That works," Tye said. "Let's have coffee first."

16

Penny and the rest were surprised to see them walk back into camp. Grace made a beeline for Robin while Tye explained about the disabled truck.

He'd taken a larger backpack from the bed of his truck, and as he talked, he unloaded it, placing a tin of coffee and a couple bags of beans and rice next to the cook fire. The coffee was cheap grocery store stuff, not his prized Pull Caffé.

"You'd be welcome to stay even without the food," Penny said, "but we do appreciate it."

She gave him an appraising look he couldn't quite read. He was made uncomfortable by the attraction he felt for her. It seemed out of place considering how recently he'd met her. He wondered if she felt the same way.

Tye didn't realize how famished he was until they all sat down to share a meal. He chewed his food and thought about the day, trying to put it all into perspective. Penny sat next to him, not saying anything, but he was aware of her presence the whole time.

Tye pitched in to clean up the dishes without being asked. Leif ran the camp kitchen like a benign drill sergeant, which Tye could appreciate. When people thought about the risks associated with living in the backcountry, they often thought of bears and mountain lions, but failed to account for the risk of illness from dishes poorly washed without the benefit of running water.

Once everything was washed and dried to Leif's satisfaction, folks started gathering around a central firepit. Somebody produced a guitar and started singing.

Tye wandered off from the camp. They were nice people, and welcoming enough, but spending a couple of hours in the lively presence of a bunch of strangers left him feeling a bit overwhelmed. Tye had come to accept his extreme introversion. He could be happy with his own company for weeks. He craved connection with a handful of like-minded people but could happily avoid small talk and social interaction forever. He'd long ago realized he'd never be considered a "fun" person and had made peace with it.

The faint trail he'd been following ended at a small lake. The Indian Heaven wilderness was potholed with dozens of lakes. The bigger ones had names and were on established hiking trails, but there were plenty of smaller lakes like this one that were unnamed.

Only a faint sliver of sun peeked over the mountains. It would be dark in twenty minutes or so, he reckoned. He was grateful for his wool pullover. Cool air was already descending from the higher elevations. The breeze rustled the surrounding trees.

Tye skirted the edge of the lake, staying close to the cover offered by the trees and shadows. He did that out of subconscious habit, born of years of hunting with a bow and arrow. When he was in the woods, he rarely stepped out into the open or crossed an exposed area.

He found a spot to sit among a cluster of ferns and watched the lake. Apparently, he wasn't the first to enjoy this spot. The vegetation was pressed down in a circle. At first, he assumed it was where a deer had bedded down, but he saw the imprint of two heel marks. A human had definitely sat here and watched the lake, just as he was about to do.

It was his habit to just sit quietly in the woods at sunset and sunrise as often as he could. It was his way of clearing his head and connecting with the world around him. Dawn and dusk were excellent times to see animals as well.

A belted kingfisher cruised low over the water. The stocky little bird was one of Tye's favorites. It zoomed back and forth, looking for bugs.

To his right, some gray jays hopped from branch to branch, clearly watching something move through the forest below them.

Penny scuffed her foot in the forest duff when she was still about fifteen yards from him. He suspected she did it out of politeness, to let him know she was coming.

He nodded and motioned her over. She was silent, moving through the woods as she walked over, then sat down next to him.

"You found my spot," she murmured, just loud enough to hear.

"It's a good spot," he said. "I can leave if you want it to yourself."

"I'd rather sit here with you," she said.

He felt like there were quite a few things implied in that sentence, but he didn't say anything. They sat there for a while, her shoulder lightly pressed against his, and watched the lake. The fact that she chose to sit so close to him seemed like an invitation, but he always felt unsure of himself when he tried to read situations like this.

"I wanted to kick Chris out," she said after a few minutes. "But the others wouldn't let me."

The breeze blew across the lake, bringing with it the rich smell of the mud on the shoreline.

"Why?"

"We knew about the work he was doing for the environmental law firm. That's why we're up here at this elevation in November. He wanted us all to join in with him. He had this vision that we would become this group of environmentalist guerilla freedom fighters, spying on logging companies. I can't do that."

"Why not?"

"I'm a convicted felon."

"I didn't see that coming," Tye said.

"Most people don't," she said. "It was when I was in college. I was a member of the Cascade Forest Freedom Fighters. You've heard of it?"

He nodded. "That's the group that protested that big timber sale in Southern Oregon?"

"That's the one."

"What did you do?"

"Some bulldozers burned in the middle of the night."

The kingfisher was no longer flying over the lake. It had retired to its night roost. In its place, he saw a bat flittering about, looking for bugs.

"How long?" he asked.

"I did eighteen months in a federal correctional institution in Ashland, Kentucky, then a year of post-prison supervision after that. I got off lucky. It was a weak case. I could have rolled the dice on a trial, but I could have wound up with twenty years. That's more than most rapists get."

"Wow," he said. The thought of being locked up in a cage for twenty years made his skin crawl.

"I have to be careful. During my post-prison time, I could have been sent back inside for associating with anybody in the environmental movement. Some of them blackballed me because they thought I must have been an informant because I received such a light sentence."

He nodded.

"I can't go back inside. My days as an environmental freedom fighter are over. If I get caught again, the FBI will crucify me, even if they have to make up most of the evidence. The rest of the world can go to hell. I just want to live in the woods and be left alone."

"How did the rest of the group feel about that?"

"Most of them felt the same way I do. The compromise was we'd stay up here and let Chris play commando, while the rest of us went about our normal routine. His little mission dragged on for weeks, and now we're stuck at four thousand feet in November, and Robin doesn't want to move until the baby is born."

He sat there for a minute, letting everything she's said sink in.

Movement on the other side of the lake caught his eye. At first, he thought it was deer, or elk, then he realized he was watching two people walking toward each other on the lake shore.

Tye nudged Penny and nodded in the direction of the two figures. Tye and Penny both hunched down to hide more of their silhouettes behind the ferns.

The sun was mostly set, with just a faint glow in the western sky. The moon had not quite risen, so everything was dim and indistinct. Tye turned his head slightly, so he could watch the two in his peripheral vision, which worked better in the dim light. He noticed Penny doing the same.

One figure was taller than the other, and he got the impression the person was wearing a broad-brimmed hat. The wind was blowing intermittently across the lake, and for a few seconds, Tye caught a snatch of conversation, but not enough to recognize the voices.

They talked for several minutes. The smaller figure gesticulated wildly, and Tye heard raised voices. Then things seemed to settle. He was acutely aware of Penny's hip and shoulder pressed against his, and the smell of her hair.

The two figures broke apart, the taller going off to the east, the smaller to the west. Tye knew there was a disused hiking trail over on that side that would eventually lead to a trailhead a couple miles away.

"That was Weasel," Penny whispered in his ear.

"How do you know?"

"I could just tell by the body language," she said. "Did you recognize the other person?"

"Didn't."

That wasn't entirely true. As they'd crouched behind the ferns, spying on the pair across the lake, the skies had cleared. The moon was just past full and was barely starting to rise, but the silvery light had shown him a glimpse of a lanky figure wearing a cowboy hat. He suspected he knew who it was.

"I'm going to see if I can follow Weasel," Penny said. "Do you want to go over there and see if you can find any tracks of the other person?"

He studied the situation. He'd have a walk of a few hundred yards around the perimeter of the lake, but the bank was free of vegetation, and it should be an easy walk, even without using an artificial light.

"Yup. I'll do that."

"K. Give me a few minutes to slip away before you start. Meet me back at camp and we can share what we find."

She stood slowly, then crept away. Tye was impressed at how quiet she was. He waited about five minutes, then rose himself. Two people moving away a few minutes apart would cause less disturbance than both of them getting up at once.

He elected to walk around the perimeter of the lake, sticking as close to the shadows of the trees just beyond the beach as much as he could. His other two options were to stumble blindly through the woods, making noise, or stumble through the woods with his flashlight turned on.

The night was cooling off quickly. Cloudy nights were often warmer than clear ones. The clouds trapped some heat. Tye's pack was back at the camp, and he wished he had an extra insulation layer with him. He patted his pockets, making sure his lighter and flashlight were there, and checked to make sure his Buck knife was on his belt.

He skirted around the lake, passing a spot where a bunch of elk had come down to the water's edge within the last few days.

Soon he was on the opposite side of the lake from where he and Penny had hidden. In addition to the powerful flashlight in his pocket, he had a much smaller red LED light on his key ring. He fished it out of his pocket and knelt to examine the ground.

There were two sets of prints. One was consistent with the moccasins Weasel wore. He traced the outline of the other set with his finger.

It was the clear imprint of a cowboy boot—a man's, judging by the size. Tye was willing to bet he knew exactly which skinny, shanked environmental lawyer was wearing them, too.

"Willie," he said under his breath.

He followed the trail. Willie wasn't trying to hide his sign, which wouldn't have been easy in a pair of hard-soled cowboy boots anyway. As he suspected, Willie had turned onto the abandoned hiking trail, taking long strides like he was in a hurry.

Tye followed quickly, intending to catch up to the man and demand he explain what the hell was going on. At times Willie had intimidated Tye, but now he was tired of being jerked around, with only a vague understanding of what was going on.

The trail stopped.

Tye had been flicking his red light on from time to time, verifying that the boot tracks were still there in the duff, though he doubted Willie would have stepped off the trail.

He cast about, looking for a boot track. All he saw were coyote tracks.

He debated using his more powerful white light, but instead backtracked using the dim red LED.

He found the last boot track, a half dozen feet behind where he'd stopped.

The trail just ended. He looked carefully. Willie hadn't stepped off, Tye was sure of it. Tye knew every man-tracking and counter-tracking trick in the book. A skilled tracker could puzzle them out, eventually. All they did was slow the tracker, giving the quarry time to open the gap.

What he was trying to ignore was the fact that the set of coyote tracks started at the same time the set of cowboy boot tracks ended.

Off in the distance, he heard the rumble of a big V8 engine coming to life. It idled for a few seconds, then the sound faded. Whoever was driving was going fast, working through the gears and running the engine up to full song through the glasspack mufflers.

Tye looked at the last boot track and the first coyote track one last time, then turned off his light.

"Son of a bitch," he said.

17

W hen Tye walked back into camp, things were quiet except for the heated argument Penny, Alex, and Weasel were having in hushed tones over at the edge of the firelight. Everybody else was either in bed or sitting on the opposite side of the fire from the arguing threesome, playing some kind of dice game and pretending they couldn't hear the conflict.

Penny shot Tye a look and shook her head, so he sat down on a cut round of wood next to the fire and warmed up for a few minutes. He hadn't wanted to walk into the middle of someone else's family argument anyway.

Meadow sat next to him.

"Do you know where Grace is?" Tye asked.

"She and Robin are already in their tent," she said, covering her mouth as she talked. "Robin is pretty tired these days."

The argument reached a crescendo. Weasel said something about "spying on me" and stalked off into the woods. Penny threw her hands in the air, then she and Alex walked off in the other direction.

Tye sighed. Arguments and drama exhausted him, and he wanted nothing more than to be back in his yurt by the woodstove, curled up with a book and a tumbler full of Gary's applejack. Maybe tomorrow night.

He waved good night to the folks still around the fire and a few minutes later was settled into his sleeping bag in the supply tent. He was bone tired, and a few minutes earlier would have sworn that he could fall asleep in a matter of moments, but instead he just stared at the roof of the tent, willing sleep to come. By now, the moon had fully risen, and the silver light filtered through the white tent canvas.

Finally, he drifted into that half-awake, half-asleep state where he could still hear every noise around camp. The dice game ended with murmured good nights. He thought he heard Alex's voice. He strained to hear Penny but didn't hear her voice.

He must have fallen asleep eventually, because he found himself sitting outside around the fire with Christopher. The campfire had burned down to a bed of red coals, but there was enough light for Tye to see the gaping wound in Christopher's chest. Christopher sat hunched over on a round of wood with his hands between his knees, looking forlornly at the tent where Robin and Grace slept.

When Tye opened his mouth to speak, no sound came out.

Christopher looked at Tye, then stood and walked into the woods, motioning for Tye to follow.

Tye followed Christopher through the forest. It was like following a video at a high speed. The trees blurred by. Occasionally Christopher would slow to a normal speed, look at some landmark like a fallen tree or a particular boulder, look at Tye, and then it was like he hit the fast-forward button again.

The trip ended at a jagged crack in a rock face. As he stood in front of it, Tye felt a slight breeze on his face, suggesting the crack was deep. Caves were rare in this part of Washington. The geology wasn't right.

Christopher was looking past him, like he saw someone over his shoulder.

Tye's nostrils filled with the scent of a woman's hair, and for a moment it was as if he was in two places at once, in the cold windy forest with Christopher, and in the tent, with his hands pressed against warm, smooth flesh.

"Kaity?" he mumbled.

"Who the fuck is Kaity?"

His eyes snapped open. In the moonlight, he could see Penny. She was straddling him, shirtless.

"Uh..."

"Well, whoever she is, she's not here," Penny said. She leaned forward to kiss him.

"Hang on..." He turned his head to the side.

"Seriously?" She climbed off him. As she felt around for her shirt, he tried unsuccessfully not to stare. She turned away from him, and it was all he could do not to touch her back as she pulled the shirt over her head.

"I'm sorry."

"Whatever. I thought it might be nice to just have a little time with somebody that isn't part of this group. Somebody that is halfway attractive, and most importantly, will be gone soon." There was a hitch in her voice that didn't quite match her words.

"I..."

"Never mind. You don't have to bare your soul to me. If waking up to that wasn't enough for you, I guess nothing is."

She picked up a pair of pull-on boots she'd left by the door and grabbed a sweater.

"What about Weasel?" Tye asked.

"We can talk about that in the morning. Enjoy your night. Alone."

She was gone with a blast of cold air as she moved through the flap of the tent. She left it unlaced, forcing him to crawl out of his warm sleeping bag to tie it up and keep the draft out.

After securing the door, Tye crawled back in his bag and tried to figure out what, if anything, he'd just done wrong. He was undecided if what he'd just done was foolish or virtuous. The image of Penny in the moonlight was hard to get out of his head.

At some point he must have slept, because the next thing he

knew, weak dawn light was filtering through the tent canvas, and he heard the sounds of breakfast being prepared outside.

Tye checked his satellite messenger.

On the way with stuff to fix your truck. Bringing May to check out the pregnant woman.

Tye gathered up his gear and contemplated the logistics of how to make everything work today. Part of it depended on Penny. He wasn't looking forward to the inevitable awkwardness of this morning.

Leif and Meadow were making a giant pot of oatmeal and brewing mint tea when he crawled out of the tent. Tye pitched in to help, setting out bowls and cups.

Grace and Robin crawled out of their tent. Grace helped Robin to her feet and walked beside her as she shuffled her way to the fire ring. Tye tried not to stare as she made her way over. Surely she would have the baby soon.

Meadow had a bowl fixed for Robin before she even sat down.

"My friend May, the midwife, is headed up here this morning," Tye said. "She'd be happy to check you out."

Robin nodded. "I'd like that. I think the time is getting close."

Grace opened her mouth to say something, then apparently thought better of it.

Apparently, Robin knew what she was going to say, anyway. She patted the older woman's arm. "Don't worry. Women had babies like this for thousands of years."

Tye took a sip of his tea and decided not to point out that a fair number of those women died in childbirth, and the ones that lived were typically surrounded by a tribe of people that knew how to deliver a baby. Nobody here seemed to fit that bill.

Alex came up, grabbed some food, and sat down, followed soon after by Penny. She didn't meet Tye's eyes as she ate.

"My friends are meeting me at my truck so we can fix it," Tye said to no one in particular. "May would be happy to examine Robin. I was thinking someone could walk with me to the truck, then lead May back here to camp."

"I can go with you," Penny said.

Tye nodded. He'd hoped Alex would volunteer to come along.

"It would be good to set out soon," he said, then looked at Grace. "Do you want to stay here while I fix the truck, then ride back with May after the exam?"

Grace nodded. It seemed she'd been distracted from her desire to find Christopher's killer since finding out about Robin's pregnancy.

"Then I have to go back to town for... arrangements."

Robin blinked back tears. "And then you'll bring him back here?"

"Yes." Grace turned to Tye. "Christopher will be cremated. I'll have a simple service for him in town, then I'd appreciate it if you'd help me bring his ashes up here."

"Alright."

Penny finished eating and washed her bowl. "I'll be ready to go in five minutes," she said and walked off toward her tent without saying anything else.

Alex shot him a look he couldn't quite read, then went back to eating. Tye would be glad to take a break from the social dynamics here in the woods. In theory, living a wild life with a tribe of friends in the woods had always sounded attractive. But experience had taught him it was usually going to be more complicated than that.

It had drizzled overnight, and the trees were wet and glistening. But the sky was cloudless, and the sun was warm. Tye tried to forget about all the human drama around him, and just stood there and enjoyed the cloudless November sky. This could be the last clear day for a long time.

As promised, Penny was ready in a few minutes. She came back with her bow, a small haversack, and a pair of sunglasses that hid her eyes.

"Let's go." She took off into the woods, forcing him to hurry to keep up.

Despite the morning chill, Penny was wearing a pair of camouflage pants cut off just below the knee. He found himself trying very hard not to stare at the skin of her calves as they walked. The part of his brain that was just a mammal looking for a mate wondered if there was a chance she'd take a rain check for last night.

He shook his head to clear it.

"Did y'all kick Weasel out of the tribe or something? I didn't see him at breakfast."

She slowed and looked relieved, perhaps because he was going to talk about something other than what had happened between them last night.

"No. He got angry and stalked off into the woods. He's done it before. He'll be out a night or two, then come back."

"Did he explain himself?"

"He said he was continuing Christopher's work, whatever that means. He said he'd never do anything that would endanger the tribe, then clammed up and refused to talk anymore. What did you find?"

The forest here was open enough they could walk side by side. They kept their voices low, but they weren't trying to be stealthy otherwise.

"I followed a man wearing boots down that old hiking trail that leads to the trailhead. I reckon the person Weasel was meeting parked there and hiked in to meet him."

That was true enough, although it left out some salient details.

"I just wonder how they knew to meet at that time and place," Penny said.

"I've considered that myself," he said. "He wouldn't tell you?"

She shook her head. "No. He just kept saying he would handle it. It's like everybody is keeping secrets all of a sudden."

Tye thought of all the things he hadn't told her about Willie and figured she had a point.

18

They walked the rest of the way in silence. Penny seemed content not to bring up the night before, so Tye decided to let it be. By the time they'd walked for half an hour or so, he felt much more settled in his mind about her. At one point in his life, this would have driven him crazy. He wasn't sure if his current state of mind was a sign of maturity or what, but it made life much easier.

Tye had marked the spot where his truck sat on his GPS, but he didn't need to turn it on. He'd described the road junction to her, and she was navigating to the spot perfectly, as far as he could tell.

"How long have you all been here?"

"Since early September. We came in time for the archery deer-hunting season, then elk season. About half of us have Washington state IDs, so we pay the in-state rate for hunting licenses."

That made sense. If you could show a Washington state residency, hunting licenses weren't that costly. They were ruinously expensive for people from out of state.

"Seems like you've been successful."

He'd seen the bags of dried jerky and canned meat stacked in the supply tent. A pressure canner could work just fine over an open fire.

She shrugged. "I guess. I don't think we'll ever be totally food independent. But it's a start."

"Where will you all go next?"

"We should have left already. We're in danger of getting stuck by snow right now. But as soon as Robin has the baby and can travel, we'll head south. Probably Utah. Maybe New Mexico or Arizona."

"That will get you out of the rain. I've been thinking about taking a trip down there myself."

As soon as he said it, he realized he'd opened the door for her to invite him to join them. Instead, she just kept walking, saying nothing, and plotting a course for the road.

They paused just inside the tree line. Tye could see his truck through the brush. It didn't look any the worse for wear than it had when he'd left it. They both stood in the shadows for a moment, listening.

"Seems pretty quiet," she said.

"Yup."

They stepped out into the sunshine and Tye walked around the truck, confirming there had been no new damage. Apparently, whoever had slashed the tires had been content to render him immobile. He still felt an itch between his shoulder blades as he unlocked the back and took off his pack. The person who had shot Christopher was still out there somewhere.

He'd just finished pulling out a pair of folding camp chairs and was trying to figure out how to sit and make small talk with a woman he'd turned down for sex when he heard an engine approaching. Kaity's Jeep crested the hill. Apparently, she wasn't slowing down for potholes, and Tye had to admit the heavy suspension was doing a good job of soaking up the bumps.

She slid to a stop in the wet gravel beside Tye's truck, and May popped out of the passenger door almost before the vehicle completely halted.

"That was quite a ride," she said. She saw Penny sitting there and looked from Tye to Penny and back with an expression on her face that Tye found hard to read.

Gary extricated himself from the vestigial back seat just as Kaity walked around the front bumper.

"I think we may have left my kidneys back a mile or two," Gary said.

Kaity looked from Tye to Penny and back, with the same exact expression as May.

"Hi. I'm Kaity," she said and stuck out her hand.

Penny introduced herself, and there was an awkward silence.

"I was thinking we could leave your satellite messenger with Robin," May said. "That way, if she goes into labor, she'll have a way to contact me."

"Great idea," Tye said, relieved for something to do.

"I'll get the tools out of the back," Gary said as Tye walked to the back of his truck and pulled the InReach from his backpack.

By the time he pulled it out, Kaity was back in the Jeep, with Penny in the passenger seat behind her. He handed the InReach to May, and Kaity drove off without a word.

Tye stood there, watching the Jeep disappear into the distance.

"Please tell me you didn't hook up with the primitive-skills intentional-community woman who was carrying a bow and arrow," Gary said from behind him.

Tye sighed. "I didn't. But judging by their facial expressions, I think both Kaity and May think I did, so I wonder if I might as well have." He turned to walk back to the truck.

"I bet the atmosphere in that Jeep is a mite tense at the moment. Why don't you tell me what happened while we get started?"

Tye's truck had a full-size spare, so they only had to fix three tires right away. As they lowered the spare from where it was stored under the truck's bed, Tye explained last night.

Gary grunted. "That was some admirable self-control."

"I have to admit, I second-guessed myself. I'm a bit tired of unresolved sexual tension."

Gary rolled the tire around to the right rear, while Tye loosened the lug nuts on the flat.

They jacked up the truck and swapped the spare for the flat. Then, with a combination of tire irons, ratchet straps, and profanity, they managed to break the bead on one side wall and install a new valve.

Tye started the truck, hooked his air compressor up to the battery, and started filling the repaired tire with air. They both stepped away from the racket of the compressor and into the shade.

"You know, if a fellow was looking to settle down with somebody, he could do a lot worse than Kaity," Gary said as he took a pull from his water bottle.

"That's been on my mind a bit."

"She's pretty darn smart," Gary said.

"Yup."

"Nice to look at."

"There is that."

"I admire her choices in life. I've seen her at the library, helping some confused soul on a computer apply for something like unemployment more times than I can count. She didn't hesitate to charge into the woods after that lost little girl a couple months back, either."

Tye stared off toward the west. It was warm and sunny right now, but in the distance, he saw dark clouds gathering. It would rain by nightfall.

"Thank you," he said to Gary.

"For what?"

"For helping me articulate why I didn't sleep with Penny last night, and why I'm really hoping this isn't going to screw things up with Kaity."

"Well, I'm sure if you explain that you turned down the half-nekkid woman who was straddling you in her favor, that might help," Gary said. "Let's check that tire. It looks pretty full to me."

They repeated the process three more times until each corner of the truck rested on a freshly inflated tire.

"That was a little bit like work," Gary said. "Let's take a breather and we'll fix this last one. No sense driving around with a bum spare."

Tye stretched his aching shoulders. Breaking the bead on a truck tire was a five-minute job in a shop with the right tools. He reckoned they'd spent the better part of half an hour on each one. The sun had wheeled around in the sky, and his stomach was starting to rumble.

They both looked up at the sound of an engine. Kaity's driving was much more sedate. They all circled up around the hood of Tye's freshly repaired truck.

"I'm pretty sure that baby is breach," May said. "She won't come down into town for an ultrasound. She's determined to do it her way. I left her the InReach, and she knows how to use it."

"So I guess you'll come back up here when she goes into labor," Gary said. It wasn't really a question.

"Of course."

Gary sighed. "Well, maybe they can pay us in woven baskets or something. Thing is, my Scout is still disabled, and your little car won't make it up here."

Tye started to open his mouth, but Kaity beat him to it.

"You could keep Tye's truck on standby. There's more room for her than in my Jeep. If Tye and I need to go somewhere, we can use my Jeep."

He was heartened by the word "we" and not the least bit bothered by the fact that she offered up his truck without asking him.

"That works," he said. "I'll give May the spare keys to my truck."

"I want to thank all of you for the help you've given me," Grace said. She looked at May. "I will pay whatever you charge for helping deliver the baby. That child is my grandchild."

She looked at Tye and Kaity. "I want your help to figure out who killed my son."

Tye hesitated. Strictly speaking, he'd done what they'd agreed. He'd found Christopher and his friends. Investigating murders was the job of the cops.

But he'd seen Christopher. Things had proceeded at such a breakneck pace that he'd not had a chance to process the apparition on the side of the road, or the dream from the night before. Over the last few months, Tye had had visions of dead people. He was finally beginning to accept it for what it was. He thought back to his visit with Hattie. Apparently, he wasn't the first person to deal with this, which gave him some comfort.

He looked at Kaity. She gave him a nod.

"We'll stay with this for a while longer," Tye said. "Investigating murders is a job for the cops, but we'll do what we can."

"The police think it was a hunting accident," Grace said. "I'm not buying it." She wrung her hands and looked around at all of them for a moment, then burst into tears.

It was May who stepped forward and wrapped Grace up in a big hug, letting the woman sob for a few minutes.

Finally, Grace pulled back and wiped her face. Tye pulled a handkerchief from his back pocket and handed it to her, glad to find a way to help.

Grace blew her nose. "I'm sorry." She looked around the circle, then focused on Tye. "I have one last favor to ask."

"Sure," Tye said.

"I'm having a memorial for Christopher tonight at my gallery. Since you are the one that found him, it seems like you should be there."

"Sure," he said, even though it was the last thing he wanted to do.

"Thank you. Now, can we please leave? I need to get back to town in time to get ready."

She got in Tye's truck, and the others climbed into Kaity's Jeep. Again, Kaity said nothing to him, just pulled out ahead of him and started driving, leaving him in her dust cloud.

At the road junction that headed to the logging site, she slowed and pulled over. A Tompkin Resources panel truck was bouncing up the rough road. The truck really wasn't made for roads such as these, and it was struggling with the ruts and potholes. Again, Tye wondered what it was doing up here. He didn't recognize the driver, and it didn't look like the driver recognized them.

After the truck made a wide turn onto the even more rutted logging road, Kaity sped away.

Tye sat there for a minute, watching the panel truck lumber up the road. He had a feeling at least some of the answers they sought were in that truck, and he was developing a plan to find them.

19

Tye dropped off Grace at her car, then drove home. As he pulled up the driveway, he saw Kaity leaning against the hood of her Jeep, her face inscrutable behind her sunglasses. He took a few minutes to square away his gear, leaving the spare keys to the truck on the front seat in case Gary and May had to use it.

"Hey," he said as he walked up to Kaity.

"Hey," she said.

He stood there looking at her, not sure what to say.

"First things first," she said. "Our work has to continue, regardless of anything else. Finding people is important."

"I agree," he said.

"Second, I'm not even sure if I have a right to ask you this. It's not like we have a thing going."

He cocked an eyebrow at her. "Do you really think we don't have a thing going?"

He'd decided on the drive home it was time to cut through all the shit and get things out in the open.

She crossed her arms over her chest. "Well... okay then. Did you sleep with her?"

"Nope. Almost did."

"How do you almost sleep with somebody?"

"She wanted to, but I demurred."

"Are you sure she wanted to?"

"I woke up with her in my tent. She'd taken her shirt off and was straddling me. I'm not the best at picking up on subtle hints, but that seemed pretty clear."

"You didn't do it because of me?"

He stood next to her and leaned against the hood of the Jeep. Their shoulders weren't quite touching, but they weren't that far away either. She didn't move away from him.

"Mostly it was because of you. Even if I didn't know you, it would have been a bad idea to sleep with Penny. But I might have been more tempted to find out for sure."

"She's younger than me."

"Yup. Probably five years or so."

"Bustier."

He didn't say anything, just watched a bald eagle soar over the river valley.

"You're not going to respond to that?" she asked.

"I don't see any response that would end well for me." Out of the corner of his eye, he saw her mouth quirk up in a smile.

"Why me and not her?" she asked.

"I've been thinking about that a bunch these last few hours. I've got a pretty strong physical attraction to Penny. It's probably pheromones or genetics or something like that. The thing is, that's it. I'm thirty years old. I don't have the romantic experience that some guys have, but there really aren't any mysteries left there either."

Over in the river valley, the first eagle was joined by a second. They circled a spot for a while, then took off down the valley with each other.

"Being with Penny might have been fun until we exhausted the physical part," Tye said. "But she's only concerned with herself. There are some reasons for that, and it's not my place to tell her story."

Kaity had turned her head to look at him now.

"You're attractive, and you're smart," Tye said. "And I value both those things. But the world is full of attractive, smart women. The night I met you, you charged into the woods after a lost little girl, even though you weren't equipped and didn't know what you were doing. Penny never would have done that. She would have convinced herself not to get involved. I want the people in my life to be the kind that will try to help out when bad things happen."

He realized she was laughing. "What?" he asked.

"That is the longest group of sentences I have ever heard you string together. You didn't get monosyllabic even once."

"Oh. Well. I've been thinking about this a bunch."

It was her turn to be quiet for a while. Tye just let her be, aware of how vulnerable he had just made himself and wondering if he was about to regret it.

"I think I always assumed you and I would be together eventually," she said.

"That's good to know," he said.

"I think I just don't know how to get from point A to point B sometimes."

"I've always struggled with that, too."

"I think I'm also resisting the idea that knowing another woman finds you attractive should fill me with a sense of urgency to make a move."

He thought about that one for a while. The two eagles were back, flying upriver this time and looking for fish.

"Well, I guess I can understand that. I'm not going anywhere. Besides, I think Penny found me convenient as much as she found me attractive."

She pulled her phone out of her pocket. "If we're going to the funeral, you need to change, and we need to get moving so I can stop by my house and change. I have packed a tremendous amount of contingency equipment in my Jeep, but funeral attire is not on the list."

She put her hand on his chest. "I'm glad we talked," she said. "I want to talk more later, but we still have a job to do. Go change and we'll get going."

He wanted to kiss her, but he didn't. Instead, he nodded and walked toward his yurt.

"Wear the blue shirt again," she called after him. "You look good in it."

His head was spinning as he changed clothes. He tried to shift gears from thinking about Kaity to the funeral. A funeral at a Portland art gallery was exactly the sort of thing Tye worked very hard to avoid.

Kaity was waiting for him in the Jeep with the engine running. When he climbed in, he barely got the door shut before she rolled down the driveway. She hit the accelerator so hard his head snapped back.

"We don't have to hurry this much, do we?"

There was a long curve in the driveway. At the apex, the Jeep couldn't be seen from the road or the house. She stopped in exactly that spot, took the Jeep out of gear, and pushed in the parking brake.

"What's wrong?" Tye asked.

"Absolutely nothing."

She undid her seat belt, twisted in her seat, grabbed his face in both hands, and kissed him.

At first he was surprised, then he kissed her back hungrily. His hand fell to her hip, then found the bare skin at the base of her back, and she gave a little moan in the back of her throat. She pressed tighter against him and ran a hand down his arm.

Tye lost track of time, and for the first time in a long time, forgot about visions, dead people in the woods, and all the things that were making him question the way the world worked. He just lost himself in Kaity.

Finally, she pulled back. He wanted to pull her back to him but didn't.

"Whew," she said.

"Yeah."

She sat back in her seat, put her seat belt on, and drove.

"I wanted to do that back there at the top of the driveway," she said. "But your yurt was right there, and I don't want to wind up knocked up like Robin."

"Less chance of that happening in the Jeep, I suppose," he said, pleased and surprised he could string together a sentence.

"I wouldn't want the first time to be in my Jeep."

"I agree, it being a Chrysler product and all."

She laughed and held his hand in between shifting gears. Tye felt a giddiness he hadn't felt since he was in high school.

The Jeep's suspension made it ride like a pogo stick. Worse, at certain speeds, the front end vibrated. Tye recognized it as something the off-road vehicle community called "death wobble." It was caused by poorly matched suspension and steering components.

"This thing has a shimmy at some speeds," Kaity said. "Gary is going to help me figure it out after he gets his Scout put back together."

Tye silently thanked his friend. "He'd be the guy you'd want to help you out."

"Is there enough blood going to your brain that we can talk about the case?" Kaity asked after a mile or two.

"I think so."

"Good. It took me longer than I expected to become coherent again. Must be those pheromones you were talking about earlier. Tell me everything that happened."

He shut his eyes and talked her through it step by step, from meeting Penny and the other members of the tribe, up to the moment Kaity had rolled up in her Jeep.

"Wow. She's a felon."

"Yep."

"So, let's go down the list of suspects. Let's start with Weasel. Motive?"

"Jealousy? There's something off about that guy, but I'm not sure he's a killer. He's a possible, but I don't think so."

"What about the guy who runs the outdoors school? The one that fired Christopher?" Kaity asked.

"Dylan Hart?" Tye thought about that one for a moment. "You know, I can see Dylan killing somebody in the heat of the moment. But stalking Christopher and sniping him with a rifle? I don't think so."

"Also, he said he was on a hunting trip when Christopher was killed. I wonder if we can verify that. He had a motive. It sounds like Christopher got him sued."

"Yeah."

"How about Penny?" Kaity asked.

He sat with that question for a while.

"It sounds like she and Christopher didn't agree about the activism," she said. "Maybe she was afraid he would draw attention to the group, maybe even get her thrown back in prison again."

"Maybe."

"And in case you're wondering, I've fully considered that my thinking might be biased because I consider her a romantic rival."

"She's really not, though," Tye said.

"She may not realize that." Kaity put her turn signal on and exited the freeway. He'd lost track of time while they were talking. She drove on surface streets through the town of Vancouver, Washington for a while. The sun was low in the sky. It was hard to believe another day was over already.

She parked in the driveway of an older craftsman-style home. It was small and neatly kept. He unbuckled his seat belt, but she put a hand on his arm before he could get out.

"Will you listen to me for a second?"

"Sure."

"We're going to go in my house, and I'm going to shower and change clothes. That is all we are going to do. We are under no circumstances going to have sex."

"I wasn't really presuming."

"I'm saying this as much for my benefit as yours."

"Oh. Well, that's nice to know."

She undid her own seatbelt. "Several times I've almost made an appointment with my primary care to discuss going back on birth control, but I could never decide if that was premature or not. I let it all lapse after my last breakup."

"I could... you know... handle that."

She wagged a finger at him. "I will control that aspect of this relationship, thank you very much. I saw that poor pregnant girl up there in the mountains, and I do not want to deal with that yet."

He didn't know quite what to say to that.

"It seems like this is all moving very fast for you," she said.

"All of a sudden, yes."

She leaned over and gave him a peck on the cheek. "Let's go."

He followed her to the door. He liked her place. It was sparsely furnished and decorated, but it still felt inviting and relaxing. There was no television, but one whole wall of the living room was lined with bookcases. He found himself tilting his head to read the book spines.

She laughed. "I do that same thing when I go into somebody's house."

"You did it the first time you came in my yurt."

"Feel free to browse. I'll just be a minute."

She disappeared down the hall, and a minute later, he heard the sound of water running. He looked at the books to keep his mind off the fact that Kaity was naked, not more than a dozen feet from him.

The books showed her eclectic taste. Quite a few dealt with lock picking, safecracking, and codebreaking. Others covered the history of intelligence agencies and spy memoirs. The fiction was all over the map, lots of lit-fic, and he saw well-worn copies of all three books of *The Lord of the Rings* trilogy.

The bathroom door popped open, and he got a brief glimpse of her in a towel as she went from bathroom to bedroom.

"There's juice and filtered water in the fridge if you're thirsty."

He was fine drinking water from the tap. There was a fiendishly complicated lock partially disassembled on the kitchen table, surrounded by small delicate tools. He didn't dare touch it, for fear of disturbing something. It made his head hurt just to look at it.

"Oh. That's my Banham M2002. Only half a dozen people have picked that one."

She stood in the doorway wearing a modest black dress.

"I'm not sure if you're supposed to tell people they look great when you're going to a funeral, but you look great."

"Thank you. That's really nice." She looked away from him and actually blushed.

She turned toward the door. "Let's go."

She seemed nervous and eager to leave, so he followed.

20

The sun was setting as they crossed the river into Oregon. To Tye it seemed like all he'd done lately was drive. At least the road was paved, and Kaity was behind the wheel. He stared out the window, his head spinning from the events of the last few days.

They had fallen into a companionable silence. It was like the old tension between them had eased a bit. He just enjoyed looking at her as she drove barefoot in her black dress. The flat dress shoes she'd worn kept slipping off the clutch pedal, so she'd taken them off and pitched them behind the seat in exasperation.

The gallery was in Northwest Portland, on a side street full of boutiques, bars, and coffee shops. Kaity squeezed the Jeep between two other cars, shut off the engine, and dug her shoes out.

"I never wear shoes like this," she said. "Why did I do this? Anyway. I'm really not sure what we're going to do here besides just show up and support our client. I think we should leave at the earliest opportunity."

"Agreed."

Tye stepped out onto the street. He hated cities. There was noise and concrete everywhere. He felt suffocated and trapped. Portland didn't smell as bad as many cities, but there was still the odor of garbage, car exhaust, and human urine that made him long for the woods.

"Well, here we go," Kaity said and took his hand.

The inside of the gallery was a bright white space. Paintings hung on the walls and soft, ambient music played just loud enough to be heard, but not loud enough to identify the song. Several knots of people stood around talking. They all were much more fashionably dressed than Tye. As he and Kaity walked in, people looked them up and down, then looked away. Nobody so much as nodded or said hello.

"Well," Kaity said under her breath, "this is... nice."

"May I interest you in wine?"

Tye jumped at the voice in his ear. A server stood there holding a tray of wine glasses.

"Sure," Kaity said. She took two and handed one to Tye.

"I'm probably not going to drink this," Kaity said. "But I just feel better having something in my hands during socially awkward situations. This has led to me getting unintentionally drunk a couple of times."

"I know the feeling," Tye said. He had an urge to stand in a corner with his back to the wall, where he could see everyone.

"Oh, that must be him," Kaity said and walked away without waiting for him to answer. He followed and saw she was walking toward an urn sitting on a dais against the far wall. A single spotlight shone down on it.

Tye looked at the plain black urn, trying hard to connect it with the body of the young man he'd found a few days before.

"I've never really thought about it before," Kaity said, "but I guess I'd rather be cremated than planted in a hole in the ground."

"I'd just like to be left out in the forest for the animals," Tye said.

Kaity looked at him out of the corner of her eye. "I guess you have put some thought into it."

Before he could answer, Grace walked up.

"Thank you both for coming." She was glassy-eyed, and Tye

wondered if she'd been hitting something a little harder than the wine.

Grace scanned the crowd and took a big gulp from the glass in her hand. "I put all this together in a hurry, and as soon as people started arriving, I realized this probably isn't what Christopher would have wanted. These people are my friends, not his."

Tye had been thinking exactly that same thing from the moment he walked in the door. There was nothing of Christopher in this place. This bright, sterile room, hung with abstract art prints worth enough money to feed his tribe of friends for a year, would have been anathema to him.

"Maybe you could do this again with his people up in the mountains," Tye said.

"I keep thinking of Robin up there in those cold mountains, sleeping on the ground. I tried to get her to stay with me, at least until she has the baby, but she just won't do it."

"This isn't her world," Tye said.

Before Grace could reply, the room went silent. Tye turned to see Wade and Anna Lee Tompkin striding across the room. Wade wore a somber, dark suit. Anna Lee wore a loud, flower-print dress that even Tye knew was inappropriate for a funeral. The only sound in the room other than the soft music was the sound of her heels clicking on the hard white floor.

The other attendees didn't even try to hide their stares. Tye got the feeling most of them were looking forward to some kind of show.

Wade stopped in front of the urn, clasped his hands in front of his chest, and bowed his head.

"My boy," he said. The tears on his cheeks looked genuine to Tye.

Grace's mouth set in a hard line. She opened her mouth to say something, then apparently thought better of it.

Wade looked at Grace. "I'm sorry. I should have done better."

Her face softened. She reached out and put a hand on his shoulder.

Behind him, Anna Lee snorted. "I don't know that it was ever firmly established that he was your boy," she said.

Grace's face drained of color. Wade turned to his mother. "Momma, don't..."

She was undeterred. "Even if he was your get, he stopped being a member of this family the second he started working with those damn environmental lawyers, trying to ruin our family business."

Anna Lee took a step toward Grace. "Maybe if I had raised him, that boy would have turned out to be something other than a hippie playing Indian out in the woods. It doesn't matter now, though. The only thing that matters now is that you understand you aren't getting any money out of this family. That agreement still stands. I talked to lawyers."

Grace dropped her hand from Wade's arm. "I don't want your money. It's filthy."

Anna Lee smirked. "It's more honest work than selling the shit you've got on your walls. This stuff looks like something a third-grader could have painted. Come on, Wade. You've paid your respects. Now it's time to get back to work."

She turned toward the door without waiting to see if Wade was going to follow. He gave Grace and the urn one last long look and followed his mother out the door.

Grace said nothing. As if in a daze, she marched mechanically across the room and disappeared through a doorway in the back of the gallery.

Tye saw that everyone else was standing around talking and shooting them glances, but no one made a move to follow Grace.

Kaity sighed. "I guess it's up to us." She grabbed Tye's hand, and they followed Grace through the door.

On the other side of the door was a small office, furnished in warm colors and wood paneling Tye found refreshing after the oper-ating-room sterility of the gallery. Grace stood in the middle of the room, hugging herself and staring at a framed picture of Christopher as a boy.

"I signed an agreement with them," she said as soon as they walked into the room. "In return for sole custody and the ability to make all the parenting decisions, I wouldn't take a dime from the Tompkins."

"Seems like a wise choice," Tye said.

"Was it? I've been wondering if maybe he'd had access to different experiences, things would have been different."

"He could have turned out just like Wade," Tye said. As soon as the words left his mouth, he wondered if it was the right thing to say.

Grace nodded. "Wade is weak."

Tye thought of Wade scuttling along behind his mother and had to agree.

"I spent so many years thinking that the way Christopher wanted to live was wrong," Grace said. "I argued with him so much. But the only people who walked in here to check on me after that awful exchange were you two. I just realized that none of those people out there are really my friends. They are people I socialize with, and do business with, but I wonder how many of them are here tonight for the free wine and hors d'oeuvres, and maybe the promise of a little scandal."

She looked at Tye. "You're right. I should be doing this with his people up in the mountains," she said.

"We can help you get up there again, with his ashes," Tye said. "We can work out the logistics."

"Would it be wrong if I just walked out there and told all those people to leave?"

"I don't think so," Tye said. "It's your gallery. Your rules."

Grace took a deep breath and squared her shoulders. "I guess I better do it before I talk myself out of it."

All eyes turned to her when she stepped back out into the gallery, but again, no one approached her to offer comfort.

"Thank you all for coming," Grace said. "I would like very much to be alone right now. Good night."

People shuffled out, draining the last swallows from bottles of wine first. Again, no one offered so much as a word to Grace.

"Wow," Kaity said under her breath. Apparently, Tye wasn't the only one that found it odd that nobody said anything.

Grace turned her back on all of them, just stood there staring at the urn that held Christopher's ashes. A few minutes later, there was no one in the stark, white space but the three of them.

"We'd be happy to take you back up into the mountains," Kaity said.

"I'd like that. Tomorrow I have to take care of a bunch of legal details. Day after tomorrow."

Kaity hesitated, and for a second Tye thought she was going to hug the older woman.

"Well, we'll see ourselves out," Kaity said instead.

Grace didn't reply, and Tye followed Kaity out the door.

It was colder outside than when they had gone in. Kaity wrapped her arms around herself, and Tye regretted not bringing a jacket.

"I'm trying to decide if we're getting too personally involved in this," Kaity said. "I wonder if we should maintain a more professional distance."

"It's personal for her," Tye said. "I've always had a problem with that distance. Like I'm supposed to care enough about finding somebody to go spend days out in the woods looking for them, but not care about them or their family personally? I dunno. I think one of the problems with the modern world is people don't take things personally when they should."

"I don't just check out books at work," Kaity said. "People walk into the library looking for help to find a job, trying to figure out their new medical diagnosis. Stuff that's much more important than finding the latest bodice-ripper romance. Last week I helped a woman design and print posters for her runaway daughter. I've been told I get too personally involved with some patrons."

"You mean like charging into the woods after a missing little girl?"

"Yeah, that."

"Well, that little girl would be dead if it wasn't for you."

They rounded the corner and Kaity's Jeep came into sight. A tall, dark figure was standing by the driver's-side door. Tye let go of Kaity's hand and took a half-step in front of her. The whole time they'd been talking, he'd been alert to their surroundings, watching other people on the street and looking into the shadows.

"It looks like I missed the funeral."

It was Willie. He stepped into the half-light of a streetlamp. He was wearing a dark jacket, bolo tie, pressed jeans, and cowboy boots. Even from twenty feet away, Tye could see a bulge under Willie's jacket he suspected was the Colt Single Action Army Willie always carried.

"Yep," Tye said. "The festivities are over."

"We could talk a little closer," Willie said. "I won't bite."

"I reckon." Tye took a few steps forward, and Willie met him halfway.

"I was running a little late, and by the time I arrived, it was over. I saw the Tompkins leaving. Anna Lee's facial expression could have curdled milk."

"There was family drama," Tye said.

"Terrible when that happens at a funeral. Christopher was a fine young man. I'm sorry I didn't get to pay my respects."

"You'll have a second chance," Tye said. "His mother is planning on having another service up in the mountains. Your friend Weasel can let you know the details."

Willie smiled. His mouth looked like it had too many teeth in it.

"Thought that was you up by the lake," Willie said.

"Yup. Want to tell me what's going on up there?" Tye asked.

Willie shrugged. "Not sure myself, but I have my suspicions. I'm sure intrigued about why Tompkin Construction took such an interest in logging all of a sudden. It really isn't their forte."

Willie made a show of looking at his wrist, which didn't have a watch on it. "Well, look at the time. I need to get going."

He strode off with a wave over his shoulder. Tye stuck his hands in his pockets against the cold and watched him go.

"That old man creeps me out," Kaity said.

"Yup. Me too sometimes."

21

"So I've been thinking," Tye said as they crossed the Columbia River back into Washington state. "Why did they cut the valves on my tires?"

"And more importantly, who are they?" Kaity asked as she signaled to change lanes.

"Right. One question kind of leads to the other. I think somebody wanted me fixed in place because they didn't want me to see something. It took away my mobility and forced me to work on my truck for hours."

"Why?"

"I think there was something going on at the logging site."

"What? Cutting too many trees?"

Tye rubbed his chin. "Exactly. What's going on at a logging site worth shooting somebody? Never mind slashing my tires."

She drove in silence for a while, drumming her fingers on the wheel. "Do you think it's the same people that shot Christopher?"

"Great question. I felt awful exposed out there, knowing there was a killer with a rifle. But all they did was mess up my truck, so maybe not."

"There won't be anybody at the logging site at night, will there?"

"Most likely not. Some big outfits will pay a guy to stay overnight and watch the equipment, but it's rare."

Kaity looked at the clock on the dash. "I have to work early tomorrow morning, but that means I'm off early in the afternoon. Plenty of time to sneak into position before dark."

He was tired and hadn't thought far enough ahead, or he would have guessed where her thinking would go.

"There's somebody out there with a rifle," Tye said.

"Yes, and you were thinking about going up there alone at night, weren't you?"

"I guess I was kind of headed that way, yes."

"Are you going to try to be chivalrous or something and suggest I not go because it's too dangerous?"

He sighed. "I know better than to waste my time."

"Perfect. I'll be at your place after work."

They spent the rest of the way talking about Christopher's murder, proposing theories, analyzing them, and throwing them out. More than once, Tye wondered if the whole thing had been a crazy accident. Maybe someone had been out poaching, saw a flash of movement, and shot Christopher by accident. But it seemed unlikely. He'd been standing in the middle of a forest road when he'd been hit, wearing a bright blue backpack. Another possibility was someone had meant to shoot at a game animal, missed, and the bullet had traveled and hit Christopher. That seemed like such an astronomically bad stroke of bad luck, Tye had trouble believing it could have happened that way.

The other thing that stuck in Tye's mind was the placement of the bullet in the dead center of the logo on the back of the pack. Experienced shooters picked the smallest spot they could as their aiming point. Tye envisioned someone looking through a magnified rifle scope, settling the crosshairs on that distinctive logo, and squeezing the trigger.

He shuddered. He'd been in more than his fair share of fights. But the thought of deliberately killing someone as they ran away was hard to wrap his head around.

At some point, he must have dozed off, because the next thing he knew, they were bumping up the driveway. The trailer was dark, and he figured Gary and May were asleep.

"I'll set a timer for five minutes." She pulled out her phone and started fiddling with it.

"What happens in five minutes?"

"That's when I have to stop kissing you and start driving home."

"Oh."

She sat the phone on the dash then kissed him. He wrapped her up in his arms and forget about everything else. This had been missing from his life for far too long, but he realized he was glad he'd given things with Kaity the time they needed to happen.

The timer dinged all too soon, and she pulled back.

"Whew," she said. "That was nice."

"It was."

"I was afraid my skills were a little rusty."

"Nope."

She laughed. "This makes me happy," she said.

"The kissing-me part, or the part where we're heading out into the woods to figure out a murder, even though we're not cops and there's somebody out there with a rifle with no compunction about killing people?"

"Umm... yes? I feel like it's a kind of package deal."

"I hadn't thought of it that way, but I guess you have a point." Reluctantly, he opened the door of the Jeep.

"Oh, hang on," she said as she twisted to dig around in the back of the Jeep. "I have something for you."

She pulled out a cloth tote full of books. "All the books on shamanism. I checked them out to your account."

"Isn't that breaking the librarian's code or something?"

"What happens at the circulation desk, stays at the circulation desk. My heart was in the right place." She pulled a second bag out of the back. "And these are for Doyle."

He took the books and made himself get out of the Jeep. Bone-tired as he was, he felt drunk and giddy with the turn in their relationship. She gave him a wave, and he watched her taillights disappear down the driveway.

Soon all he could hear was the soft patter of the cold rain on the treetops as he walked the short path to his yurt. It was only after he squatted in front of the wood stove to light a fire that he saw the envelope on his bed.

It was from Hattie. She didn't have a phone, much less internet, so if she wanted to get in touch with someone, she'd walk the mile down her driveway to the county road and drop a letter in the mail.

Still in his coat until the stove had a chance to drive the chill out of the yurt, he tore the envelope open. Hattie's handwriting was neat and precise. His own writing was laborious and sloppy, and he was often embarrassed when he corresponded with her.

I've passed word to my mother's cousin's ex-husband, Fred, and he's promised to get word to someone who can help you. The fellow in question lives in the bush near the boundary waters in Minnesota, sometimes Canada, and only comes to town a couple of times a year. Assuming Fred doesn't miss him on his next trip into town, they'll have a chat. Maybe the fellow will head your way sometime when it's convenient, maybe he won't. Most likely you won't hear about it ahead of time, and he'll just show up.

That probably isn't a satisfactory answer, but that's the way these things go sometimes. If I hear anything else, I'll either send you a letter or try to run into Kaity at the library.

The letter ended with Hattie's neat signature at the bottom. The old woman was a little gruff and hard to know, but she seemed glad to have Tye and Kaity in her life. Tye put the letter on the bed beside him and looked at it. All his life, he'd seen visions of people who weren't there, people who were dead. Sometimes he had strange, prophetic dreams. For years, he'd kept his mouth shut about them. The only person who knew was Gary. Now it seemed like everyone knew: May, Hattie, most of all, Kaity. None of them had shunned him like he'd been afraid they would.

The letter offered promise and fear in equal amounts. All his life, he'd hoped for someone who could help him with this curse, or was it a gift. He needed someone who could tell him he wasn't crazy, and maybe offer a little guidance.

Kaity wasn't far from his mind. Her scent still clung to him. She didn't wear perfume. He thought it was her shampoo, something floral with a hint of something spicy underneath. The yurt was warming up, but he found himself not wanting to take his jacket off, lest the scent go away.

He turned his attention to the books she'd given him. There was a sticky note on each cover. One heavy tome with a sedate cover had a note that said, "Very academic. PhD anthropologist. Zzz..." Another had a lurid cover of a man soaring over mountains. That note read: "Very New Age. But maybe a little helpful?"

It looked like she'd at least skimmed each book, but he wouldn't have been surprised to find out she'd read each one cover to cover.

Except for his friendship with Gary, Tye had been a loner all his life. He'd lived out of the back of his truck, moving from job to job as a hunting guide, commercial fisherman, logger, and search-and-rescue technician. Now he found himself settled in one place, surrounded by people who wanted to help him and didn't expect anything in return.

His finger traced the outline of Kaity's writing on the sticky note. He was afraid that if they went up in the mountains together, she'd get hurt. He was tempted to gather up his gear, strap on his gun belt, and drive up to the logging site himself. He could be in place before sunrise, build a little blind out of brush, and spend the day spying on the activity. Gary had a good camera with a long lens he could borrow. He could be back tomorrow evening with pictures of whatever shenanigans were going on up there.

If he did that, he knew things between him and Kaity would never be the same. She was determined to be an equal partner in all this, and he had to admit she had every right to be. She'd worked hard to set up the business side of things and was busy hustling new clients. Clearly, she was putting in the work to learn new woods skills. She definitely wasn't up to Tye and Gary's level, but she was progressing quickly, especially for somebody that had a full-time job that kept them in a building.

He knew he should wait and go with her like they'd planned, but he couldn't shake the image of her with a bullet in her back like Christopher.

In the pocket of his coat, his cheap cellphone buzzed. He pulled it out to find a text message from Kaity.

Just in case you were thinking about going without me, out of some chivalrous notion of protecting me, I'd just like to remind you that would really piss me off. We're either equal partners in this, or we're not.

He laughed, despite himself. He pecked a reply. *Thought about it. Don't want to see you get hurt. But I'll go with you.*

The yurt was warming up quickly, thanks to the stove. He shrugged out of his jacket and was pleased to find he could still smell her a little.

His phone buzzed again. *Good answer.*

He picked the phone up, trying to think of a reply. But before he could tap out a message, another from Kaity came in.

I worry about you getting hurt, too.

What was the right thing to say to that? "Thank you" didn't seem to cut it. Before he could decide, she messaged him again. He knew she used voice-to-text, something he didn't think his phone could do, and he was chronically a few messages behind.

I just saw you, but I already miss you.

I miss you too, he managed to type before another message could come in. "And I think I love you," he said out loud, but he didn't type it. Not yet.

Good night, she sent.

Good night.

He sat there for a few minutes with the phone in his hands in case she said something else, but nothing came.

22

In his dreams, Tye was racing through the cold forest. For some reason, one of his shoes was missing its laces and threatened to fly off his foot. He charged aimlessly through the underbrush in a panicked flight to get away.

Tye saw a figure ahead. For a second, he thought it was another threat, then the figure stepped forward into a band of moonlight, and Tye saw it was Christopher. His face was pale, and he was mute. He held up a hand and motioned for Tye to follow him.

Christopher stayed just ahead of him, sliding effortlessly through the underbrush. He seemed to know where he was going, so Tye followed. He realized with a start that the dream was silent. They moved soundlessly through the leaf litter and trees around them.

Christopher led him to the base of a cliff. There among the jumbled rocks at the bottom was a deep crack, shoulder-wide and head-high. Christopher gestured for Tye to go inside. He was insubstantial in the moonlight. Tye could see the branches behind him waving in the wind.

Tye tried to speak, but no words came out. It was like his lips were glued together. Christopher gestured again, impatient. He was fading as Tye watched, like the wind was blowing him away.

The temperature dropped, and Tye felt his skin stung by pellets of ice. Snow whirled around him, silent, but still wet and cold. He charged through the crack to get out of the wind.

He looked back and all he saw was a wall of swirling snow. Tye's shoulders brushed either side of the stone passage. Instead of the inky blackness he expected, he saw a soft red glow ahead of him, and felt warmth on his face.

The floor of the cave was rough and uneven. He crept forward, around a bend, and found himself in a chamber lit by a fire. The smoke was drawn up through a natural chimney in the rock. The walls glittered with veins of quartz, and as Tye looked more closely, he realized there were thick threads of gold in the rock as well.

There were hundreds of symbols painted on the walls: elk, human figures carrying spears, the sun, birds. Some were so faded as to be barely discernable. Others looked like they could have been painted yesterday.

Tye's breath caught in his throat. He saw a figure he recognized. The Dark Man. It was merely a silhouette of a dark figure, probably drawn with charcoal, but in his gut he knew it was the same one that chased him in his dreams. The Dark Man was surrounded by a ring of other figures wielding spears and knives. Without thinking, he walked over to the drawing, tracing the lines without touching the rock. For reasons he couldn't explain, he felt kinship with the figures in the circle, holding the Dark Man at bay.

He took in the rest of the room. There was a bough bed with a pile of blankets in one corner. Waves of fatigue washed over him. It felt like he had followed Christopher through the forest for hours. He took a few steps out toward the entrance of the cave, enough to see that the weather outside was worse. Visibility was only a few feet from the entrance.

Somehow, he knew in this place he would be safe. From the neat stack of wood next to the fire, he selected a few sticks, and once they were burning brightly, he settled into the bough bed under the blankets. The sounds of the storm outside seemed far off, and all he could hear was the pop of the wood in the fire and the steady drip of water like a heartbeat.

Tye woke up, not sure where he was. It took him a minute to realize he was in his yurt, not the cave. The drip was from a branch that hung over the yurt. Water dripped off and landed on the taut fabric of the roof. He kept procrastinating on climbing the tree and cutting the branch down.

Tye hated mornings like this. There was a sense of unreality about everything around him. Sometimes he was unsure if he was still dreaming, or he was really in his yurt.

"Nothing weird is happening. Must be the real thing," he mumbled after a while. He threw off the bedclothes and decided to face the day. Out the window, he saw a cold drizzle falling. The inside of the yurt was chilly, so he stirred up the hot coals in the bottom of the wood stove and threw in a few split pieces of kindling so he'd have some warmth while he made coffee and got dressed.

The night before, he'd remembered to plug in his phone before going to sleep. It buzzed. Kaity.

Hey. How was your night?

Reflexively, he typed out *fine,* but didn't send it. He deliberated for a few seconds, then erased it.

Weird dreams, he sent instead.

About the case?

He thought about that for a few seconds.

Maybe? Could just be my weird head.

Either way, I'd like to hear about it. I'm headed into downtown for a meeting. Yuck. See you after work. I'll bring dinner.

Sounds good. Almost as soon as he was finished tapping out those two words, another message from Kaity came in.

Remember what I said about not going without me?

He laughed. *Promise I won't.*

K. Miss you. Don't forget Doyle's books.

Miss you too. I'm headed out to see him soon.

Nothing else came. He sat there for a moment, hoping for one last message, then had to laugh at himself for acting like a lovesick teenager. He found he didn't mind it all that badly. It was nice to have someone to be lovesick about.

After coffee, he gathered up Doyle's books and headed out. May and Gary had taken his truck in case Robin messaged them that she was in labor, so he folded himself into May's subcompact.

As he drove into the city of Vancouver, he found himself glancing from time to time at the cell phone on the seat next to him.

"So those kids just live up in the woods full-time?" Doyle asked as he swirled his applejack around in his glass. The only things that had changed since Tye's last visit was Doyle was wearing a different shirt, and books had been shifted from the "to be read" pile to the "read" pile.

"Yup. They move from national forest to national forest."

"Doesn't sound half bad. No bills. No boss. Just hunt, fish, and gather berries all the time."

It was a little more complicated than that, but in principle, Tye had to agree. "It didn't work out too well for Christopher Tompkin, though."

"Tompkin? Is that the same Tompkin as the construction company?"

"Yup. Same one."

"I worked the case when old man Tompkin died."

"Case? What case?"

"Lord, when was it?" Doyle stared off into space for a moment, his eyes unfocused. "It was the summer I bought my first brand-new car. Overtime money. So just over forty years ago. Yes, that's right."

Tye was doing math in his head. Wade would have been an early teen at most. Probably not that.

"You know the medical examiner and the sheriff's department have to investigate any medically unattended death?"

Tye nodded.

"Usually, it's pretty cursory. If a fellow dies straining one out on the toilet, we tried not to inconvenience the family too much. This one was a little different, though. One bright summer morning, I got called out to the Tompkin residence. Big spread up on a hill. The medical examiner and I arrived at more or less the same time."

He held out his empty glass, and Tye poured in a little more applejack. Doyle raised an eyebrow, so Tye poured in a little more.

"Mrs. Tompkin, hell. What was her name? Mary Beth? Something like that?"

"Anna Lee."

"That's it. Anna Lee. Seems Anna Lee had found Mr. Tompkin, Wade Senior, floating in the pool and made a 911 call. One of our junior deputies was the first to arrive and got himself quite wet pulling the elder Wade Tompkin out of the pool. I arrived to find the volunteer fire department packing up their gear and Wade lying on the pool tiles wearing nothing but a blue Speedo."

"What killed him?"

"Undetermined. No sign of any trauma. Didn't smell of alcohol or marijuana. Just an unexplained sudden death."

"What did the autopsy show?"

"There wasn't one. Unlike what the TV would have you believe, autopsies are pretty rare and expensive. The medical examiner chalked it up to most likely a sudden cardiac event. Not uncommon for a man in his fifties."

"His fifties? Anna Lee isn't that old. She's maybe seventy now?"

"Nope. It was definitely a May-December romance. I don't believe she was even quite thirty at the time. I actually pushed for an autopsy, but the medical examiner and my boss all but laughed at me. There was no way to justify one. Like I said, there wasn't a mark on the man, or anything the least bit suspicious about the physical evidence."

"Why did you want one?"

"Anna Lee. Here was this young woman, suddenly widowed, barely out of high school when she'd married a much older man. When I arrived, she was in the kitchen with a cup of coffee and a pack of Chesterfields, making phone calls. Lawyers. Wade's business associates. Already had a funeral home picked out. She was working her way down a list she'd written on a piece of Tompkin Construction stationary."

"Wow."

"Yep. She was cool as a cucumber the whole time I interviewed her. Stuck to the same story. Wade liked to swim in the mornings. He'd get up before her, do some laps, and by the time she woke up, he'd be done and in the shower. She said that morning she got up and found him floating."

"Where was Wade Junior?"

"Away at wrestling camp. So it was just the two of them in the house."

"Interesting timing."

"I thought so too. So, I argued with my boss and the medical examiner to at least do an autopsy on Wade Senior, but I got shot down. To be fair, I didn't have a shred of evidence, just a creepy feeling from her demeanor."

"So that was it? Case closed?"

"That was it. Case closed. I always wished I'd just flat-out asked her if she'd drawn up that list the night before, though."

23

T ye left Doyle with his bag of new books and a jar of applejack. Tye genuinely enjoyed his visits, and he could tell they were a highlight of Doyle's week, particularly when Tye had a new case he needed to discuss. The old detective was still sharp. His agile mind was stuck inside an increasingly failing body. Doyle seemed to relish an opportunity to help them out.

As he drove away from the retirement community, Tye stopped at an intersection. A left turn would take him back toward home. A right turn would take him south, back toward the river and the bridge that would take him into Portland. He turned right, committing to a course of action that he'd been considering for hours.

It was Sunday, so traffic was light as he wound through surface streets on his way to the Nature's Way school building. He drove past without stopping, verifying that the parking lot was empty, before leaving the car in a grocery store lot a few blocks away. A light drizzle was falling, and he pulled up the hood on his windcheater jacket.

He walked around to the backside of the Nature's Way building, near the loading dock and dumpsters. Next to the metal roll-up garage door was a smaller person-sized door. Just like it had years before when Tye worked here, the door was set crooked in the frame, leaving a gap where he could insert his driver's license. He wiggled it back and forth and the door popped open.

Originally, the three-story brick building had housed a commercial printer. The presses had been in the warren of basement rooms. The concrete floors still had blue-black ink stains, and after the building had been shut up for a while, the air smelled faintly of machine oil. Tye stepped behind boxes of office supplies and listened for a moment. All was quiet. The building was empty.

As he walked toward the stairs, he passed canoes, stacks of bows and arrows, tents, and other outdoor equipment. This place had a complicated history for him. He'd taken the job out of desperation, just after he, Gary, and May had mortgaged themselves to buy their property. At first it had seemed like a great job: teach kids and adults wilderness skills, like tracking, plant identification, and archery. But very quickly, it had become a grind. Dylan had changed over the years. Instead of creating a revolution that made people want to connect with nature, now he seemed more interested in sitting in his office, crunching numbers and plotting how to expand his business.

Tye paused again at the top of the stairs. Still quiet. He pulled on gloves as he walked toward Dylan's office. He was surprised to see the rifle case still there on the floor.

"I thought you were supposed to be out hunting," Tye muttered as he squatted in front of the case.

He expected the latches to be locked, but they weren't. Nestled in the egg crate foam was a 6.5mm Creedmoor Kimber Mountain Ascent rifle. It weighed under five pounds and was worth more than all of Tye's guns combined. The Leupold scope on top would easily fetch a house payment.

There were two boxes of ammo resting in a cut-out in the foam. One was full, the other was missing three rounds. He picked up the rifle and opened the bolt to make sure it was empty. Using the penlight from his pocket, he looked in the bore. It was slightly fouled with powder residue, and there was the faint smell of burnt gunpowder. The rifle had been fired and put away without being cleaned.

That meant nothing. Some guns were more accurate with a

slightly fouled bore, and hunters would leave the gun a little dirty before cleaning it at the end of the season. Tye squatted there holding the rifle in his hands, wondering if this was the gun that had killed Christopher, if Dylan was capable of such a thing.

The cartridge was certainly powerful enough to kill a grown man. Designed for long-range shooting with low recoil, the Creedmoor round was capable of killing an elk from several hundred yards away.

Tye replaced the rifle and closed the case, careful to put it all back just like he'd found it. He stood and looked around the office, not sure of what else to do. Coming here hadn't been an impulse, exactly, so much as an action driven by intuition. He wasn't exactly sure what he was looking for, but he figured he'd know it when he found it.

The computer screen on Dylan's desk was dark. Tye realized there was no actual computer, just a docking station for a missing laptop, not that Tye would have been able to hack into it, anyway.

The shelves held books and pictures. The books were naturalist field guides and volumes about primitive-living skills. They all had dust on them. They clearly hadn't been opened in a while. Tye recognized some of the people in the pictures. They had been fellow students at different primitive-skills schools. One photo caught his eye. It showed Tye and Dylan sitting in a pit house they'd dug together, their faces dark with mud and woodsmoke.

There were piles of books and bound reports on the desk. They looked like titles of academic research papers and government reports. Tye saw titles like *Remediation of Polychlorinated Biphenyl Contaminated Soil* and *PCB Groundwater Infiltration*. At one time, Dylan had been active in a couple of different environmental movements, protesting logging, habitat destruction, that sort of thing. Tye wondered if he was involved in something like that now. He flipped open one of the reports and was greeted with dense text and incomprehensible graphs.

The sound of a car door slamming outside caught his attention. He glanced out the window to see a black Land Cruiser in the lot. Dylan and Isaac were headed toward the front door.

Tye swore under his breath and put the report back. At the doorway, he paused long enough to look back and make sure nothing was out of place.

The building had two stairwells; one at the front, connecting to the lobby, and one in the back, which Tye had taken from the basement. He heard the front door open and then there were steps ascending the front stairs. There was no way he'd make it down the long hallway to the back stairs before someone saw him.

He ducked into the fiber arts room, hoping Isaac and Dylan weren't here to felt some wool hats on a rainy Sunday afternoon. He ducked behind an organizer full of wool yarn and hoped for the best.

At first the voices were indistinct, then he made out Isaac and Dylan's voices.

"Yeah, I lost my deposit on the trip," Dylan said. "But I didn't think I could leave town with everything that was going on. I was actually on my way to the airport when I got the call."

"Will the cops think we're involved?" Isaac asked.

"Shouldn't. It sounds like a hunting accident to me."

"I wish I could say I'm sorry about Chris, but he was such a pain in the ass."

"Yeah. I have mixed feelings about it, too."

"If I'd known, I would have never told Caine where to look for him."

"Can't be helped now. Let's just get my rifle and I'll help you load the truck so you can get to the site."

"You stashed it here in your office?" Isaac asked.

"Yeah, I was going to leave on my hunting trip, but when I found out they discovered the body, I was worried my name would come up. It was probably stupid to stash it here, but I guess I sort of panicked."

"Freakin' Tye Caine. I should have done more than mess up his tires."

"This has already gotten too far out of control," Dylan said.

Their voices faded as they walked down the stairs. Tye sat there listening to the sound of doors shutting, his nose itching from the wool in the air. Finally, after five minutes by his watch, he risked crawling over to the window and peeking over the sill. The lot was once again empty.

The hallway where Dylan and Isaac had just walked was full of an oily, chemical smell. Tye wondered if they'd been working on a vehicle or something. As he crept down the back stairs, Tye thought about what he'd just heard. There was nothing that definitively led him to believe they'd shot Christopher, but it didn't exactly rule it out either. The only thing he'd established for sure was Isaac owed him for a set of valve stems and the hours of backbreaking labor to replace them.

It felt like eyes were watching him the whole way back to the car. He slid behind the wheel, started the engine, and locked the doors. Drumming his fingers on the wheel, he tried to figure out if he'd learned anything that was worth the risk he'd taken.

He felt like something was just out of his grasp, but he didn't know what. He put the car in gear and started toward home.

24

"Wow, that was illegal," Kaity said around a mouthful of garlic tofu from the Thai restaurant in town. "Like super-duper illegal."

"Yeah," he said. He was having trouble concentrating on his own food. She was sitting cross-legged on his bed, deftly eating with chopsticks out of a waxed container. She was wearing outdoor clothing in muted colors, and a shock of dark hair stuck out from the watch cap she was wearing. He kept sneaking glances at her and thinking about how attractive she was.

"Maybe we should talk to each other before one of us goes and does any breaking and entering," she said.

"I suppose that's a fair point."

He took a bite of his own food with a fork. He'd given up on chopsticks. He was sitting at his workbench, his food next to the parts of the disassembled rifle he'd shoved out of the way. He made a mental note to get a second chair.

"You keep looking at me all googly-eyed," she said.

He took another bite to give himself a moment to think of an answer. "It's just... you know... nice to have you here."

She smiled at him. "You are such a dork sometimes."

She folded up the container, looked around for a place to put it, and finally settled on the floor.

"You've definitely got the minimalist thing going on in here." She leaned over and gave him a peck on the lips. "I really need to rethink my garlic consumption now that there's somebody I'm kissing on the regular. But right now, let's talk about we're doing here."

"The logging site is here," he said, tapping the map he spread out on the bed. "I was thinking we could head up this road over here. It's a little off the beaten path, but we would be able to park the Jeep and just walk a half-mile or so along this ridgeline, and we'd be able to scope out the site before we walk down into it. There's a full moon tonight, so we'll see well enough to get around once we're in the open. Do you have a headlamp with a red light for when we're walking through the trees?"

She nodded. She turned her head and a stray strand of hair brushed against his cheek.

"So we'll sneak in, see if anyone is there. If there isn't, we can check out the logging site more closely," she said.

"Yep."

"And then sneak back into the woods before daylight. I have my good camera with me and a long lens, so once the sun comes up, we can get some photos."

"Perfect."

"The sun rises late this time of year, so we have plenty of time."

"We do."

"All right. Let's get in the Jeep. My gear is already packed."

As Kaity drove, Tye split his time between navigating with the paper map and watching the road ahead for animals. The Jeep was old enough that it lacked a navigation system. Tye had found most of them useless in national forests anyway. They often showed roads that no longer existed, sometimes didn't show roads that had been added, and were frequently prone to picking a route that was either closed by snow, or so badly maintained as to be impassable.

Twice they spooked deer on the side of the road, once close enough that Kaity had to slam on the brakes to keep from hitting it.

She was doing a good job of picking a line around the ruts and potholes, but still Tye felt a little seasick after a while. The heavily sprung Jeep swayed back and forth, and his inner ear didn't care for it.

"This is our turn," he said. "We're about a mile from where I'd like to park."

The road to their right was rough and steep, but passable. The Jeep was equipped with a set of yellow fog lights mounted low on the bumper. Kaity turned those on and switched off the headlights. It gave enough illumination to creep up the road, but hopefully would make them less visible.

"Good call," he said. He switched on his handheld GPS and dimmed the display.

In the dim light of the fog lamps, he saw tire tracks in the mud.

"Somebody has been up here ahead of us," she said, just as he opened his mouth to comment on the tracks.

"Yep."

She steered so her wheels were in the tracks of the other vehicle. "Huh. About the same width as us. Maybe another Jeep?"

"Or something similar." The Jeep was narrower than the big trucks frequently seen on these roads.

"Maybe somebody up here hunting?"

"Maybe." He looked at the GPS. "Not much farther now." The road switch-backed its way up the side of a slope. At the top, it would follow the top of a ridgeline that ran roughly north-south. Tye wanted to park at the spot where it connected to an east-west ridge-line. That would lead them to the logging site.

"There's somebody here already," Kaity said. "I was right. It's another Jeep."

"I think that's Isaac's Jeep," Tye said.

"Isaac? The guy from Nature's Way school?"

"Yeah." Tye leaned forward and squinted through the windshield. Same spare tire cover with the elk picture. Same "If you can read this, flip me over" upside-down sticker on the rear bumper.

"What's he doing here?" Kaity asked.

"Dunno." The hair on the back of Tye's neck stood up, and it felt like he was missing something just out of his grasp. Earlier, he'd tried to make all the pieces of this puzzle fit together, and now all he could see were more pieces.

"Is he in it?" Kaity asked.

"Not sure." Tye's hand found the door handle, and he stepped out. Without even thinking about it, he buckled the pistol belt around his hips and palmed his flashlight. The damp night cold was bone-chilling. Mist hung in the air, diffusing the light of the flashlight.

The Jeep was empty. Tye felt the hood. Still warm. The inside of the Jeep was full of gear and trash. Amid the fast-food wrappers and dirty socks, Tye saw the long black shape of a rifle case. It was not the same as the one in Dylan's office. It was battered and covered with stickers. Tye remembered it from a hunting trip he'd taken with Isaac.

Tye looked around for footprints in the gravel, found a couple, and stopped.

He dropped to one knee and pulled a measuring tape out of the thigh pocket of his cargo pants. The tracks in the gravel had roughly the same measurements as the tracks he'd followed in the gravel behind Grace's house after it was burglarized.

He walked to the far edge of a road and found a clear print of a Vibram sole, headed in the direction of the ridge Tye had wanted to follow. The edges of the track were still crisp. He walked back to the Jeep. The width of the tires looked like a pretty good match for the vehicle that had burned rubber getting away from Grace's house.

"Huh," he said. He walked back to the warm cocoon of the jeep.

"What's going on?" Kaity asked.

"I wish I knew," he said. "I don't understand what Isaac is doing up here. This can't just be a coincidence."

The map was spread out in Kaity's lap. "If we drive past the Jeep, there's another way into the logging site."

He followed her finger as she traced the route. It would be more difficult navigation, and they wouldn't be on the highest ridge, but they would still be above the site and able to look down into the valley.

"That works." He was grateful she'd taken the time to figure that out. He hadn't had a Plan B in mind, and his head was swimming, trying to figure out why Isaac's Jeep was sitting in the exact spot where he'd intended to park.

"Dylan had a rifle case in the corner of his office the day I went to see him," Tye said, as much to himself as to Kaity.

"Dylan. The head of the Nature's Way school?" Kaity asked.

"Yup. That's the guy."

"I think it all comes down to figuring out the motive," Kaity said, as she steered around the end of a fallen log that jutted out into the road.

"Christopher caused trouble with the parents of Dylan's students."

"Big trouble," Kaity said.

"Yeah. That poor kid killed himself, and now there's a lawsuit," Tye said. "But what does the logging contract have to do with it?"

"Maybe we'll find out tonight."

"I think we need to be careful. Isaac is out here somewhere. It looked like he was headed in the same direction we were going to go originally." As he said this, Tye wondered if they should back out and head home. But once he grabbed hold of something like this, it was hard to let go. He'd never met Christopher, but he thought if he had, he would have been talking to a younger version of himself.

"Well, I want to find out what is going on," Kaity said in the tone he'd come to recognize meant her mind was made up and wasn't likely to change. He figured if he tried to bow out, there was a pretty good chance she'd go without him.

"Here?" she asked. There was a wide spot by the side of the road where they could park the Jeep.

He consulted his map and GPS. "I reckon that's as good as any."

She shut the Jeep down, and they spent a few minutes gathering gear. True to her word, Kaity was dressed in muted browns and grays, and had a green Hill People Gear backpack, the same brand as Tye's, but a different model. Tye was wearing faded brown pants and a camouflage hunting coat. As long as they moved slowly and were careful with their lights, they shouldn't have much trouble blending in with the nighttime shadows.

He shouldered his own pack and made sure his headlamp was set to emit a dim red light. It was just enough for him to navigate the woods without tripping or getting a branch in the eye, but the red light wouldn't ruin his night vision and wouldn't be visible from more than fifty yards away.

Last, he checked the load on his Ruger. The cylinder was full of .357 Magnum jacketed soft points and he had two speed loaders full of the same on his belt, along with some extra ammo in his pockets.

"After our little adventure last month, I'm reconsidering my stance on firearms," Kaity said as she watched him re-holster the pistol and make sure the thumb strap was snapped.

"Yeah? Well, we can go plink some tin cans out in the forest if you want to make an informed decision."

"It's a date. I hope we don't need that tonight, though," she said.

"That makes two of us," Tye said as he led them into the forest.

25

They fell into a rhythm as they moved through the woods. Tye would lead for a hundred yards or so, then they would stop to listen and consult his GPS. Kaity had her own GPS unit, apparently a new purchase since the last time they'd been in the woods together. She'd plugged the location of the Jeep into her unit, which was a relief to Tye. That way, if they were separated, she could find her way back without having to depend on dead reckoning.

Over the decades, Tye had stalked through the woods with quite a few people of various skill levels. Gary was his most constant companion. They'd grown up together and been adventure buddies since. Gary was almost as much of a ghost in the woods as Tye.

Kaity wasn't, but he was impressed anyway. They had practiced moving slowly through the woods a couple of times. With each step, Tye moved his front foot forward, felt, touched down with the ball of his foot, and then slowly transferred his weight off the back leg. It was a slow, monotonous way to walk, but Tye found it almost like a moving meditation. He had to give up thoughts of the destination and focus on the process of getting there.

Clearly, Kaity had been practicing. When he'd first met her, only a few months ago, she'd been clumsy in the woods. Each time he saw her, it was clear she'd been working on skills, and often showed up with a new piece of gear, too. He suspected she'd taken some formal classes in bushcraft and survival skills as well, but she'd never offered the information, and he'd never asked. She was determined to learn things her own way, and only tolerated his attempts to teach so much.

It took just over an hour to traverse the mile to the spot Tye had marked on the GPS. During daylight, they could have walked it in less than half that. Tye smelled the logging site as they approached the tree line. The fresh evening breeze brought with it the smell of sap from the freshly cut trees, along with diesel fuel and grease.

He settled behind a chest-high stump and turned off the headlamp. Now that they were out from under the forest canopy, there was enough moonlight to see the dark hulks of logging machinery and the slash piles of cut-off branches and treetops. The machines looked like evil robots from a science-fiction movie. The industry was more reliant on machines and less on people every year. Tye had done some summer logging work in his late teens, and even then, the crews had been almost twice the size they were now. Tye counted two feller-bunchers, insectile-looking machines that could grasp a tree and cut it off at the base, a forwarder, and a few other miscellaneous pieces of equipment like an excavator, a fuel truck, and a maintenance trailer.

The night was silent but for the sound of the wind on the ridges above. Kaity was squatting shoulder-to-shoulder with him, but looking in a different direction, which he appreciated. It was something he and Gary did automatically after years of long practice. Apparently, she'd picked up on it.

He squatted there behind the stump, listening. He heard nothing but couldn't shake the feeling that something was wrong. If he'd actually seen or heard Isaac, he would have been much relieved.

Beside him, Kaity shifted minutely, and turned to look at him in the darkness. She jerked her head toward the mass of machinery.

Tye nodded and rose. He led the way to where they could take cover behind a dormant excavator about twenty yards away. His plan was to move from cover to cover, stopping to listen each time.

As he pressed against the metal of the excavator, Tye wondered if there was any point to this. He wasn't seeing anything other than heavy equipment, cut logs, and piles of slash. He listened again, straining to hear the faintest scuff of a boot on the ground, or the rustle of clothing against vegetation.

Instead, he heard the faint tick of the engine of the excavator as it cooled, and an occasional drip as oil drained down into the oil pan. He frowned. It was well after midnight, and the sun had set at 4:30 PM. The engine should have been long cooled by now. Why was someone up here running heavy equipment in the dark?

He felt his way along the treads of the excavator until he reached the engine compartment. He pulled off a glove and put his hand against the metal grill. It was still hot enough that it was uncomfortable to touch for more than a few seconds.

"What?" Kaity whispered in his ear.

By way of answer, he took her hand and held it in front of the grate. She nodded.

The heat of the excavator was welcome against the cold night. He stood there warming his hands and trying to figure out why someone would be running machinery up here at night. Apparently, it had been shut down recently, but they'd not seen a truck hauling out logs on their drive in. The day's production was still stacked neatly next to the road, ready to be picked up and loaded in the morning.

Something else tickled at his subconscious, but before he could grab on to it, a cry broke the silence. At first Tye wasn't sure it was human, then he heard it a second time, followed by the heavy thump of something striking flesh.

It was close, on the other side of the excavator and a big pile of logging slash. Tye pulled his flashlight from his pocket with his left hand but didn't turn it on yet. He could see well enough to make his way around the slash pile without tripping. He heard the rustle of movement from behind him as Kaity followed.

There were two dark figures. One was on the ground, raising its arms to ward off a blow. The other towered over him.

"Stop!" Tye yelled and turned on the light. There in the frozen

tableau were Weasel, on the ground and bleeding from the head, and
Isaac, poised to strike with a shovel. A smashed camera was on the
ground between them.

Isaac blinked in the light, snarled, and turned toward them,
shovel still raised.

Oh shit, he'll hurt Kaity, went through Tye's mind as his revolver
appeared in his hand, unbidden. He realized the sights were centered
on Isaac's chest, then jerked the gun to point at the dirt by Isaac's feet.

"Stop!" Tye yelled again.

"Or what?" Isaac asked with a sneer.

The blast of the heavy Magnum load was like thunder, and the
bright white muzzle flash was like lightning. A spray of dirt peppered
Isaac's legs.

"Shit!" he yelled and dropped the shovel. He ran off into the
woods. Tye tracked him with the muzzle of the gun until he vanished
into the trees. There was a giant purple after-image of the muzzle
flash burned into Tye's retina.

"That was really crazy," Kaity said.

"Yeah." Tye realized he was still standing there with the gun in his
hand. He shoved it back in the holster and snapped the strap. He
wondered if he kept up this line of work, if eventually he was going to
wind up shooting somebody.

Weasel moaned, and Tye ran up to him. Blood ran down his face
from a scalp wound, and there were boot marks all over Weasel's
dirty white shirt. He tried to sit up, then winced and grabbed his ribs.

"Hold on," Tye said. He turned to Kaity and handed her the flashlight. Tye had trained as a Wilderness First Responder, and he knew
getting an accurate assessment of Weasel's injuries was vital before
they made any decisions about how to proceed. He decided to make
sure Weasel wasn't going to die right away, then get him to safety,
before doing a more in-depth examination of his wounds.

The scalp wound was superficial, but bloody. Weasel's lip was
split, and he spit out a chip of a tooth. When Tye probed his sides,
Weasel winced and pulled away.

"You've got busted ribs," Tye said as he wrapped a bandage

around Weasel's head. "But I don't think your lung is punctured. This is going to suck, but I need you to try to walk. Isaac has a rifle in his Jeep, and I'd like to get among the trees in case he decides to fetch it and come back."

Weasel nodded and held up a hand. Tye hoisted him to his feet. Weasel nodded and shuffled, half bent over, but he was making it under his own power. Kaity scooped up the remains of the camera and they made a beeline for the trees. Tye knew it was impossible for Isaac to make it to his Jeep and back, even at a dead run, before they were under cover, but he still felt an itch between his shoulder blades. He couldn't get the image of the gaping exit wound in Christopher's chest out of his mind.

Well inside the tree line, Tye found a little depression where they could turn on a light without it being seen.

The gauze had soaked through. Tye replaced it with a heavy combat dressing he carried in the case of someone suffering an accidental gunshot while out hunting. Weasel's eyes were focused and reactive to light, which was a good sign, but a brain injury had to be presumed after a blow like he'd received.

"What were you doing here?" Tye asked as he fixed the combat dressing on Weasel's head, as much to gauge the man's level of responsiveness as to get an answer.

"Willie wanted me to pick up where Christopher left off," Weasel said. "He gave me that camera the night you followed me to the lake."

Kaity was fiddling with the camera. "This is a nice rig. Well... it was. This is a night-vision lens."

Weasel nodded, stymieing Tye's efforts at tying a knot. "Yeah, he wanted me to get pictures of what's going on at the logging site."

"Hold still," Tye said. "Why is everybody so all fired interested in this logging project, anyway?"

"Willie wouldn't tell me. He likes to play it close to the vest. It's a bogus project, man. The forest service shouldn't be allowing logging this close to a riparian area. It's just such a small cut that the big environmental organizations think it's not worth worrying about. They have bigger fish to fry."

Tye finished with the bandage. "This will hold you until we can get you looked at."

"I don't have health insurance."

"Our friend May is a nurse. She can at least tell you if your brains are likely to run out of your ears."

"What did you see tonight?" Kaity asked.

"I snuck in through the woods. I heard heavy machinery running the whole time, but they were finished before I got within sight. I waited long enough. I thought everyone had left, and I decided to look around and take some pictures. That's when Isaac hit me from behind."

"Lucky he didn't kill you," Tye said.

"He didn't say anything, just hit me from behind and started beating me. I think he would have killed me if you two hadn't shown up."

In his mind, Tye replayed what he'd seen in the glare in his flashlight. He had to agree with Weasel. There was a difference between a fight and a beating, and this had definitely been a beating.

"What the hell is going on up here?" he wondered aloud.

"I dunno, man. I thought we might do some direct action, drain the oil out of the equipment, maybe spike some trees, but apparently Willie wants evidence of some kind. He's a lawyer."

"Yeah, but I don't think that's all he is." Tye reached down and helped Weasel to his feet again. "I've done all I can do. Let's get you out of here."

They made better time on the way back. Kaity led the way back, only consulting the GPS a couple of times. Tye kept one eye on Weasel and one eye out in the darkness, hoping they wouldn't be ambushed. The more time that passed, the less worried Tye was about Weasel having a brain bleed, but he was realistic enough to know there was little he could do about it out here in the forest.

The biggest threat of being ambushed was back at Kaity's Jeep. There were multiple routes they could take, but they all led back to their only way out of the woods. About a quarter-mile before the road, Tye had the other two stay put, then sneaked the rest of the way, his reloaded revolver in hand.

On the way, Tye had plenty of time to consider what he'd do if he found Isaac waiting for him. He was surprised to find he had little problem with the idea of killing the man. He didn't want the fury he'd seen back at the logging site unleashed on Kaity. There had been a coldness to the violence that had unnerved him. He resolved that if Isaac was waiting at the Jeep with a rifle, he would shoot him.

A light rain started. If it had been only a couple of degrees colder, it would have been snowing. All the more reason to get to the vehicle and get out of here. This was miserable, dangerous weather. Getting wet would turn them hypothermic in minutes.

All Tye's caution and planning turned out to be for naught. Kaity's Jeep sat there in the darkness. Tye crept around it, making a complete circle, conscious all the while of the time ticking away. Finally satisfied all was clear, he hurried back for the others.

They loaded Weasel into the back. Kaity started the engine and turned up the heater. Tye sighed in relief, knowing the cabin of the little vehicle would soon be warm.

"I appreciate you going ahead," Kaity said as she turned the Jeep around.

"Welcome," Tye said.

"What were you going to do if Isaac had been here waiting for you?"

"Shoot him."

She was driving slowly and carefully, trying not to jostle Weasel, who moaned at every bump.

"I feel like I should make disapproving noises at that idea, but I can't make myself do it after seeing him beat Weasel like that."

"Yup. That was quite a sight."

"I guess we're starting to realize the downside to this whole business of getting involved in other people's affairs."

"Yup, I reckon we are."

26

Isaac's Jeep was gone. Tye had Kaity park down the road, and he again crept up on foot, revolver in hand. She'd looked like she wanted to object but didn't. Instead of waiting, she did pull up as he was walking back. He was grateful because now the rain had turned to pellets of ice and the wind was biting.

"Do you think Isaac killed Christopher?" Kaity asked once they were back on a paved road.

"He sure seems capable," Tye said. "But what I don't understand is, if Isaac is willing to shoot people over what is going on up there, why was his rifle in the Jeep? Once you've shot one person, I reckon you might as well keep on going."

"I guess that's one way to look at it," Kaity said, and fell silent.

Tye half-dozed on the way back. Something was pulling at his mind. He felt like he was missing something, but he was just too tired to see it.

Gary and May were in bed when they pulled up, but they were both used to being roused from sleep for one emergency or another. May went to work on Weasel in the kitchen while Tye and Kaity went into the spare bedroom that served as Gary's office. Kaity had pulled her laptop out of the Jeep.

"Isaac," Gary said as he unscrewed the lid of a bottle of applejack. "Why am I not surprised?"

He held the bottle up and cocked an eyebrow at Tye. He shook his head. Tye felt better after half a ham sandwich he'd found in the fridge and water, but he still felt a mind-crushing migraine lurking in the background like some kind of horror movie monster. He decided to just stick with water.

"He sounds skeezy," Kaity said from where she was digging through the complicated array of adapters and cords that she carried in her computer bag so she could hook her laptop up to Gary's monitor. They wanted to look at the pictures on a bigger screen.

Tye and Gary looked at each other.

"We've never been exactly friends with Isaac," Tye said.

"Always rubbed me the wrong way," Gary said. He pointed at the screen, which was now displaying a picture. "I think you found the right combination."

"Perfect," she said. "What's your Wi-Fi password?"

"Don't have one."

"You're kidding."

"Nobody else lives within range. I reckon the raccoons might steal our signal and start ordering stuff off the internet, but it's a risk we take."

She muttered something under her breath about "the boonies" and slid the memory card from Weasel's camera into her computer. They all crowded around the screen.

"Not the best pictures," Gary said.

"No." She adjusted the pictures, lightening them and changing the contrast.

"Looks like a logging site to me. Harvester. Excavator. Cut-down trees," Gary said.

Kaity switched to another picture.

Gary frowned. "What is that box truck doing out there? They're lucky they didn't bust an axle on those roads."

Kaity zoomed in on the truck. "That's the Tompkin Construction logo on the side."

"Maybe they are using it for parts delivery or something?" Tye said.

"Got a perfectly good four-wheel-drive pickup truck sitting there. Doesn't make sense to me. Besides, why did a construction company get into the logging business?" Gary asked.

Kaity closed the window on her screen and opened a web browser. "I'm confused about the logging thing, too."

As she talked, her fingers flew across the keyboard. Windows were opening on the screen at an alarming rate.

"Your internet is really slow," she said.

"We can only get it via satellite out here," Gary said.

Kaity was switching between windows so fast it was making Tye's eyes hurt trying to follow her.

"Here. The Tompkin Natural Resources Management was created six months ago. It's a completely different company than Tompkin Construction. They bid on that timber sale just a week later. There were only two other companies bidding, and Tompkin way underbid them."

"You found all that out that quickly?" Tye asked.

"I'm a librarian, bud, it's what I do. You find the real footprints; I'll find the digital ones."

Gary tapped on the screen. "Can you open that document? I think it's the actual timber sale."

She clicked on the file, and they waited for it to load. Outside the trailer, Tye heard a great horned owl calling. He tilted back in his chair and closed his eyes, only halfway listening to Kaity and Gary. He was replaying the events of the last few days in his head, trying to figure out what he'd missed.

Gary whistled. "That's all they bid? They can't be making any money on that timber sale. That's way too low."

"You know something about logging?"

"Tye and I worked as choker setters one summer. I can't say I know everything about the business, but I do know that's not even enough money to cover expenses on a job like that."

"Let's pretend for a minute I know what a choker setter is and move on. Why would somebody form a logging company, even though they have no logging experience, and then grossly underbid on a timber sale?"

"Is it some kind of tax dodge?" Gary asked. "I wish I knew more about this kind of thing. We're trying to decide whether to incorporate the farm as an LLC, or a non-profit or whatever. It's confusing."

There was more typing. Kaity and Gary were quiet. Tye replayed the scene back at the logging site in his head. Something was off, but he couldn't quite figure out what it was.

"So, Tompkin Development used to have projects all over Oregon and Washington. But right now, it looks like they only have one. It's right here in Clark County."

"Wait a minute. Tompkin Development? I thought it was Tompkin Construction."

"Tompkin Development manages the projects. Tompkin Construction always gets the bids to do the actual work."

"So, one company hires the other, but they are both owned by the same person?"

"Technically Tompkin Construction is owned by Anna Lee. They get some kind of incentive from the state for using a woman-owned business."

"Rich people are complicated," Gary said.

"Guess what? Here's an article from almost two years ago. They are building an eco-friendly education center on an eighty-acre parcel on the outskirts of Vancouver, Washington. Any guesses who the client is?"

"Nature's Way," Tye said without opening his eyes. "Dylan's school. There's a big display in the lobby about their new property."

"There's our connection," Kaity said.

Tye finally realized what was bugging him. His eyes flew open, and he stood up so fast, Kaity jumped.

"Sorry," he mumbled. "Show me the pictures Weasel took of the logging site again?"

She switched back to the pictures.

"Scroll back to the very first one," Tye said.

"There," Tye said. "The excavator. Why would there be an excavator at a logging site? The engine was still warm when we got there."

"Because uhhh... They wanted something excavated?" Kaity asked.

Gary sat up straight in his chair. "That's a good question. Are they just using it to move slash around?"

The excavator was a squat, tracked vehicle with a claw on the end of a long, articulated boom. It was primarily used for digging, but the claw could also be used to grasp and manipulate heavy objects. Slash was the term used for all the limbs stripped off a tree in the process of making it into a straight log to be shipped out and milled into lumber. At the end of a logging operation, giant piles would be left behind.

"Anything you bury out in the middle of the forest under a giant pile of logging slash ain't likely to be discovered," Gary said.

"Yeah. But what is it?" Tye asked.

Kaity went back to some of the documents she'd retrieved earlier and sat there, tapping her teeth with her finger.

"I have a theory," she said. She swiveled in her chair to face Tye. "How do you feel about sneaking around in the dark at a construction site?"

"I'll make coffee."

27

"The Tompkins are broke," Kaity said as she downshifted. The roads were deserted this time of night. A heavy fog had settled, and Kaity was taking it slow.

"They don't look broke," Tye said. "Fancy clothes. Fancy cars."

"For starters, they paid a huge fine to Washington Department of Fish and Wildlife. Apparently Anna Lee was caught poaching elk. She shot two bulls and only took the antlers and something called a backstrap. She left the rest of the meat to rot."

"The backstrap is like the filet mignon on an elk," Tye said. "You're only allowed to kill one elk a year, and you're supposed to take all the meat. It was Anna Lee and not Wade?"

"I'm certain. The news article was about her. She was lucky not to go to prison.

"That's a really terrible thing to do." As a life long hunter, Tye was offended by wasting wild game meat.

"It gets worse. They negotiated a bankruptcy settlement about eighteen months ago. It's all public record. They are also still entangled in a giant sexual harassment lawsuit that started six months ago. Apparently, Wade can get a little handsy."

"They were going broke doing construction, and they decided to start logging instead? That doesn't make sense."

"Bear with me. The article that said Nature's Way was going to build on the parcel in North Vancouver is over two years old. It dates from just before the bankruptcy proceedings."

"So?"

"So I looked at satellite images of the property. Not much has changed in two years. They've moved some dirt around and set up a temporary structure. That's it."

Tye frowned. "It seems like Dylan would want to get the place up and running as quick as he could so he could start recouping on that investment."

"Exactly. The parcel has been bought and sold numerous times over the last twelve years, but no one has developed it."

"That seems strange. Every time I drive into town, I see a new strip mall or apartment complex where there used to be an empty field."

"Dylan paid well under market value for the land."

"Why? We bought our land about that same time and paid dearly for it. Land ain't cheap out here."

"Prior to all the buying and selling, the land was owned by an electrical supply company for decades. It was zoned as light indus-trial, and Dylan had to get it changed before they could start construction on the new school building."

"All of this is very much out of my wheelhouse."

"I have a theory," Kaity said. "What do you know about PCBs?"

"Is that the stuff people sprinkle on weed that makes them think they can fly when they smoke it?"

"That's PCP. Different. PCBs are polychlorinated biphenyls. It's a really toxic chemical that was used in electrical transformers. There are places all over the country where PCBs have leaked out of old electrical transformers and seeped into the groundwater. It can cost millions of dollars to clean up."

"So?"

"So, what if Dylan found this sweet deal on a piece of property for his school, then found out it was contaminated? He wouldn't be able to build, and the property would be useless."

"Wow. I found a bunch of books in Dylan's office about PCBs."

"And what if Tompkin Construction was so hard up for clients that they cooked up a scheme to haul the transformers into the national forest and bury them?"

Tye thought about that one for a minute.

"I don't know. Dylan and I went to the same primitive-skills schools. Every one of them revolved around caring for the earth. I feel really guilty driving a full-size pickup truck."

"Dylan is a millionaire. You are... kind of the opposite of a millionaire."

"Really? He's a millionaire? I knew he was doing pretty well, but I didn't know he was a millionaire."

"I did some back-of-the-envelope math on the number of classes he runs, the admission prices, and some likely overhead costs. Millionaire."

"Wow. I'm in the wrong line of work."

"I think you're in exactly the right line of work."

Kaity pulled over, consulted the map on her phone for a moment, then pulled back out onto the road.

"So, if we get there and find evidence they are hiding toxic waste, then what?"

"I have the number for the Washington Attorney General's Environmental Protection Division on my phone. There's a place where we can park, sneak through the woods, and look around."

Tye checked his watch. They still had hours of darkness left. The sun set early and rose late this time of year.

The headlights washed over a sign that read "Future home of Nature's Way School!" It was sun-faded, and someone had spray-painted an obscene word in the bottom right-hand corner.

Kaity pulled over and got out, carrying a full-size camera. Tye followed her across the road. He'd left his gun and other gear back at the house, deciding that getting arrested for armed trespassing wasn't something he wanted to risk. He carried a compact monocular and his headlamp.

Gary had offered to come along, but Tye was reluctant to involve his friend in trespassing and possibly breaking and entering. Gary and May were also planning on going up into the forest early in the morning so they could return Weasel to camp and May could tend to Robin. Tye had no idea how long this little wild goose chase was going to take.

The red LEDs on the headlamps were dim, giving just enough light for them to make their way through the thicket slowly without tripping. On the other side of the trees, Tye could hear the rumble of machinery and the whine of a crane or winch. He was surprised that anyone would be working this late, but the houses were far apart out here. At least they would be until everyone sold their properties off to be subdivided.

They came to the edge of the tree cover and could see lights ahead. They crouched behind some bushes, and Kaity raised the camera. Earlier, she'd made sure the flash was disabled. Tye looked through his monocular. The moon was almost full, and there were few clouds. He could see reasonably well. The field in front of them was a muddy, churned-up mess. There were stakes driven into the ground with flagging tape tied to them, probably to mark future roadways and utility lines. A couple of big pieces of earth-moving equipment were parked in different spots.

About halfway across the field was a long, prefab building with a pair of sliding garage doors in front. The doors were open, and as they watched, the panel truck they'd seen at the logging site rolled out. A person hopped out of the truck, pushed the sliding doors shut, locked them, and got back in the truck. Tye and Kaity huddled behind the brush, listening to the sound of the truck's engine fading in the distance.

After a while, Kaity stood up. "I'm going in."

He'd figured doing something illegal tonight was inevitable, and he'd come to terms with it. There was no one in sight, but he still felt horribly exposed as they trotted across the muddy field. It was like a moonscape, with holes and trenches everywhere. There were lots of places where it seemed like big rectangular holes had been filled in.

There was a man door on the side of the building. Kaity ran up to it and squatted down.

"Hold the light," she said and pulled a black case out of her back pocket. The lock popped open much quicker than Tye expected. She straightened and pushed the door open and walked in without hesitation. Tye followed.

"Stop!" she said, and he froze. "Look."

She shone her light into the deep pit only a few feet in front of the door.

"That has to be an OSHA violation. What's down there?" he asked.

Gingerly, she took a few steps forward. "Just what I thought. Transformers."

"Wow," Tye said. He shone his light down into the hole. It reminded him of an archeological dig, with portions of big electrical transformers sticking up out of the dirt. "This building is sitting on skids. I bet they just move it around and dig up the transformers so nobody can see."

"And then haul them out to the logging site, where they bury them under the slash piles. If somebody finds out about this, they won't be able to build their school."

"So it's worth taking a loss on the logging operation," Tye said.

"Or killing Christopher."

Tye shone his flashlight around the room. There were tools scattered around the dirt floor. Over in a corner, he saw a pair of twelve-volt car batteries connected to a power inverter. He followed the power cables to a round camera mounted near the ceiling.

"Oh no," he said. "We need to get out of here."

The door behind them crashed open. Tye nearly jumped out of his skin. He turned around just as a bright light clicked on, blinding him.

"Both of you put your hands up. Do it now."

28

All Tye could see was the bright light. He didn't know for sure that the person holding the light was holding a gun, but they certainly sounded like they might be. Tye put his hands up.

Kaity didn't.

"Who are you?" she asked.

"I'm the person who is going to shoot you in the face if you don't put your hands up." Tye recognized Isaac's voice.

"Are you a cop?" Kaity asked before Tye could say anything.

By way of reply, Isaac pulled the trigger. There was a bright flash. Inside the building, the sound of the shot was like an icepick in the ears.

Kaity flinched but didn't fall over.

"Next one goes in your face, sweet cheeks."

She put her hands up.

"It's Isaac," Tye said. "I recognize his voice. Do what he says."

"Good advice," Isaac said from behind them. He snickered.

From out on the paved road, they heard the roar of an engine. It got closer until it stopped right in front of the doors, then they rolled open, and now Kaity and Tye were illuminated by the headlights of the truck as well.

A figure stepped out of the truck. Tye could just see a silhouette, but he knew who it was.

"Hello, Dylan," Tye said.

"Shit," Dylan breathed.

"We're out of options, now," Isaac said.

"I guess," Dylan said. His voice quavered.

Tye's hands were pulled behind him and bound with tape. He felt a rising sense of panic. Gary would probably know some fancy martial arts move that would at least give him a chance at defeating two people while he was having his hands bound. Tye had a folding Buck knife in a pouch on his belt, but by the time he could've unsnapped the pouch, used both hands to open the knife, and got close enough to use it, he had little doubt he'd have been shot a half a dozen times.

Then it was a moot point. He felt rough hands unsnap the pouch and pull the knife out. His wallet and car keys were next.

Tye heard the ripping sound of duct tape being pulled off a roll. He fought the urge to pull away. After Isaac was done with Tye, he moved on to Kaity.

"Turn around."

They did, and there was Dylan, looking out of place in stained coveralls with a smudge of dirt on his cheek. He held a complicated-looking combat shotgun in his hands. Isaac was wearing work clothes too, but he had a pair of night-vision goggles dangling by a strap around his neck and a large handgun.

Isaac looked relaxed, like he'd done this sort of thing before. In the harsh glare of the headlights, Tye could see that Dylan was pale and shaking.

"You look scared, Dylan," Tye said. "I guess shooting somebody with a rifle isn't quite the same as being up close where you have to look them in the eye, huh?"

He swallowed hard. "Shut up. You don't know what you're talking about. I didn't shoot anybody." But he still didn't meet his eye.

Isaac gestured with the gun. "In the truck."

Tye tensed. He didn't know exactly what he was going to do with his hands tied behind his back, but he didn't want to get in the back of that truck. During his search-and-rescue days, he'd attended training about recovering kidnapping victims, and a clean-cut FBI agent had talked about secondary crime scenes, where an abductor took his victims so they could do whatever they wanted in privacy. The slide presentation had given Tye nightmares for a week.

Kaity turned and started walking toward the truck, carefully picking her way along the edge of the pit. Tye found himself following her.

Dylan unlatched and pushed up on the rolling door covering the back of the truck. In the light of Wade's flashlight, Tye could see the back of the truck was three quarters full of old rusty transformers haphazardly tied down.

Kaity started to climb in. It was difficult with her hands behind her back. Isaac reached out a hand, but instead of helping her, he stuck a hand up her shirt. Kaity froze. When he saw the look on her face, Tye heard an animal growl that he realized was coming from him.

He charged, hands behind his back, meaning to headbutt Isaac in the side of the jaw, but his feet slipped in the gooey mud, and he wound up crashing into Isaac's shoulder instead. All three of them, Tye, Kaity, and Isaac, crashed to the ground. Tye tried to pull his hands around and scrabble for Isaac's pistol, but before he could do anything, a heavy blow fell on the side of his neck.

Tye grunted and saw stars. He looked up to see Dylan raising the butt of the shotgun, threatening another blow.

"Enough!" Dylan said.

Isaac scrambled to his feet, murder in his eyes. He grabbed the pistol, but Dylan leveled the shotgun at him.

"Leave them alone. Don't touch her again," Dylan said.

For a moment, Tye thought they were going to shoot each other, and wondered if that would work out to his and Kaity's favor.

Instead, Isaac stuck the pistol in his waistband and shrugged. It was like he'd turned his anger off with a switch.

"Whatever you say, boss. You drive the truck with these two in the back. I'll lead the way in my Jeep."

Dylan turned to them. "Just get in. We don't want to hurt you. We just need to figure out what to do with you for a little while. We can make it worth your while to be quiet."

Kaity nodded. "We'll do what you say." She bumped Tye's hip with hers.

Fighting a rising panic, Tye followed Kaity into the back of the truck. He sat beside her in a small space between two transformers. The sliding door rolled shut, plunging them into darkness. Tye fought against the sound building in his throat that was half scream, half growl.

"Don't worry," Kaity said. "I have a plan."

29

Tye tried to control his breathing to fight the rising panic he felt. All his life, he'd hated being confined or restrained. When other kids would want to wrestle, he'd try to beg off, knowing that if he got pinned to the ground, he would be liable to go into full-blown berserker mode until somebody got hurt. He wasn't afraid of the dark, but right now, the inside of the truck felt like a tomb. The truck's cargo box swayed back and forth on the suspension, and he heard the transformers shift. The last thing they needed was for one of the heavy transformers to break free and land on them.

Beside him, Kaity squirmed around.

"Now would be a great time to tell me your plan," Tye said.

"I'm trying to get my hands over my feet so they are in front of me."

"You can do that?"

"Lots of yoga."

She squirmed and grunted, pressing against them, then away as the truck rolled back and forth.

"Is there a way I can help?"

"Not really. I don't suppose you have a knife on you?"

"No, Isaac took my Buck knife."

"Anything else?"

"He took my wallet and car keys. I might still have a lighter in the bottom of my pocket. I don't think he reached all the way in."

"Let's save burning through the duct tape as a last resort. Anything else?"

He wasn't sure if she really wanted to know what he had in his pockets, or if it was just a way to take his mind off things.

"Uh... A have a handkerchief in my back pocket."

"What else? Think of what we can do to improvise."

In the wilderness and survival community, adapting everyday objects to a new purpose was a staple skill. He'd never considered it in quite this context, though.

"I've still got my belt. And my shoelaces. They are parachute cord."

Parachute cord, also known as 550 cord, was thin and light but would still hold 550 pounds, hence the name. It was made with a tough outer mantle and seven individual strands inside.

"That's clever, swapping shoelaces for parachute cord like that," she said

"Actually, I just broke a shoelace and didn't want to drive into town."

She gave a grunt. "There. That hurt."

He felt her hands on his wrists, picking at the duct tape.

"Wow. You're really flexible," he said.

"Yes. And it hurt. I'm trying to find the end of the duct tape that's wrapped around your hands, but the circulation is cut off in my fingers. Now what?"

The inside of the truck lit up for a bare second, then was plunged into darkness, then lit up again.

"What's that?" she asked.

"We're driving under streetlights. The top of the truck is translucent plastic. It's less weight, and it lets some light in so you can see back here in the daytime."

"Is it breakable?" she asked.

"I bet it is. I have an idea."

He felt a glimmer of hope for the first time since he'd turned around to find a gun shoved in his face. This wasn't different from any of the other survival situations he'd found himself in over the years. He just needed to keep working on the problem and doing the next right thing.

"I'm all ears," Kaity said. Her voice was shaky.

"Can you undo one of my shoelaces?"

"Look, Buster, this is no time to be coming on to me."

"I'm serious. It will help."

"I'm kidding, dummy." As she spoke, he felt her tugging at the laces on his right shoe.

"I pulled it out of your shoe. Now what?"

"Loop it around that railing about halfway up the side of the truck."

There was a wood railing that ran around the inside of the truck for lashing items down. In the flash of a streetlight, he saw her struggling to feed the end of the line behind the rail.

"My fingers feel like sausages. He put this tape on too tight. I got it."

He scooted toward the middle of the floor. "Put the ends in my hand."

Her fingers felt cold against his as she shoved the ends of the shoelace into his hand. He held on as hard as he could and scooted forward some more, pulling the lines taut.

"Now saw away at the duct tape on the cord."

"Won't it break?" she asked. Despite the question, he saw her pushing her hands against the cord so it was between her wrists.

"It might. But I've got another shoelace. I don't have any other ideas."

She pressed against him and started sawing back and forth on the cord.

"Is it working?"

"A little," she said. "It's cut a notch in the tape, but it's slow."

They went on like that for long, agonizing minutes. They had to stop twice because the cord pulled through Tye's fingers, which were going numb too.

"How long do you think we have?" she asked after they got the cord set up the second time.

Tye had been sitting there thinking about exactly that. "The logging site is about an hour and a half away," Tye said as he tightened his grip on the string as best as he was able. His fingers felt like pins and needles were being jabbed into them, except the very tips, which he couldn't feel anymore. After a long period of darkness, a handful of lights passed by overhead, then it was dark again.

"I think we've been in here for almost half an hour," he said. "If I'm guessing right, we're passing through the town of Battle Ground right now."

She grunted, then said, "I'm almost a third of the way through."

"The bad thing is, the roads are going to get rougher the farther we go. We're really going to get bounced around back here."

She was silent for a minute, just sawing at the tape, then she hawked and spat.

"What did you do that for?"

"DNA. That's why they didn't shoot us back at the construction site. There would be blood spatter everywhere."

He tried to summon up enough saliva to spit, but all of a sudden, his mouth was parched. He concentrated on holding the cord tight and tried to think of a way to get the roof panels off the truck. Even though the night was cool, it was surprisingly hot inside the truck. He felt sweaty, almost feverish. The pile of transformers in the front smelled of rust and dirt, with a faint oily undertone. The floor was slick in spots with patches of an oily substance, which he realized was probably the PCBs leaking out. That wasn't good for his health, he supposed, but he had more pressing concerns.

Kaity was the one doing all the work. All he had to do was sit there, hold on to the parachute cord, and think. He kept beating himself up for not connecting with Isaac's head back at the construction site. Getting shot there would have been worse, but being transported up into the national forest was even worse. Maybe back there, Kaity could have figured out a way to escape.

"Halfway," she said.

"Try pulling your hands apart."

She pulled with a grunt. "I think I felt some strands pop," she said. "It's got to be an inch thick. He put half the roll on there."

"And the other half on me."

She attacked the tape with renewed vigor. The road had become curvier, and it had been a long time since they'd seen a streetlight. Suddenly, the van lurched right, then rolled left. Kaity tipped into him, and they both went sprawling.

"These are the curves on state route 503, I bet. Hold on. There's a few more."

He tried to wrap his legs around her as the load of transformers shifted and creaked ominously. The truck swayed through a few more sharp turns. Tye was pretty sure he knew where they were at. There was a particular stretch of road with a series of downhill, almost hairpin turns.

The truck straightened out for a little while, then stopped.

"Yep," he said. Unwrapping his legs from around her. "We should turn right here."

On cue, the truck turned right, then picked up speed.

"We're traveling along Lewis River Road," he said.

"Awesome," she said. "There's one problem. I can't find the cord. Do you have it?"

"I don't."

He forced himself to remain calm as they scrabbled around on the floor, looking for the lost piece of parachute cord. He could tell she was struggling to fight off panic with deep breathing as well. Tye was of limited use with his hands behind his back.

"I found it," she said, right as he was about to tell her to untie his other shoelace.

She made a sound that was half sob, half curse. "Oh, my fingers hurt so bad. I've got it, but I'm afraid I'll drop it."

He heard her rustle and tried to think of something he could do to help.

"Okay," she said, her voice oddly muffled. "I've got one end in my mouth in case I drop it. Scoot back."

He slid back toward the rail, and she managed to get both ends of the cord back in his hands. Her fingers were so cold he couldn't believe she was still using them. He ignored the fact that one end of the cord was wet with spit and concentrated on holding on.

She sawed back and forth frantically. He guessed her arms and shoulders were going to be sore in the morning, if they lived that long.

Suddenly, she stopped.

"What?"

"Hold on. Yes!"

He heard a ripping sound.

"I did it! I'm loose! Oh my God, my hands hurt."

He heard her flapping her arms around. He realized she was crying.

"Okay," she said. "I've had a moment. I know we're not out of this yet, but it felt good to get a win. Now turn around."

He still had a death grip on the parachute cord. She pulled it out of his hands and started sawing away at the tape. They made much quicker progress using it that way than she had rubbing her hands against the line.

"It's getting hot," he said.

"Yeah. I'm going to have pretty good blisters on the insides of my wrists."

"You didn't say anything."

"What was the point? I couldn't stop."

So he sat there and gritted his teeth against the burning pain in his wrists. He couldn't pull his wrists apart against the resistance of the tape, so the parachute cord was rubbing against his skin as well as the tape. He figured if she could hack it, he could.

He pulled his hands apart as hard as he could.

"I'm halfway through," she said. "Give it a tug."

She pulled the cord out and he pushed his hands together, then jerked as hard as he could.

"Nothing," he said.

"We'll keep going."

The truck made a sharp turn, and they slid toward the back. The ride became much rougher.

"We just turned onto the forest service road on the way to Indian Heaven," Tye said.

"How much longer?"

"Maybe forty-five minutes."

She kept going, and Tye kept pulling. Sweat was running down his forehead, even though she was doing most of the work. The air in the back of the truck seemed close and stale. He didn't know if it was due to a real lack of ventilation, or if it was because of the panic he felt edging up on him from all directions.

To take his mind off things, he relaxed his shoulders, then gave a jerk. He felt a pop, and suddenly his hand was free. Even though he couldn't see in the blackness, he held his hands up in front of his face and flexed his fingers. Despite the burning pain as the blood rushed back in, he found himself laughing.

Kaity was laughing, too. She wrapped her arms around him in a brief hug. "We did it!"

Tye felt the panic recede. Just a little. He took hold of the wooden railing and pulled himself up on shaky legs.

"Yep. Now let's figure out how to get out of here."

30

"Just see if you can steady my legs and keep me from swinging," Tye said.

"Easier said than done," Kaity said.

Their plan made sense if Tye didn't think about it too much. The back of the truck had a ceiling a little less than eight feet high, by Tye's estimation. The roof was constructed of translucent panels that spanned the top of the box from side to side. They had rooted around the pile of transformers and Kaity came up with a loose mounting bracket, a flat metal bar about two feet long and a few inches wide.

In addition to the wooden rail about halfway up the wall, there was a row of metal rings attached to the wall every few feet, about a foot or so below the ceiling. Tye was dangling from one of the rings by the parachute cord, which he'd tied through the ring on the wall, then through his rigger's belt. He was trying to steady himself by putting his feet on the rail, with little success because of the rough road.

Kaity wrapped her arms around his legs and pushed, essentially pinning him with his right shoulder against the wall. Now his hands were free. The panels were fastened at the corners. He pushed up in the middle and it flexed, giving him just enough room to stick the metal bar between the edge of the panel and the frame of the truck box.

"Can you just break it?"

"Maybe. I'm afraid it will make so much noise he'll hear it up front, though."

He worked the bar forward. There was some kind of weather stripping, sealing the gap between the panel and the top of the truck box. It was giving way slowly. He pushed the bar forward an inch at a time, then levered up, breaking the seal. A faint trickle of cool night air blew in through the crack.

"I've been thinking," Kaity said, her voice muffled as her cheek was pressed against Tye's leg. "If we don't get out before they stop, we should just rush them. Then we should split up and go in separate directions. I think they only have one set of night-vision goggles."

"Yep," Tye said. The truck lurched as it went over a particularly bad pothole, and the bar slipped out of the crack. He forced himself not to give in to frustration. Instead, he took a deep breath and started over again, pushing up on the panel and wedging the bar in near the center to work it forward bit by bit.

"Once you get that off, what do we do?" she asked. "The truck is still moving."

"We need to go up and over the back of the truck. Don't go over the side or you might fall under the wheels. You're shorter than me, so I'm going to help you climb up. Then we hang off the back. If you can drop to the bumper, then the ground first, that'll be best."

"That sounds pretty sketchy," she said.

"It beats getting shot in the back of the head. Dylan was lying to either us or himself when he said they weren't going to hurt us."

He'd reached the forward edge of the panel. It was held in place by a bolt or screw a quarter of an inch thick. He had no way of unscrewing it, especially from the inside, so he attacked the translucent panel around it, working the bar back and forth. He was rewarded by a cracking and crunching sound, and the panel popped free. He pushed it up a hand's breadth and just hung there for a moment, enjoying the cold night air.

"That was good, right?"

"Yeah. Halfway there."

Now he had to turn around, so he was facing the back of the truck, with his left side pressed against the wall. His legs were going numb from the belt pressing into his hips, and he had a crick in his neck that felt like it was going to be permanent. He attacked the second half of the panel. He hadn't kept good track of the turns, so he was disoriented. He didn't think they had much time left.

The second half was going well when the truck bottomed out its suspension in a particularly nasty rut. Kaity fell, letting go of his legs. He swung out away from the wall. The belt bit cruelly into his hips and back. His feet slid off the rail, and he heard the ring holding him creak ominously as it took all of his weight.

He went back to work on the roof panel while she braced his legs again. The truck slowed, giving him a little warning before they bottomed out in another rut. His head slammed against the roof, but he managed not to drop the pry bar. In fact, the impact popped the panel loose from the rest of the adhesive, leaving only one bolt holding it down.

"I'm almost through. Get ready," Tye said.

"Would now be a good time to mention how much I hate the idea of jumping off a moving truck?"

The truck made a turn, and despite slowing to a crawl, the ride became horrible. Tye realized they'd turned on the temporary road to the logging site. Instead of answering Kaity, he stuck the bar deep into the joint between the panel and the frame and twisted. The panel popped loose and started flapping up and down with each bump. He handed Kaity the bar, then pushed up with one hand. The panel flexed up at least a foot. Plenty of room.

"It's loose. Let's go. They're going to stop soon."

She climbed up onto the rail. Tye helped her get over the top of the edge. She nearly pitched out headfirst at a particularly bad bump, but he held onto her belt. She swung a leg over, hung by her fingers, and then was gone. He heard a crunch of gravel when she hit, but didn't hear her scream, so he figured she'd either avoided the wheels or had been killed instantly.

He pulled his head and shoulders out of the truck. The air was chilly, and the moon gave some decent illumination. He held on to the wildly bucking frame with one hand and managed to untie the knot holding him to the railing with the other. The cord slipped through his fingers and was gone.

He swung a leg over like Kaity had done and managed to lower himself until he was dangling by his fingers. It was too far for his toes to reach the bumper. He held on with one hand, the muscles in his arm screaming, and felt for some kind of handhold on the locking bar of the door. The truck took a particularly nasty bump. The roof panel slammed down on his fingers, and he dropped. His feet hit the bumper, and he pitched backwards. He had the presence of mind to tuck his chin before he hit.

All the air left his lungs and he saw stars. He managed to sit upright and tried to fight off the sense of panic that came with not being able to breathe.

After a moment he was able to take a short, hitching breath, then he could breathe again. His left hand was wet and sticky, and he realized blood was running down his arm. He'd skinned his elbow up pretty good, but he flexed the arm and it still worked. He ran his hands over himself experimentally and found a big raw scrape on the point of his hip, but otherwise everything seemed to work. He also realized he was missing his shoe.

"This is going to hurt in the morning," he said. That made him remember Dylan and Isaac. The taillights of the Isaac's Jeep and the truck Dylan was driving were visible a hundred yards away. The truck was bouncing down the rough road at a snail's pace, and it didn't seem that they realized anything was amiss.

He heard the crunch of feet on gravel. Kaity walked up and thrust something at him.

He realized it was his shoe.

"I can't believe that worked," she said. "Holy crap. We just jumped off a moving truck. That was epic." She was talking way too fast, like someone who had just taken a hit of speed.

"Yep. We need to get in the trees. Those night vision-goggles won't work too well if we get into some cover."

She reached down a hand, and he took it. She jerked him to his feet. Nothing felt broken, but plenty of things hurt.

"Then again, maybe it will just start hurting now," he said under his breath.

"Yeah. Me too. Which way?"

"That way."

He was hobbling a little, and the laceless shoe didn't help, but they made decent time toward the tree line. He had a rough idea of where they were. The tribe's camp was only a few miles away.

"I thought we were dead," she said. "Things are looking up."

"Yep. Sure wish I had a shoelace, though."

31

It was darker inside the tree line, and every step risked tripping or getting a branch in the eye. Tye found himself trying to keep up with Kaity, who was all but running. Finally, the inevitable happened, and she crashed to the ground. Now it was his turn to help her up.

"You okay?" he asked as he helped her to her feet.

"Yeah."

He realized she was shivering. They were both lightly dressed and covered in sweat. He guessed the temperature was in the upper forties, and likely to drop at least a few more degrees.

"We need to come up with a plan here. It's cold," Tye said.

She wrapped her arms around herself. "We could get hypothermia, right?"

"You're shivering. You're already mildly hypothermic. I have a lighter. We can probably make a fire. I think we need to get farther away from the road. Eventually, they're going to figure out we aren't in the back of the truck."

She gestured for him to go ahead. He picked his way carefully forward, keeping track of his pace count, and taking frequent breaks to listen. The temperature was dropping as the cold air on top of the ridges settled into the valley below. He could picture a topographical map of the area where they were. The sky was cloudless, and the moon was three-quarters full, so he'd had a few reference points to work with before they plunged into the trees. He had a reasonably good feeling he knew where they were. He took them up a little draw, staying mid-slope, away from the worst of the winds on the ridge top and out of the cold air that would sink to the bottom.

They had changed clothes before going into town, figuring that wearing camouflage and hiking clothes might look suspicious. He was wearing jeans, a t-shirt, and a light windbreaker, all of which had gotten sweaty during the escape from the truck. Kaity was also wearing jeans and a synthetic hoodie. Even with temperatures in the forties, there was a non-trivial chance that they could become significantly hypothermic in short order. It was still early in the evening, and the overnight low temperature up here was likely to be below freezing.

Tye was worried about Kaity. They were about the same height, but she probably weighed fifty pounds less than him and would shed heat much faster.

Their progress was slowed by his need to keep his shoe on, and the heavy vegetation. It was impossible to be quiet. They just had to settle for not crashing through the brush like elephants. They would pause for listening breaks at irregular intervals. Even if Dylan and Isaac found their trail, they couldn't follow at night without noise.

"I'm shivering pretty bad," Kaity said after a few minutes. He could hear her teeth chattering. He was starting to shiver as well.

Tye was leading them as much by feel as by sight. They managed to navigate around a particularly dense stand of vine maple without tripping, but Tye felt almost suffocated by the dozens of little branches all around him that he could barely see.

"Also, I'm really only pretending that I can see," Kaity said. Her tone was measured and even. He knew she wasn't complaining, just giving him information he needed to know. Another shiver wracked her body.

"Here," he said as he pulled off his windbreaker. "We can take turns wearing this."

He expected her to argue, but she didn't. Kaity had trouble getting her arms in the jacket. Her movements were clumsy.

"This sucks," she said, teeth chattering.

As soon as Tye took off the jacket, he felt even more chilled. "Let's keep moving. We need to find someplace to make a shelter."

"Lead the way. From now on, I'm not leaving the house unless I'm dressed for the elements. Not even for the mailbox."

Tye laughed a bitter laugh. He'd just been thinking about the trunk full of outdoor clothing back in his yurt. He skimped on groceries sometimes, buying the dented cans, but he bought the best gear he could find. But instead of his merino-wool base layers and high-tech breathable outer shells, he found himself wandering the woods with all cotton clothing, jeans, a t-shirt, and a plaid flannel.

The full moon was the only thing working for them right now. Currently, it was free of clouds, but he could see a wall of clouds moving in from the west. Kaity looked in the same direction as him.

"It's going to rain, isn't it?" she asked. "The forecast said it would rain after midnight."

"Yep. It's going to rain."

"I thought we'd be in and out by now," she said. "I pictured us getting the evidence, going back to your place, and drafting an email to the attorney general."

"Me too."

"I'm scared," she said.

"Me too."

"That's not what you're supposed to say. You're supposed to say something encouraging about how you've done stuff like this a million times, and you are about to build a structure out of twigs with hot and cold running water."

"I want to find a place like a rock overhang, or even a good-sized fallen tree. We can make a debris shelter using some tree limbs and some boughs to shed the rain. Then I'll work on making a fire."

"Much better. I understand the shelter part. I don't understand the fire part. Everything is wet."

"That's going to be a challenge. Let's get moving while we still have some light."

They were following a game trail. Tye couldn't trust it to take them to any particular place, but animals would generally follow the path of least resistance through any terrain. They were headed up a narrow valley, away from the road. He'd considered heading back toward the road, but the likelihood of anyone other than Dylan and Isaac driving by at this time of night was infinitesimal. There were no structures nearby that Tye knew of.

They were about halfway up the slope, right where Tye wanted to be. That would keep them out of the pocket of cold air that would settle in the bottom of the valley, and away from the winds that would blow across the top of the ridges.

He looked for some place to construct a hasty shelter. It was going to be harder than he'd made it out to Kaity. This was tall, old timber. The forest floor was almost exclusively fir needle duff, devoid of the piles of leaves they would need to build a shelter that would shed some of the oncoming rain.

Briefly, he wondered if they should go lower down the slope. If there was a creek down there, there would be different vegetation, perhaps some willow and alder trees with lower-growing branches, and piles of dead leaves they could use to build a nest to burrow into.

He opened his mouth to suggest this when movement caught his eye. A human figure moved through the trees, then stood in a patch of moonlight, looking over his shoulder.

He was probably almost a hundred yards away, but Tye was pretty sure it was Christopher.

"What are you looking at?" Kaity asked. She leaned to look past him and squinted. "I don't see anything."

He almost told her what he saw but stopped himself. "I think there's a pretty clear path through the trees. Let's head up that way."

As soon as he started walking, the figure ahead started moving, too. Tye never managed to get any closer. Every time Tye was afraid the figure was going to get too far ahead, it would stop and wait for Tye to catch up.

"What about there?" Kaity asked from behind him. He stopped and looked where she pointed. There was a downed Douglas fir tree not far from them. The trunk was easily chest-high to Tye, and there was a riot of broken and shattered branches on the ground all around.

Ahead, the figure pointed up the slope.

"Let's keep this spot in mind," Tye said. "If we don't find anything better in the next few minutes, we can come back."

She looked skeptical but nodded.

Ahead, the figure was gone. Tye marked the spot where he'd stood when he'd pointed up-slope and walked toward it.

The light faded as the clouds moved in. Tye found the spot where Christopher had stood and pointed, or at least he thought so. Out of habit, he checked the ground. In the dim light, he didn't see any obvious tracks, but he was willing to bet there wouldn't have been any.

There was a faint game trail headed straight up the slope, or at least Tye could convince himself there was. He bent at the waist to see the trail through the duff, halfway convinced he was imagining it.

"Where are you going?" Kaity asked. "I think we should go back to that fallen tree."

Her speech was slurred. It reminded Tye of somebody who was trying to talk after being numbed at the dentist's office.

The skies finally opened up, but instead of the rain he'd been dreading, it was sleet, little frozen pellets that stung his skin.

A few more feet. He wasn't sure if he said it out loud or just thought about it.

"Or I guess instead of going back, we could just go inside that cave you just found," Kaity said from behind him.

He'd been so intent on following the trail through the duff, he hadn't been looking up. Now he straightened and saw the jagged narrow crack in the cliff face in front of him.

Just like the one in his dream.

32

"At least I think that's a cave," Kaity mumbled. "Like, somewhere we can go inside and be warm. Do you think so? Please say yes." Her teeth were chattering, and she shivered violently.

"I saw this place in a dream," he said.

"You dreamed of it? I'm not sure if that's good or bad."

"Me neither."

"I don't care. I'm going inside."

Just like in his dream, the entry was narrow enough he had to turn sideways to get his shoulders through. He bumped into Kaity, who had stopped just inside.

"Of course it's dark. I can't see a thing. It's warmer, though."

She was right. On a hot summer day, the air wafting into his face would have been delightfully cool, but now it felt warm. Tye had read somewhere that caves tended to stay at the average year-round temperature of the region where they were located. If that was true, this was about to save their lives.

His fingers were barely coordinated enough to get the lighter out of his pocket and strike the wheel, but he managed. The weak flame cast enough light to see for only a few feet.

"Careful," he said. "The floor will be rough. Keep going. It should open soon."

He stayed close behind Kaity. She was shivering so badly it was almost like she was vibrating.

"What's all this?" she asked and stopped again. In the faint glow of the lighter, the figures painted on the walls and ceiling seemed to dance.

Tye tried not to think too hard about the fact that the cave was identical to the one in his dream. Instead, he walked over to where he knew the little hearth would be. There was already a fire laid. He put lighter's flame to the pile of wood shavings at the bottom, and soon the tinder and the smaller pieces of kindling were alight, casting a glow through the cave.

"Oh. A fire."

She moved over to the fire and put her hands as close to the flames as she could without burning her skin.

"I've never been so grateful for heat," she said. "You just take it for granted, you know? You adjust the thermostat in the house and the heat just turns on."

He nodded and joined her by the fire, feeling a giant weight lift off him. Apparently, he wasn't going to get her killed tonight.

"You knew this place was here?" she asked.

"I had a dream about this place," he said.

"You mean dream about a cave in general, or this exact place?"

"This exact place." Tye had to fight to get the words out. He had this fear that eventually Kaity would decide that this whole thing was too weird for her, and that she didn't want anything to do with him.

Instead, she leaned into him and put an arm around his waist. "I never believed in visions and things like that until I met you. What now?"

Outside, he could hear the wind picking up. It sounded like the sleet had turned to rain, for the moment. "I think we should stay here for the night. The rain is going to wash away our tracks, so I'm not worried about Isaac and Dylan tracking us down. Let's look around."

The stack of firewood probably wouldn't last all night, but it wouldn't have to. The cave's natural warmth would have been enough to keep them from dying, and now that the rock was starting to heat up from the fire, it was downright comfortable.

In Tye's dream, there had been a bough bed over by the fire. In reality, there was a big black trash bag instead. Kaity opened it and pulled out a self-inflating sleeping pad, a sleeping bag, and a wool blanket.

"Yes!" she said as she pulled out the blanket. She was shivering less, and her words were no longer slurred. Tye felt chilled, but he wasn't shivering anymore. His hands burned and ached as warm blood began to circulate again.

Kaity busied herself setting up the mattress while Tye took a burning branch from the fire and walked back out to the cave opening. Frigid air blew into the opening, and it was raining hard outside. He shivered, but this time it wasn't from the cold. If they had tried to survive in a makeshift shelter, they'd be well on their way to severe hypothermia by now.

He couldn't see more than a few feet past the cave entrance. There was no way Isaac and Dylan could track them through this. They were safe, for now.

Back inside the cave, Kaity was on the mattress. She'd unzipped the sleeping bag into a quilt and was burrowed into it and the blanket, so all that showed were her eyes and nose.

"There's room for you," she said.

Tye stopped by the woodpile. He added more fuel to the fire and kept one wrist-thick piece of firewood. It would do as a club. It was a poor answer to the pistol and the giant shotgun Isaac and Dylan had been carrying, but it was something.

He slid underneath the covers beside Kaity. He could still feel the faint tremors as her body sought to warm itself by shivering. She pressed against him and pulled his hand under her hoodie, against the warm, soft skin of her belly.

"This isn't how I envisioned our first night together," she said.

"Me neither."

"I mean, ordinarily, if you told me 'we need to cuddle to fight off hypothermia,' I would think you were feeding me a line."

He laughed. "I've never been terribly good at feeding women lines."

"I can tell. It's one of the things I like about you." She yawned. "I am so incredibly tired I can barely keep my eyes open, despite the fact that we escaped from being kidnapped and are on the run from two guys who might be murderers."

"Normal," he said. "Your body burned a bunch of energy trying to keep warm."

"If I go to sleep, I'm gonna wake up, right? I'm feeling much better than I was."

"Yeah. You're fine. I was a little worried about you for a while, but I think you're out of the woods."

"Good," she said. She gave his hand a squeeze. "Thank you."

Her breathing slowed, and after a few minutes, Tye was pretty sure she was asleep.

Tye's head was spinning. First, there was the new intimacy with Kaity, which felt both novel and completely natural at the same time. He wanted to just lie there with her and enjoy it, but he couldn't get Dylan and Isaac out of his head.

Had they killed Christopher? It seemed like a leap to go from a shady real estate deal to shooting somebody in the back with a rifle. But there was an air of desperation about Dylan that Tye couldn't quite understand.

Isaac just scared him. Tye hadn't realized how far the streak of coldness ran in him. With a flush of hot shame, he remembered how he'd stood there helpless while Isaac touched Kaity. There had been a casual cruelty to Isaac's actions that had shocked Tye. He'd certainly seen similar things in his life, but not from someone he thought he knew.

Then there was the cave. In the flickering firelight, his eyes were drawn to the drawing of the Dark Man. Somehow, despite the drawing, he felt safe here, like this was a place he was supposed to be. The Dark Man seemed contained by the surrounding people.

He smelled Kaity's hair, felt her curves pressed against him, and listened to the pop and crackle of the fire. He'd expected to have trouble sleeping but found his eyelids drooping. There was a thudding sound, like a heartbeat, that he felt as much as heard.

In his mind, he felt himself back out in the forest, in the rain and wind. It was like two tracks were playing in his mind: one where he was here, wrapped up in blankets with Kaity, the other where he was alone and in danger of freezing again.

He stepped back into the familiar glow of the cave. Only, instead of Kaity's face lit by the fire, he saw someone else he recognized. A small, wizened old man, clad only in a skin around his loins. He squatted in front of the fire, bending an arrow shaft to straighten it.

"You again?" the old man said. "You just left a few minutes ago."

Tye blinked. He'd met the man in another dream, in another cave on an island in Puget Sound. He called himself the First Man.

"That was another cave," Tye said.

The First Man shrugged. "They are all the same." He gestured at the floor beside him. "Sit. The air is damp this time of year and makes my arrow shafts bend."

Bemused, Tye sat cross-legged on the ground near the fire and watched as the old man sighted down the arrow and turned it. He grunted and held the high side of the bend nearest the fire.

"So. Here you are again. How did you find your way back?"

"I followed a dead man."

He nodded. Tye wasn't sure if it was because of what he'd just said, or because he was satisfied that the arrow was hot enough, because he drew it away from the fire, bent it with his thumbs, and sighted down the shaft again.

"Almost there," the First Man said. "A dead man? You seem to talk to them quite a bit. That's rare these days." He again held the arrow up to the fire.

That opened up so many questions in Tye's head, he didn't know which one to ask first.

"Why me?" was the one that finally came out.

The old man shrugged. "Why not? Maybe it is good for everyone that you do these things. Have you done good things?"

Tye blinked. "I guess. I found a lost child."

"Mmm. This is good. Children should not be lost. And you fought?"

Tye pointed at the ceiling. "Yes. The Dark Man, over there on the ceiling."

The First Man glanced up at the drawing, looked away, and shook his head.

"He is no good, that one."

"Who is he?"

"He is you. He is me. He is all of us when we want too much."

Tye didn't know what to say to that. The old man sighted down his arrow, and apparently satisfied by the results, slid it back into the skin quiver on the floor next to his bow. He drew out another arrow and sighted down that one.

"I don't understand," Tye said.

"I have this many arrows," the First Man said, and held up three fingers. "I could look at my arrows and be happy. Or I could look at my arrows and decide I want this many." He held up another finger, making four. "Maybe that's when I start becoming the Dark Man."

"Four arrows?"

The old man sighed and held his new arrow up to the fire. "You found the lost girl, and fought the Dark Man, before you met me?"

"Yes."

"You were fighting someone else when you met me. Who?"

Tye tried to put it into words that he thought the old man would understand. "They were tech people. They were trying to control everyone."

"And what did all these people want? All these people you have fought?"

"More." The word came out of Tye's mouth before he had a chance to think.

The First Man nodded, and this time Tye knew it was because of what he'd said, because the arrow was still crooked.

"Yes. More. This many arrows is enough. Maybe a few more would be nice. Too many become hard to carry. But there are people in your world who would carry more arrows than stars in the sky, and would still want yours, even if it meant you wouldn't be able to feed yourself."

Tye felt a wave of fatigue wash over him, and a sensation of being *pulled* like there was a rope around his waist, dragging him toward the cave entrance.

The First Man must have seen something cross his face.

"Mmm. Your time here is growing short, I think. You have been here a long time, especially for one such as you. It takes great energy to do this."

Again, Tye had a million questions he wanted to ask all at once. "What should I do?" was the one that came out.

"Protect the weak," the old man said. "That is what is best for everyone."

There was more Tye wanted to ask, but he felt himself being jerked backward into the darkness. The thud of the heartbeat grew louder, until, with a sudden intake of breath, he found himself back in bed with Kaity.

When Tye had last looked, the fire had been blazing a foot high. Now it had burned down to barely glowing coals.

"It felt like you weren't there," Kaity mumbled. "Where did you go?"

Tye almost said "nowhere," but he wasn't exactly sure that was true.

"I'm here now," he said instead. "I'm going to put some wood on the fire."

He scooted away from her, stacked the rest of the firewood on the coals, and blew the fire back to life. Outside, it was quiet. It had quit raining.

Kaity fitted herself against him again when he crawled back under the covers.

"This is nice," she said. "We should do this more often."

"I agree."

She was asleep again in minutes, but Tye spent a long time staring at the flames.

33

Tye looked out of the cave entrance, into the weak gray light of dawn. There was a light snow on the ground, less than an inch. It was undisturbed by any tracks. In the treetops above, ruby-crowned kinglets were flitting from branch to branch, chirping at each other without a care in the world. Tye sat his makeshift club by the opening and turned to go back in the cave.

Kaity stirred and mumbled.

"Morning, sleepyhead."

She sat up and rubbed her eyes. "What time is it?"

"Right around daybreak. We should probably head out soon."

"Is there coffee? I would feel better about this whole surviving-in-the-woods-while-fleeing-murderers thing if there was coffee."

In spite of his worries, he smiled. "I'll buy you a cup when we get back to town."

"And a chocolate croissant?"

"And a chocolate croissant."

"Deal."

She stood up and brushed herself off. They both looked terrible. They were covered in dirt, and in some places, blood. Tye's jeans were shredded over his left hip, and he had a good patch of road rash. It hurt, but he didn't think anything was broken. They both had a skinned elbow and various other bumps and bruises.

"I guess the advantage to traveling light is we don't have to pack up," she said.

Kaity had a point. Tye was a big believer in minimalist gear, but even then, he usually had to take a few minutes and pack up his camp. Now all he had to do was make sure his lighter was in his pocket.

The sky had cleared up, promising some warmer temperatures once the sun was fully up. But it was still cold. He picked up the sleeping bag and blanket. The bag was dark brown, and the blanket was a dull gray color. Insulation and camouflage.

Kaity managed to drape the sleeping bag around herself so it would keep her warm and not trip her.

Tye tore a thin strip off one end of the blanket and fashioned a makeshift shoelace. It wasn't perfect but it was better than nothing. Then he draped the blanket around himself.

"I reckon I'm ready to go," he said.

"We're not going to win any fashion awards. Which way?" she asked.

"I've been thinking about that. The tribe is that way. But I wonder if it might be a good idea to get a little elevation and check our back trail for a few minutes."

She looked up the slope where he was pointing and sighed. It wasn't steep enough to need a rope or other climbing equipment, but it wasn't going to be an easy stroll, either.

"Okay," she said and started trudging up the hill.

As they picked their way up the slope, Tye considered their options. Isaac and Dylan would have had plenty of time to work out a plan by now. Tye felt like it would be foolish to assume there wasn't another tracker following them.

If you wanted to catch up with someone, you had to track them faster than they were moving. Tracking was a slow, painstaking exercise. The night before, if Tye hadn't been crashing through the underbrush with one ill-fitting shoe, in the dark, with Kaity in tow, he could have hidden his sign, left false trails, and taken other measures to slow down and confuse his pursuers.

The light snow would slow Isaac down even more. It would obscure the sign Tye and Kaity had left on the ground, but it was rapidly melting. There were still things like broken branches where they had plunged through the underbrush that would be obvious.

What frightened him the most was that Isaac was likely to have a rifle, and all Tye had were rocks and sticks.

He was surprised to find he was a little out of breath as they reached the summit. Normally he would have made it up the slope with little trouble, but the combination of fatigue, hunger, and dehydration left him winded.

He sat in an open spot where he could see into the distance. There was still a low-hanging mist in the valleys, with the ridgelines poking up like ships on an ocean. He took a few minutes to orient himself. From this spot, he could see the terrain they had traversed the night before. The logging road was a barely discernible break in the trees.

The birds were still singing their morning chorus and flitting about. In just a few minutes, he saw or heard robins, Steller's jays, varied thrushes, crows, and a solitary raven that flew directly overhead and roosted in the trees somewhere behind them. Kaity came over and sat silently beside him.

He sat there, studying the terrain and watching their back trail.

"What are we doing?" Kaity asked.

"Just a second," he said. In the distance, a pair of birds took flight. It was too far away to be sure, but he was fairly sure they were Steller's jays.

"There." He pointed. "See that?"

"The birds? So what?"

Another bird took off.

"There goes another one." He pointed again. "See that little clearing just ahead of where those birds took off? We crossed that last night. Watch what happens."

After a couple of minutes, two figures broke out of the tree line.

They were too far away to recognize, but one of them squatted in a posture Tye recognized all too well as that of a man bending over to study tracks. The other seemed to be carrying something. Tye was pretty sure it was a long gun.

"Isaac," Kaity said.

"Yep. I reckon that's Dylan with him."

The two figures moved forward a little at a time, with the one in the lead stopping for a few seconds every couple of paces to check for sign on the ground.

"I have an idea," he said. "I think we're gonna go pay Isaac back for my tires."

34

They watched Isaac's Jeep for several minutes. Tye and Kaity squatted in a vine maple thicket, watching and listening.

"I think we should do it," she said.

Tye considered. They'd changed course, doubling back toward the road. They'd been careful to leave as little sign as possible considering he was limping on one foot and Kaity was still a neophyte at counter-tracking. It wouldn't be a terribly difficult trail for Isaac to follow, but Tye had left enough false trails that he'd have to slow down, buying Tye and Kaity time.

"I wonder if we can hotwire it?" he asked.

She shook her head. "Nope. It's too new. It has a microchipped key and ignition system. It takes really specialized equipment to steal a Jeep from that model year."

"They teach you that in librarian school?"

"Internet video. I did my research before I bought my Jeep. Look, we should just do this like we talked about."

They moved forward. Tye picked up a rock as they went.

"If the alarm goes off, do you think they'll hear it?" Kaity asked.

Tye considered the distance. Isaac and Dylan were at most a couple of miles away.

"They might" he said. "It's quiet up here."

"Don't break the window yet. Let's come up with a plan."

Kaity pushed her face against the glass and looked. "I see a back-pack and some shoes in the back."

"Do the shoes have shoelaces?"

"Yes."

"I'm breaking the window." He pulled his fist back with the rock sticking out.

"Hang on."

She used the sleeve of her hoodie to cover her hands.

"You break the window with the rock. I'll reach in and unlock the doors with my hands covered so I don't get cut."

"You're surprisingly good at this," he said.

"Stick with me, kid, I'll turn you into a master criminal." She said it out of the corner of her mouth like a character in an old gangster movie. He realized she was trying to cover up the same nervousness that he felt.

He smacked the window with the rock and it spiderwebbed. It took a second blow to get the glass to fall out. Kaity reached in and there was a *thunk* as all the doors unlocked. Aside from the raucous call from a crow, there was no noise.

"They didn't set the alarm," Kaity said and snickered.

She ran around to the back of the truck. Tye hunted around under the dash for the hood release. He finally got it open and started pulling at wires in the engine compartment.

"Here," Kaity said, holding out her hand with his Buck knife in it. "All our stuff is in the backpack."

She was wearing the pack, and the pair of shoes dangled from her hand.

He was glad to see the knife. It was the closest thing to a family heirloom he owned. The copper in the Jeep's wiring harness didn't do the blade any good, but he'd fix that problem when he had the time. The edge was still more than sharp enough to slice through the valve stems of all four tires.

He had to admit to a certain feeling of satisfaction as the Jeep settled on four hissing tires. It would have been even more satisfying to cut up the sidewalls, but he didn't want to take the time to hack through the tough off-road tires.

They trotted down the road for a couple hundred yards, leaving the Jeep to settle on its deflating tires.

"In here," Tye said, pointing at a gap in the salmonberries on the side of the road. They settled under a big hemlock tree. Kaity handed him the shoes and started looking through the backpack.

"All our pocket litter was in here. Your knife. Our car keys. Wallets. My cell phone."

"Does your phone have a signal?" he asked as he threaded the shoelace through the eyelets.

"No. They smashed it," she said. "They were probably going to throw our stuff in the same hole as our bodies."

The day was warming up, but Tye still shivered.

Kaity dug through the rest of the pack. "There are also sweaty gym clothes. Ew. And check this out."

She held out two protein bars, the kind body builders ate after a workout.

"Chocolate or vanilla?" she asked.

"You pick."

She opened both bars, broke both in half, and gave him half a vanilla and half a chocolate.

The bars tasted like chalk, with a hint of chocolate or vanilla. Tye was grateful for the calories. His energy levels were dragging, and his thinking had been a little fuzzy for the last couple of hours. He found himself increasingly having to force himself to focus, lest his thoughts wander off into some unrelated territory.

"There any water in that bottle in the outside pocket?" He knew he was dehydrated. They'd both gotten sweaty in the back of the truck and hadn't had anything to drink since dinner the day before.

She pulled the bottle out and shook it. "Maybe a third full. I guess we can drink it if we don't mind Isaac's backwash."

"Beggars can't be choosers."

They passed the bottle back and forth, each getting no more than a few mouthfuls of water. After that, they stowed all the gear in the backpack and set out. Tye's foot felt much better having a proper shoe.

They didn't quite run down the road, but they weren't walking either. This route was technically longer than going overland to the tribe's camp, but the road would be undoubtably quicker.

"So, if somebody drives up, are we going to try to flag them down?" Kaity asked between panting breaths as they jogged down the road. He could tell she was working hard, but she didn't seem as out of breath as he was. Maybe there was something to all that Pilates stuff after all.

"I was thinking we should hide," he huffed. "Maybe take a few minutes to see who they are, then try to flag them down."

"They could be gone by the time we decide," Kaity said.

"Could be, but I'd hate to get it wrong."

"Wait," she said. "I hear something."

After a moment, he heard it too, an engine, and tires on gravel.

They stepped back into the shadow of the vine maple thicket. Soon a Tompkin Construction truck came into view and blasted by them in a cloud of dust. Wade was driving. Tye had a brief glimpse of someone in the passenger seat.

"Well, he's in a hurry," Kaity said.

"He is. Got somebody with him, too."

"How long before he finds Isaac's Jeep?"

"Rate he's going? Fifteen minutes tops. Dylan and Isaac ain't out of the woods yet, though, I guarantee you that. Isaac will be going around in circles for a while yet."

"I wonder what Wade will do when he finds Isaac's Jeep all smashed up, but no Isaac."

"Good question. I reckon we better get a move on."

"I feel like things are going to come to a head soon," Kaity said.

"Yeah. I think you're right."

35

They walked for hours, ready to dive into the woods if they heard traffic.

"Pepperoni pizza," Kaity said.

"What?"

"When we get out of this, I'm going to get a great big pepperoni pizza. Food is all I can think about right now."

"I thought you were vegetarian?"

"Vegan. It's my fantasy, nature boy. Don't interfere."

Tye found himself zoning out, trudging along, his eyes on his feet. That wasn't good. They needed to stay alert for the sounds of traffic.

The only noise was the clink of their feet on the rocks. In some ways, Tye wished he didn't have his watch. The individual moments seemed to crawl by, and he forced himself not to look at it too often. But slowly, inexorably, they were getting closer to their destination. Tye was fantasizing about a big, juicy hamburger when Kaity raised a hand.

"Car," she said.

It was becoming increasingly clear that she had superior hearing. They ran off the road on the downhill side, dropping to their bellies in a thick stand of vine maple. They heard the engine slow to a crawl, right as the vehicle came abreast of their position, then stopped. Wildly, Tye wondered what sign they had left that gave them away so easily, then realized it didn't matter anymore. He looked around for a big stick to use as a weapon and didn't see one. His Buck knife would have to do. The four-inch blade didn't seem like much of a match for a rifle.

They heard the crunch of boots on gravel, then saw the silhouette of a man wearing a broad-brimmed hat. He was heading right toward them.

Tye was debating whether to try to stay hidden, run, or spring up and fight when he heard a voice he recognized.

"Are the two of you coming or what? I've got the heat turned all the way up."

It was Willie.

36

The water Willie stored in his truck tasted like the plastic jug it was in, but Tye didn't mind. He and Kaity passed it back and forth, drinking contentedly. The long bench seat was a little crowded, and when they climbed in, Kaity had arched an eyebrow at him to let him know she wasn't riding in the middle. The plow-handle shape of Willie's revolver grip kept digging into Tye's side, but all in all, this was a vast improvement.

Despite his other concerns, Tye marveled at Willie's truck. He wasn't a classic car aficionado, but he guessed it had to date from the late fifties, and it was immaculate, with tuck-and-roll upholstery that looked brand-new, and candy-apple-red metallic flake paint that was somehow blemish-free despite all the rocks on the back roads. The ride was surprisingly smooth.

Just a few minutes in the heated cab, coupled with some water, was enough to make Tye feel like a new man. His stomach rumbled.

"There's food in that bag down at your feet."

Kaity rummaged around in the grocery sack on the floorboards of the truck. "Jerky. Pepperoni sticks. Canned ham. It's all meat."

"Sorry," Willie said. "I don't usually hang out with vegetarians."

Tye looked at the speedometer and realized they were driving ridiculously fast considering the conditions of the road. There was no way this truck had stock suspension, as it seemed to glide right over all the potholes and ruts.

"Left here?" Willie asked, jerking his chin at the road junction ahead of them.

Kaity looked up from the package of beef jerky she was examining with a skeptical eye. "How do you know where we're going?"

He gave her a toothy grin as he navigated a turn at a speed that should have put the truck up on two wheels. Instead, it glided around the corner like it was on rails.

"Just guessing. You want to go join up with Christopher's friends?"

"What do you know about Christopher?"

Willie concentrated on his driving for a minute. "He was a good man," Willie said. "I wish there were more like him. He understood the right way to live."

"Do you know who killed him?"

Willie shook his head. "I didn't have any more insight than you," he said. "Who is it?"

Kaity explained about the transformers and the logging site, then told him about how they'd been abducted by Dylan and Isaac.

"That's quite a tale," he said. "Now what?"

"We need to warn the tribe," Tye said. "Now that Dylan and Isaac are found out, they have zero reason not to clean up this mess by killing everybody."

"Do you really think they'll do that?" Kaity asked.

"I don't know that they won't," he said.

"The big question is, do you go to the police?" Willie asked.

"And explain to them how we were abducted by Dylan and Isaac after we illegally broke into their construction site?" Kaity asked.

"Yeah, but they killed Christopher," Tye said. "And we were just trespassing. Kidnapping us is a much bigger deal."

Kaity cocked an eyebrow at him. "Show me some proof they killed Christopher. And show me some proof they abducted us. Who are the cops going to believe? The rich businessman and his loyal retainer, or the hippie and the librarian?"

"I'm not a hippie, I'm a left neck," Tye said automatically, but the wheels in his head were turning as he said it. She had a point.

"But now that we know that they are dumping PCBs in the middle of the national forest, there are ways we can officially find that out, that are admissible in court," Willie said. He muttered it under his breath, as if he was talking to himself as much as he was to them.

"One thing at a time," Kaity said. "Let's go warn the tribe, and then we'll take it from there."

"I need to get back to town pretty damn quick so I can talk to my partner," Willie said.

"Can you at least stick around long enough for us to warn them, then take us back to town?" Kaity asked.

Willie nodded. "We'll make sure it all works out. One way or another."

Tye realized that wasn't exactly an answer, but neither he nor Kaity pushed it for now.

"You can let us out right up here," Tye said.

"You mean right up here by your truck?"

It was several seconds before Tye realized that the dot on the side of the road was actually his truck. The old man apparently still had pretty sharp eyes.

"What's that doing up here?" Kaity asked.

"May was going to come up here to check on Robin, remember?"

Willie's truck glided to a stop right behind Tye's. "Here we go. End of the line. Baggage claim to your left," the old man said.

"I guess we won't need you to stick around for us after all," Tye said. He reached into his pants pocket to confirm his truck keys were still there. Kaity was out almost before the truck stopped moving. Tye followed.

"Thanks," he said.

Willie tipped his hat, and Tye shut the passenger door. The old guy executed a three-point turn and sped off in the direction they'd come from. The truck seemed oddly quiet.

"There's something about that guy that creeps me out," Kaity said.

"Yeah." Tye unlocked the back of the truck and climbed in. He handed out a plastic bag of emergency food.

"There's some dried fruit, nuts, some crackers. They're vegetarian, but I can't vouch for them being vegan."

"I'll take it," she said.

Several of May's medical bags were on the floor of the truck bed. He lifted up the sleeping pad and unlocked the compartment underneath. His gun belt was inside, as well as Gary's. He took the gun belt with him when he climbed out of the back of the truck. He buckled it around his hips, then pulled the Ruger out and dropped six rounds in the cylinder, then he took a swig of water and pulled out some fruit leather. What he really wanted was a steak dinner, but this would have to do.

Movement caught his eye. He dropped the fruit leather and his hand dipped to his gun before he even thought about it.

It was Gary, stepping out of the trees. He put his hands up and stopped short. "Whoa! Easy there, Ace. What the hell happened to you? You look like you got dragged by a horse or something."

Behind him, Leif and Penny stepped out of the woods. Penny had her bow and clearly hadn't expected to see anyone there. She stopped short when she saw Kaity standing there, and looked her up and down. After a second the two gave each other a nod.

"I don't even know where to start," Tye said. "Can you just trust me that I'd feel a bunch better if you'd buckle on your pistol? If Isaac or Dylan show up, things are probably going to get a little Western. I can fill you in after that."

It took quite a bit to disturb Gary's usual unflappable calm. This earned Tye only an eyebrow lift.

"You better make it quick," Gary said as he climbed into the back of the truck. "We're here to get May's equipment. That gal is about to have her baby."

"What?" Kaity asked. "Wow."

"That's really bad timing," Tye said.

"Things like this usually are," Gary said. He handed one bag to Leif, then the other to Penny. After buckling on his own gun belt, he dropped a moon clip full of fat .45 rounds into the cylinder of his old 1917 Smith and Wesson.

"Long story short," Tye said. "Isaac and Dylan are dumping toxic waste in the forest. They captured us and drove us up here, but we got loose. Now they are tracking us."

"Did they kill Christopher?" Gary asked as he opened his backpack. He pulled out his long kukri knife and thrust it through his belt.

"I think it's a good guess," Tye said.

"And to cover it up, they might as well kill anybody they need to, because once you go down for one murder, what's a couple more?" Gary said, with a grim expression on his face.

"That's about the size of it."

"She's really about to have the baby?" Kaity asked. She was standing there with a box of crackers in her hand, blinking. Tye had been wondering if there would be a moment when all the events of the last couple of days would catch up to Kaity and she would shut down. He could feel that moment coming for himself. Soon, he would need to just go find a quiet place and stare off into the distance for a while.

"Yup," Gary said. "May says it's maybe a couple of hours off, but definitely on the way."

She put the box of crackers down and donned the backpack again. "Let's go," she said.

Penny led the way, carrying her bow and a medical oxygen tank on her back like it was nothing. May built her business on providing natural, home-based births, but she was also a trained nurse, so she carried modern medical equipment with her as well.

As they walked, Tye brought Gary up to date on everything that had happened. When he finished, Gary gave a low whistle.

"I wondered what was going on with you two. I really hated to take your truck, but I can't get that Scout running right."

"It all worked out in the end," Tye said. He opened his mouth to say something else but stopped. From the direction of the road, he heard the rumble of an engine and the crunch of tires on gravel.

"Company," Gary said.

"Surprised it took them this long. Isaac knows where the camp is. Won't take long for them to trail us."

"Won't," Gary said.

They all stopped and looked at each other.

"I guess a couple of us should go on with the medical equipment, and the rest should stay behind as a welcoming committee," Tye said.

"I'm staying," Kaity said and crossed her arms across her chest. Tye thought about pointing out that she didn't have a weapon and decided that it wouldn't be a particularly good use of his time.

"I'm staying too," Penny said, speaking for the first time. She'd been listening intently as Tye described events to Gary, but hadn't offered any comment until now. "These are my people," Penny said. "And I have my bow."

"If that was Isaac we heard pulling up, he's got a rifle," Tye said.

"We need to take them here in the dense forest," Penny said. "By the time he sees me, he'll be within bow range."

To Tye, it almost sounded like she was planning an assassination.

"I can carry both these bags," Leif said. He looked scared and relieved to have a reason to keep going. Wordlessly, Penny shrugged out of the backpack with the oxygen kit, and the broad-shouldered cook donned it and picked up the other kit.

"Tell Alex everything," Penny said.

Leif swallowed and nodded, then took off at a pace that wasn't quite a run, but not quite walking either.

"Now what?" Kaity asked.

"I reckon we need to arrange ourselves a little ambush," Gary said.

"I know just the place," Penny said.

37

P enny led them to a stand of older trees, where the Douglas firs grew tall and broad, with little undergrowth. They followed Leif's tracks as far as they could before diverting away, leaving plenty of sign of their own. They figured their pursuers would follow the trail with the most tracks, and if they didn't, that would give Tye and the rest an opportunity to sneak up behind them.

They left an obvious trail through an open area with little cover, then doubled back, taking up their positions. Tye found a spot to hide behind the giant root ball of a fallen tree and got comfortable. The whole thing reminded him of a surreal way of hunting deer. He knew the secret to staying still was to find a place where he wouldn't have to shift around, but now the quarry was human instead of animal.

Kaity stayed with him. She did a good job of staying still and quiet.

He resisted the urge to look at his watch, knowing it was at most half an hour since they'd stopped and set up the ambush. It was mid-afternoon, and it seemed like the day had taken forever to unfold, yet at the same time, it felt like he and Kaity had just left the cave.

Tye listened hard for bird alarms and similar disturbances, but this time, there was nothing. One second, he was looking at a quiet, empty forest, and the next there they were: Isaac halfway bent over, and Dylan following behind. Isaac carried a big pistol on his belt, but Dylan was carrying a shotgun.

When he saw them, his mouth went dry and his stomach went cold. He gripped the Ruger so hard he wondered in the back of his mind if it was possible to crack the wooden grip.

There was a huckleberry bush in the middle of the small clearing. Much abused by browsing elk, it was their trip line for triggering the ambush. As soon as Isaac passed the bush, Gary stepped out from his tree and raised his worn old Smith and Wesson at Dylan.

"Dylan. Stop."

Dylan jumped, and for a heart-stopping second, Tye thought he was going to raise the shotgun at Gary. Tye brought the revolver up at eye level. He was looking at Dylan's left side. The Ruger's front sight had a light-gathering, fiber optic tube installed. Tye put the glowing red dot on Dylan's ribcage. He had to fight to hold it on target, like he was forcing two magnets together. Tye had spent a substantial portion of his life with a gun in his hand, and he had an ironclad rule not to point it at another person.

"I should have known," Isaac said. "Oh, and the little forest princess too," he said when Penny stepped out into the open, her bow drawn.

"Put the gun down," Gary said.

"Or what?"

"Or I will cut you down. You're headed in the direction of my wife with a loaded gun and bad intentions. There's a shovel in the back of my friend's truck and plenty of country out here to bury you in."

There was no doubt in Tye's mind that Gary meant it. Gone was no longer the affable, thoughtful poet and farmer he knew. It was like some dark, avenging angel had taken Gary's place. Tye had seen Gary this way once before, the night he'd killed a man.

"Will you let me go if I put it down?" Isaac asked.

"I will. Whatever Wade Tompkin is paying you, it's not enough. I'm going to take your guns and let you walk out of here."

At the mention of Wade's name, a funny look passed across Isaac's face. He seemed to consider for a moment, then, still holding his right hand high, he pulled the shotgun off from around his neck and let it fall to the ground.

"Keep your hands away from that pistol and get on your knees," Gary said.

Isaac complied, and Tye let go the breath he'd been holding. He and Kaity stepped out of the bushes.

"You too, Dylan."

Gary plucked Isaac's pistol out of his holster, then pulled the sling of the shotgun over Dylan's head. He patted both men down, confiscating car keys, wallets, and everything else.

Finally, he stepped back and surveyed the pile of stuff on the ground.

"Kaity, would you mind putting all this stuff in the backpack?"

Tye picked up Dylan's shotgun, made sure the safety was on, and slung it over his back.

"Now what?" Dylan asked.

Nobody answered him for a moment.

"Walk over to the other side of the clearing with me," Tye said. "If you try to run, I'll shoot you in the ass with a load of buckshot. I'm in no mood to fool around."

Dylan hung his head and marched like a condemned man to the base of a tree on the other side of the clearing.

"That's far enough," Tye said. He wanted Dylan out of earshot of Isaac. "Did you kill Christopher?" Tye asked.

Dylan shook his head. "Nope."

"Who did? Wade? Isaac?"

"I don't know," Dylan said. Tye realized there were tears streaming down his face. "Isaac said he didn't. I guess I believe him."

"What the hell happened to you?" Tye asked. "A few years ago, you wanted to change the world by getting kids out into nature. Now you're dumping toxic waste in the forest and kidnapping people."

"I don't know." Dylan's voice broke. "I was asking myself that on the drive up here last night. It was just so much money to buy that property, then we found out we couldn't use it. Wade was supposed to solve it for me."

"Where is Wade right now?" Tye asked.

Dylan just shook his head and looked at the ground.

"Unless you're planning on pulling out fingernails and such, I don't think you're going to get more out of him," Gary said. Tye had been so focused on Dylan he hadn't heard Gary walk up.

"Do we have time for that?" Tye asked. Dylan shot him a look, as if to see if he was serious. Tye wasn't sure that he wasn't.

"Not really," Gary said.

Tye jerked his head, and Dylan obediently walked back to the center of the clearing.

"Are we just going to let them go, then?" Kaity asked.

"I don't particularly care for the idea of trying to march them around. We know who they are. What they've done will catch up with them sooner or later."

"Guess it's time for us to part company then," Isaac said with a smirk.

"I guess it is," Tye said. "Take off your shoes."

"What?"

"Your shoes. Take them off."

"You can't do that," Isaac said.

"We're the ones holding the guns. So take off your shoes. I'll be generous and let you keep your socks."

"No."

Rattlesnake quick, Gary unsheathed the kukri and put the tip against Isaac's nose. "You were hunting my woman with a gun in your hands. I wasn't kidding about the shovel."

Isaac fought at the knots in his boot laces with trembling fingers. There was a look on Isaac's face that Tye found familiar but couldn't quite place. Then he remembered a kid he'd known in middle school that liked to bully people around. He was big for his age and took it for granted that people would be cowed into submission. He'd shoved Tye once, on the playground, and Tye had hit him as hard as he could, knocking him down. The look on Isaac's face was just like the look on the face of that boy when he hit the ground.

"This isn't over," Isaac mumbled as he undid his boots. Tye's temper was up, and he was tempted to hand the shotgun and revolver to Gary and invite Isaac to go for it, but they needed to get out of here, so he held his tongue.

Now shoeless, both men stood.

Kaity walked up to Isaac. She punched him. It was a sloppy punch, and she didn't get much of her weight into it, but it landed square, her fist flattening both the bottom of his nose and the top of his lip. He staggered back but didn't fall. Tye stepped forward, ready to intervene in case Isaac retaliated, but he didn't. He just stood there and bled.

"You two get out of here," Tye said.

Wordlessly, they turned and walked gingerly away on their stockinged feet.

"I've never hit anybody before," Kaity said.

"I suspected that," Tye said.

"It felt kind of good. I've been really angry since Isaac... Well, you know."

"Don't blame you."

"Except I think I hurt my hand."

"I expect you're right. No offense, but that wasn't very good form."

She massaged her knuckles. "I guess I should take classes."

"Might be a good idea if you plan on making that a habit."

"All right," Gary said. "Let's make some tracks. We need to hoof it if we're going to get there in time for the baby to be born."

"What a weird day," Kaity said.

38

They stopped a mile or so later to look at Kaity's hand. It was already swelling.

"Boxer's fracture," Gary said. "We'll have May look at it when she gets a chance. Try to keep it elevated as you walk."

"For some reason, I feel cooler having broken my hand punching a guy," Kaity said. "It's like having an interesting scar, only without the scar."

They stopped at irregular intervals to listen, and even walked along their back trail a couple of times, even though the odds of Dylan and Isaac following them at any speed were slim.

Kaity talked quite a bit at first about random things, then went silent. Tye left her alone with her thoughts and walked up beside Penny, who had been quiet the whole time.

"I think we brought some trouble down on you," he said.

She shook her head. "Not you. Christopher. Although I can't blame him, really. Was he wrong for getting involved in that dumping case? Or am I wrong for not wanting to fight it?"

"Tough call," Tye said. "Sometimes when you pick one thing to fight about, it's hard to know where to stop."

She gave him a curious glance.

Behind him, he could almost feel Kaity's eyes boring into the back of his head as he talked to Penny.

He was spared further discomfort when they walked into camp. People were milling around the central campfire, talking, and keeping one eye on the teepee.

Penny put her bow and quiver down, then went inside the teepee.

All eyes were on Tye as he unslung the shotgun and managed to unload it without blowing a hole in himself or anyone else. It was a semi-automatic gun with an extended magazine that ran the whole length of its short barrel. It was complicated, with a couple more buttons and levers than he was used to.

"Is that one of those Italian jobs?" Gary asked.

Tye handed it to him, glad to be rid of the thing, and bent to pick up the bright red shells from where they'd ejected onto the ground.

"Shame we can't keep this. It's worth a new rear end for my Scout," Gary said as he worked the controls like he knew what he was doing.

"Here," Tye said, handing him the handful of shells. "You hang on to it in case the excitement isn't over."

Gary nodded and fed the shells back into the magazine but left the chamber empty. He propped the shotgun carefully next to his pack.

May came out of the teepee, wiping her hands on a towel. She gave Gary a peck on the lips.

"Leif said something was wrong?" she asked.

By answer, Gary walked over to Kaity's backpack, pulled out Dylan's pistol, and checked the chamber. He handed it to May butt first.

"That bad?" she asked as she tucked the pistol into the waistband of her jeans.

"You might wind up being that gal's last line of defense. I suppose moving her to where the vehicles are parked is out of the question?"

"We can't move her. The baby is coming, that's for certain. It's in a good position, head down, but her labor has slowed to a crawl. It'll pick up again, but it could still be some number of hours. Or it could be fifteen minutes. We could carry her and then find ourselves delivering on the forest floor in twenty minutes. I want to stay here. I've got light, fresh water, all my gear set up."

Gary nodded. "You do your thing. We'll do ours."

A soft moan came from inside the tent.

"Duty calls," May said. She gave Gary another kiss and ducked back inside the teepee.

"What do you reckon, Tye?" Gary asked.

He realized everyone in the camp was looking at them. Alex walked out of the teepee and gave them a nod. He looked tired and more than a little scared.

"Here's what I think we should do," Tye said. "Put out some sentries. Maybe a couple on the more obvious routes, and a couple more roving between. We can't hide this camp, but we can at least detect anybody bad before they get too close."

"You think Wade has it in him to try something?" Gary asked.

"Don't know. But Isaac does. And it's not out of the question that he'll find his way out of the woods, find some shoes and gear, and get back before this baby is born."

"I want to be a lookout," Weasel said, fingering the rifle. He was holding the rifle and practically quivering. He looked like hell. The bruises were starting to show on his face, and he was hard to understand because of the swelling in his lips, but his eyes were bright, and he was alert.

"Sounds good," Alex said. "And Penny and Nick with their bows."

Nick was a tall, quiet guy with a handmade bow and a quiver full of immaculately fletched arrows. He nodded at Alex.

"Everybody else, start packing and get ready to shift camp," Alex said. "We'll leave as soon as Penny and the baby can travel."

At most of the communal living experiments he'd seen, this would have prompted an endless round of arguments, but instead everyone snapped to, packing away gear in backpacks and bags.

"This outfit is not what I expected," Gary said.

"Right?"

Penny came out of the tent and grabbed her gear. She settled her quiver over her shoulder as she walked up to Tye.

"I was thinking of posting Weasel along the creek route, and Nick by the path that runs through the berry thicket. I can watch the old trail that runs by the road, and you can circulate around."

She looked at Gary. "I was wondering if you would stay here in camp and cover people while they pack up. My folks aren't fighters, and it would be good if someone was here with a gun."

Gary looked at Tye. "That work for you?"

"Yes. Stay here with your wife. You're the last line of defense."

Gary hefted the big shotgun and checked the load. Weasel was all but quivering with anticipation. Nick was quiet and seemed calm, which Tye took to be a good sign.

"Weasel has his rifle, and if he starts shooting, we'll hear it," Tye said. "We need to get you a noisemaker, Nick."

By way of reply, Nick reached under his shirt and pulled out a whistle carved from bone that hung around his neck on a leather thong. He blew a high, shrill note. Penny pulled an identical whistle out from under her shirt.

"We use them to communicate sometimes," she said.

"That ought to do it," Tye said. He put on his backpack. "Let's go."

Weasel took point. For all his other issues, he was quiet in the woods. He had a knack for picking routes that afforded him both visual cover and a place to put his feet where he would minimize noise. It probably took twice as long as it needed to get to the creek, but their passage was almost noiseless.

He pointed at a big deadfall that spanned the creek. "I was thinking of setting up in there," he whispered.

Tye and Penny both nodded. Weasel settled in and all but disappeared into the tangle of branches. Next, they found a spot a few hundred yards away for Nick to hide. He wasn't as good as Weasel, but Tye was still impressed by his woodsmanship.

That left Tye and Penny alone. She leaned in to murmur in his ear, and he was uncomfortable by how near she was to him.

"Let me show you the spot I had in mind, then you'll know where to find me."

She led the way, and he followed, trying hard to remember to look around at their surroundings and not stare at Penny. They followed a faint elk trail through the woods to a cluster of thick Douglas firs.

"I'm going to set up in here," she said. "How often do you think you're going to rotate around?"

He hadn't given much thought to that question. He looked at his watch and realized there was only an hour or so of daylight left. He felt like he'd been existing outside of time for a while.

"I'm going to swing through every hour or so. If I do it too often, I'll risk getting busted because I'm moving too quick."

"And if you wait too long, one of us could get taken out, and you'd never know it until they are on top of the camp."

"Right. I'll swing by camp periodically."

"Sounds good. Do you really think they'll come and try to hurt us?"

He'd been thinking about exactly that question during the walk.

"I think they aren't good people. They've already killed one person, so they've got nothing to lose by killing more."

She nodded, then drew an arrow from her quiver and put it on the string, before finding a seat behind some cover. She started scanning the woods.

Tye found himself wanting to say more to her, although he wasn't sure what. Instead, he ghosted away, picking his way silently through the forest. He found a spot about halfway between the line of sentries and the camp and stood with his back to a tree. He was tempted to sit down, but he was afraid if he did, he would fall asleep.

He considered their situation. The camp was tucked back in a steep, narrow draw that ran east to west. Technically, their pursuers could come at them from any direction, but the reality was, there were a limited number of approaches that made any sense, and they all ran from the road and up the draw. The logging road ran across the wide mouth, and the little hidden spur road where the tribe had stashed their vehicles was at the north end. There was a braided network of game trails that grew closer together the more the draw narrowed near camp.

He figured the odds of anyone trying to come in overland from the west were slim. There was nothing there but back country. By the time somebody navigated through that, Tye and the others would hopefully be long gone. Likewise, coming up over the ridges from the north and south was possible, but unlikely.

He drank a couple swallows of water and ate a handful of trail mix, then set out to check on the others. He went slowly, walking a few steps, looking around, then walking a few more, exactly as if he were stalking deer.

He slowed down even more as he approached Weasel. The guy was excited and had a rifle. Tye didn't want any unfortunate misunderstandings.

Weasel was doing a good job of being still, and it took Tye several minutes to pick out his shape among the visual clutter in the blowdown. He'd covered his bandages with a dark cloth, and he looked like hell, but he was alert. Tye caught his eye, and they exchanged a thumbs-up.

The sun was starting to set, making the shadows lengthen. Up until now, the air had been still, but now a slight breeze began blowing. The draw sloped upward toward the camp, and now that the sun was setting, the air was cooling and flowing downhill, carrying with it the faint smell of woodsmoke from the big communal fire.

Tye frowned. That would be a beacon to anyone trying to find the camp, but there was little to be done about it now. He stepped into a shadow in the trees and went still, just like when he hunted deer or elk, but now he was waiting for humans.

Tye had never killed anybody before, and he was surprised at the fatalistic acceptance he felt at the possibility. Out of habit, he checked to make sure his revolver was securely fastened in its holster. It was a good weapon, but no substitute for the rifle he wished he had.

He told himself to stay focused on the moment. Tye had no desire to get into a gunfight tonight, but if he did, he needed to have his mind on what he was doing instead of ruminating about something else.

That was when the gunshots rang out.

39

There were two heavy rifle shots in rapid secession. They echoed around the draw, but Tye was almost certain they came from Weasel's position. He took off running, revolver in hand. In some ways, it almost felt like a relief. One way or another, things were about to get resolved.

He was almost there when he realized he was running pell-mell into a middle of a gunfight. He skidded to a stop just as another shot rang out. No bullet whizzed by, so he figured it wasn't aimed at him.

The light was fading fast, and here under the trees, it was already hard to make out details. He carried a small but powerful flashlight in his pocket. He pulled it out and carried it in his left hand, his revolver in his right. Now he moved from tree to tree, pausing to look around before each step.

He heard footsteps and heavy breathing headed his way. Someone was jogging toward him, rifle in hand. They moved as if drunk, bouncing from tree to tree and almost tripping over branches and roots. As he got closer, Tye realized it was Wade. The rifle dangled from his left hand, and he was pawing at his face with his right.

After almost falling again, Wade stopped. He reached around

blindly, found a tree, and leaned the rifle against it. Tye crept up, gun in hand. Finally, he got close enough to see Wade's face in the half-light. It was covered in blood, and there were inch-long slivers of wood sticking out of his skin. He figured the man must have been taking cover behind a tree when a bullet hit close by, driving chunks of wood and maybe even fragments of bullet into his face.

Tye holstered his gun. Wade didn't have a rifle in his hands anymore, and even if he had, he couldn't see well enough to shoot anyway. Tye wondered if Weasel was lying in the underbrush some-where with a gunshot wound, and if he should go looking for him.

Tye hoped some other people would get here quick. This was all too much to take in at once.

He decided to deal with the problem right in front of him first.

"Hey, Wade, you need to settle down, man, so I can help you with your face."

Wade stopped pawing at his eyes and turned to face Tye. His face was a mess. Both eyes were shut, and Tye's stomach did a slow roll when he saw a piece of wood the size of his pinky sticking out of Wade's right eye socket. The bleeding seemed to be worse.

"Dude, you're going to bleed out. Just sit down and I'll help you."

Wade gave an inarticulate, guttural growl, lowered his head, and charged. Tye belatedly remembered Doyle mentioning Wade's trip to wrestling camp right about the time Wade wrapped his arms around Tye's waist, and they slammed into the ground.

Tye landed badly. All the air drove out of his lungs with a whoosh and his mouth clicked shut. He tasted blood from his tongue.

Wade was in a frenzy, raining blows down on Tye's head. Tye tucked his chin and covered his face with his forearms, managing to avoid enough of them to stay conscious. He wrapped his legs around Wade's waist and held on.

Tye hated fights. He wasn't terribly good at it, and right now he had a sick feeling that he was out of his league. He dropped his guard to try to punch Wade in the ribs and was promptly rewarded by a punch to his cheekbone that made him see stars. Wade's fingers scrabbled for his neck. Tye barely managed to drop his chin in time, suffering a cut from one of Wade's fingernails instead.

The thought was forming in the back of his mind that he was going to have to kill Wade. His Buck knife was sheathed on his belt behind his gun but was trapped between his hip and the ground. He'd never get it open in time anyway.

That left the revolver. At this range, the heavy .357 Magnum slugs would pass right through Wade and not even slow down that much.

Wade hit him again and used the fraction of a second where Tye was stunned to go for his neck again. Tye managed to turn his head, so Wade jabbed him in the eye instead.

Through the rush of blood in his ears, Tye realized somebody was screaming Wade's name.

Wade turned his head. "Over here!"

While he was distracted, Tye reached up and pushed on the stick jutting from Wade's eye. The other man screamed, and both hands flew up to his face. Tye bucked, and Wade flew off. Tye managed to get to his knees. Wade flailed around with his arms wide. His fingers brushed the fabric of Tye's shirt, and he launched himself at Tye again.

This time, Tye was ready. He didn't exactly win, but he did manage to turn it into a rolling tumbling fight, instead of one where he was on his back getting his head stove-in. First Tye was on top, then Wade, then Tye again. Tye managed to get some blows in, throwing an elbow here and a punch there. He knew Wade was weakening, and Tye hoped somebody else from his side showed up soon.

Wade pulled some kind of tricky little move and Tye found himself with his leg pinned to the ground. Wade's grasping fingers found the revolver in its holster, and Tye frantically tried to push them away. The bullets would go through him at this range as easily as they would Wade.

"He's over here! He has a gun!" Wade yelled. Tye tried to roll on his side so the gun was underneath him, but Wade kneed him in the groin. He heard and felt a pop as the thumb break on his holster opened, and then Wade stood with the Ruger in his hand.

Tye fought the dull ache in the pit of his stomach. In the half-light of the setting sun, he could see that Wade was prying the eyelids of his right eye open with his left hand, while the muzzle of the gun in his right sought a target. Tye shrimped to the side just as Wade pulled the trigger. The bullet hit the ground, spraying him with dirt. This close, the muzzle flash was like a flashbulb, and the report of the big Magnum was like an icepick to the ear.

Wade hadn't been ready for the recoil, and Tye could see he almost dropped the gun. Tye scrambled to pull the Buck knife out of the belt pouch, thinking he could at least take Wade with him, when another shot rang out. Tye flinched, expecting to feel a hot burning sensation in his guts, but he realized the shot had come from farther away.

Wade dropped, boneless, and Tye realized the shot had hit him instead. Tye smelled hot coppery blood. There was a bullet hole in the back of Wade's shirt. His feet kicked the ground a couple of times, and he was still.

"Wade?"

In the gloom, Tye saw a figure holding a rifle. It was Anna Lee.

"Wade?" She was louder this time, more shrill. She worked the bolt of the rifle, chambering another round.

Tye looked around for his revolver but didn't see it. He belly-crawled behind a big log, finally managing to get his Buck knife out of the case and thumb it open. He stayed there, his belly pressed into the dirt and the scent of the wet forest floor in his nose, trying to catch his breath and considering his options.

"Oh, Wade." It came out as a half sob, half yell.

Despite his predicament, he found himself feeling a little sorry for her.

"Where are you?" Her voice was hoarse and raw. "You killed my boy."

That didn't seem right to him, but he didn't think arguing with her would be a good idea right now.

Tye swallowed hard. He heard her move away from Wade's body and thrash through the underbrush. Tye risked a peek over the log, steeling himself for a bullet to the face. She was walking around in a circle, holding the rifle and muttering.

He realized the revolver was there a few feet past the end of the log. Before he had a chance to talk himself out of it, he gathered his legs under him and sprang for it. The rifle shot sounded like a clap of thunder, and he was sprayed with chips of wood, but he didn't feel a bullet hit him.

He snatched up the Ruger and pointed it at her, once again feeling the inherent wrongness of having a human body under the sights of his gun.

She had brought the rifle down and her hand was on the bolt. She froze when she saw the revolver in his hand.

"Stop!" he yelled.

She sneered at him. "You think you have the stones to shoot me, boy?"

But her hand stayed still. The rifle was across her chest, the chamber empty. She would need to chamber another round and swing the muzzle toward him while bringing it to her shoulder. All he would need to do was pull the trigger.

"Put the rifle down."

"Or what? I don't have anything left to lose. Maybe it would be a favor if you killed me."

"Why did you shoot Christopher?" The words were out of his mouth before he had a chance to even think about.

"Because he was a threat! That kid wanted to ruin us with his damn environmentalist lawyers and his pictures. He was jealous of what we had. He knew he could never have it, so he wanted to ruin us."

She seemed to change as she talked, into some twisted little creature full of hate and venom. "People have always wanted what I have. I always have to fight to keep it."

"I really don't think he wanted your money," Tye said.

That earned him another sneer. "Everybody wants something."

"Did Wade know?" Tye asked. "Did Wade know you killed his son, your grandson?"

She looked down at Wade's body. "I think Wade chose not to see certain things."

"You realize you just killed your own son, right?"

She looked back toward where Wade's body was in the ferns, and a flat, expressionless look fell over her face. Of everything that had happened so far, that was what scared him the most.

"Looked like you in this light. Same height. Same dark hair. Same color jacket. Crying about it won't help. Now I guess I have to just clean up the mess and move on."

From back toward camp came the sound of a baby crying. Anna Lee cocked her head. "Sounds like that little bitch has had her whelp."

"You can't kill us all," Tye said. "There's over a dozen people over there. Every one of them will die before they let you hurt that baby. Just put the rifle down and we'll sort this out."

She looked from him to the direction of the baby's cry, then back at him.

"Well. Isn't this a hell of a thing?" Without swinging the muzzle toward him, she reached up and worked the bolt of a rifle, driving another round into the chamber. While they'd talked, Tye's gun muzzle had sort of drifted away from her, as if of its own accord. Now he brought it back on target.

"What are you doing? Put the rifle down."

"No."

Quicker than he could react, she brought the muzzle up under her own chin and pulled the trigger. At the sound, he reflexively fired a shot, but it passed only through open air as her body fell in a boneless heap.

The sound of the heavy rifle round echoed through the hills for a long time, but it wasn't loud enough to drown out the sound of the baby crying.

Tye stood there for a while, between the two bodies of mother and son. Finally, he broke open the cylinder of his revolver, replaced the fired rounds, and went to check on Weasel.

40

They built the fire up to a head-high blaze. Gary produced a bottle of applejack and it made the rounds. The mood was oddly celebratory. But then again, Tye was the only one who had seen two people killed. He thought about what Anna Lee had looked like, shook his head, and took another sip of applejack.

Kaity popped out of the teepee, saw him, and made a beeline for him.

"The baby is fine. We heard shooting and everybody got ready to fight. I've never seen anything like it. It's like they were all willing to die to keep anything from happening to Robin or the baby."

From across the fire, Tye noticed Penny looking at the two of them, then she quickly looked away.

"Yeah," he said, his voice rough. "We were all ready to fight."

"What happened?"

He realized she'd been in the teepee the whole time, and while everyone had heard the shots, only Weasel, Penny, Gary, and he knew the whole story about what had happened.

"Anna Lee and Wade are gone," he said.

"Gone? You mean..."

He nodded.

"Did you..."

"No. Not me."

She looked around the camp, as if seeing the people there for the first time.

"I'm glad you didn't have to," she said. She gave him a one-arm hug.

He hugged back, then they both sat down, her hip touching his.

He just sat there, nursing his applejack and feeling waves of fatigue wash over him as he tried not to think about the two bodies cooling out in the forest. The members of the tribe were all in a good mood, treating Weasel like a returning hero. Penny and Alex had a long conversation at the edge of the light cast by the fire, and Gary and May stood with arms around each other's waists as they toasted another successful birth.

Tye wasn't sure exactly when Willie showed up. One minute the old guy wasn't there, the next he was walking around slapping backs and distributing cans from the six-pack that dangled from one long finger. Penny gave Willie a long look, but everyone else seemed happy to see him.

Willie finally made his way around to Tye and offered the last beer silently.

"What the hell," Tye said. He took it and popped the top. It wasn't particularly good beer, but it was cold.

Wille carefully cut the six-pack rings with a bone-handled switch-blade that appeared in his hand as if by magic, then tucked it away. He reached into a shirt pocket and held something out to Tye.

It was a brass shell casing.

"If I'm not mistaken, that goes to that young lad's rifle," he said, jerking his chin toward Weasel's rifle that sat on the ground by Tye's feet. "I wouldn't want any of you to get wrapped up in the unfortunate hunting accident that claimed the lives of Wade and Anna Lee."

"That would be bad," Tye said slowly. He reached out and took the shell casing, then tucked it into his pocket.

"Hell of a coincidence, the two of them out here hunting while you all are camped so close by. Way I see it, she must have mistaken

Wade for a bear and took a couple shots at him. Then, while she was overcome with grief, she shot herself."

"That all sounds plausible, except for the part where Anna Lee experienced grief," Tye said. His tongue felt thick in his mouth. He wondered if the beer was on top of the applejack was such a good idea.

"You were going to fight," Willie said. It was a statement, not a question.

"Tried to shoot her," he said. "But she'd already done for herself." He realized he wasn't that drunk. It just seemed like Willie had some sort of power over him to compel him to talk that he didn't quite understand.

"Why?"

"I was afraid she'd hurt the baby," he said. "And everybody else."

"Why do you care? Why was that your problem?"

Tye shrugged. "It's my job. That's what I'm supposed to do. Help people. Keep them from getting hurt."

Wilie nodded to himself, as if satisfied by something. "You'll do," he said.

"What's that supposed to mean?"

"It means that sometimes people need to do the right thing, and often, you're that person."

"I'm just glad all this is over."

"That's where you are wrong, young Tyrell Orrin Caine. For you, all of this is just starting."

41

A couple of days later, they all stood on a ridgeline overlooking the valley where Christopher had died. They were all there: the tribe, Gary, May, Kaity, and Grace. Robin held baby Willow wrapped in her father's deer hide as she shook the last of Christopher's ashes out into the wind. Everyone had scattered a little, leaving the last for Robin.

"Goodbye," she said as the last of him floated away. She didn't cry. Tye suspected she was all cried out. The baby made a happy noise, halfway between a coo and a squeak, as Robin carefully fitted the lid back on the box that had held Christopher's ashes.

After that, they all filed through the forest silently to their vehicles. The tribe's truck was loaded to the top with gear, and the big passenger van was parked behind it, as were Tye's truck and Gary's Scout. Grace walked with Robin's hand in hers.

Kaity walked over for one last goodbye with Robin and the baby. Kaity's right hand was still in a cast, so she gave Robin an awkward side hug.

Tye heard the scuff of a foot on gravel. When he turned and saw it was Penny, he knew she'd done it on purpose. She was cat quiet usually, but she probably hadn't wanted to startle him. He was still a little jittery from recent events. He wasn't wearing his gun, but his gun belt was rolled up in the back of his truck, only a few paces away.

Penny stood shoulder to shoulder with him, quite close. He could smell her hair in the warm sun.

"Sure you don't want to come?" she asked.

He could go get his backpack out of his truck, hop in the tribe's van, and have everything he needed. He could drive his truck and follow them and have most of what he wanted. He looked over and saw Gary and May leaning against the front bumper of Gary's Scout with their arms around each other's waists.

Then his eyes settled on Kaity. She stood there with her arms folded across her chest, talking to Robin and Grace, but somehow, he knew she was watching him and Penny out of the corner of her eye.

"I appreciate it." he said. "But it's not the right thing for me."

"It's hard to leave family," she said. She reached over and squeezed his hand.

She turned and walked over to the tribe's big truck and hopped in without a backward glance.

Grace buckled the baby into her brand-new car seat.

"I'll see you all in a few weeks in New Mexico," Grace said and shut the door.

With a belch of blue smoke, the van lurched forward after the truck, and they both chugged down the rough forest road at barely more than a walking speed out of deference to their youngest passenger.

Kaity gave a final wave at the van, wiped a tear from the corner of her eye, and walked over to him.

She linked an arm in one of his and they walked slowly back to the vehicles. Gary and May were helping Grace into the Scout.

"I'm exhausted. I want to get some rest before we have to give our depositions in the morning," Kaity said.

"Me too. Sounds like Dylan confessed to everything, though."

"It would make me feel better if the cops could find Isaac, though."

Tye nodded and started the truck.

"She asked you to go with her, didn't she?" Kaity asked.

"Yep."

"Why didn't you?"

"Because my family is here." He didn't even have to stop to think before he said it. It just came out.

She let go of his arm so they could climb into his truck. There was a moment when Tye thought Gary's Scout wasn't going to start, then the engine fired with a roar.

They bounced down the rough road for a while in silence.

"I'm not sure I want to have kids," Kaity said.

"Not sure I do either. I haven't always had the most stable life, with me living out of the back of my truck and all."

"You've upgraded to a yurt."

"It was an improvement. I've been thinking about building a cabin, having my own shower and such." He nodded toward Gary's vehicle ahead of them. "They're thinking about having a baby, and I wouldn't want to be underfoot all the time."

"Wow. A cabin with actual running water?"

"Yup. I'm moving up in the world."

"Hypothetically speaking, if a woman were to spend the night, it would be nice not to have to do a walk of shame over to May and Gary's place to use the shower."

He picked his way carefully around some deep ruts, then made a turn onto a paved road. Now that it was safe to drive with one hand, he put his hand on the seat between them, and she took it in hers.

"Hypothetically speaking, that would be even more motivation to start construction. Probably have to wait until spring, though."

"That works." She yawned. "I am still exhausted. I feel like curling up with a good book."

"Me too. Let's go home."

"Good idea. Let's go home."

KEEP READING!

Keep reading for a peek at *Warrior Soul,* the next Tye Caine Wilderness Mystery!

DID YOU ENJOY WILD MIND?

Please leave a review!

Would you like a free Tye Caine Wilderness Mystery short story?

Visit www.dlbarbur.com to join the Tye Caine Tracker Pack!

We'll keep you updated with developments in the world of the Tye Caine Wilderness Mysteries, plus share occasional info on tracking, wildlife, wilderness skills and more.

WARRIOR SOUL CHAPTER 1

Tye Caine shifted his shotgun into his left hand and knelt to look at the footprint.

The early-morning breeze blew up the hill, and the ever-present hiss of the river in the valley's bottom competed with the songs of black-capped chickadees. The sun was just peeking over the horizon, promising to warm the spring air that was still chilly from the night before.

Tye didn't recognize the track in the patch of bare ground, muddy from last night's rain. The track was fresh. He could see every detail of the worn lugged boot sole. He put his foot next to it. Whoever made the track was a much bigger, heavier person than him. The impression in the mud was deep.

He stood and turned a slow circle, scanning the thick forest around him. His right hand crept back onto the stock of the shotgun without him even thinking about it.

Normally, he didn't walk around his property with a shotgun, but he'd woken that morning with a sense of foreboding, and as he passed his pickup in the driveway, he'd stopped to retrieve the battered old Mossberg from the locker in the back of his truck, feeling foolish as he'd done it.

The track was at the northern border of the property where he lived. On the other side of the property line were thousands of acres of private timberland. There was no reason for anyone to be up here. It wasn't hunting season, and they were half a mile from any of the gravel roads that snaked their way through the timberland.

Other than the birds, the surrounding forest was still. He couldn't shake the feeling of unease he'd had since he awakened. It wasn't a feeling of being watched so much as a feeling of building pressure, like a storm was coming.

Tye cast about for more sign. Other than the single clear track, there was scant evidence of the person's passing. Sticks littered the forest floor, but none were broken. There were no impressions or damage in the soft patch of moss that would have been the logical next place for the person's foot to fall.

Tye was a tracker, and over the years he'd trailed hundreds of people while working search-and-rescue cases. He'd developed a sense for people who were woods-wise, people who were aware of the sign they were leaving behind. Other than the single clear track that screamed like a billboard in the middle of the forest, the person had left very little sign of their passing through. It was hard to believe that was an accident, and it was even harder to believe they hadn't left the track in the mud expressly for Tye to see.

Tye walked a wide circle around the northern edge of his property, walking slowly and quietly. There was plenty of sign where deer passed through every night, and the wide trail through the low-growing vegetation of the valley's resident black bear just awakened from her slumber, but he had to strain to follow the trail of the human. He pieced together the trail from a bent piece of vegetation here, a faint partial impression on the forest floor there.

There were motion-activated wildlife cameras strapped to several trees here on the edge of the property. Tye enjoyed keeping track of what wildlife visited his land. It was like a window to another world. The trail he was following led right to the camera.

With a last look around, Tye slung the shotgun over his shoulder and pulled the memory card out of the camera. Using a card reader attached to his cell phone, he scrolled through the pictures.

He was greeted with shots of several blacktail deer, and a good-sized black bear snuffling around in the undergrowth looking for morsels to sate her spring hunger. Normally he would have examined each picture closely, trying to identify each animal and enjoying the nuances of their behavior when they were unobserved by humans.

Now, he swiped through the pictures, glancing at each one long enough to make sure there was no human figure, until he reached the end.

There, only inches in front of the camera, was a human hand with two fingers extended in a "V" sign.

The time stamp was only an hour and a half ago.

There were no other pictures on the card. Clearly, the person had been aware of the camera and had avoided being captured by the lens, other than when they'd stuck their hand in front of it.

Tye transferred the pictures to his phone, then put the memory card back in the camera. He was debating following the trail north into the woods on the other side of his property line when he heard an engine coming up his driveway. It was several hundred yards away, but the sound carried in the still air. He thought he recognized the sound of the engine as belonging to his girlfriend Kaity's Jeep.

Frowning, he checked his phone for a message from her. Nothing.

He turned and followed the trail down the hill. There was probably nothing wrong, but he couldn't shake the feeling of dread that had been following him around all morning like an unwanted black dog.

He listened as the Jeep climbed the steep driveway, then heard the crunch of tires on the gravel of the new extension to the driveway that had just been installed. The engine cut out, and he heard a door slam.

Aside from his worries, it was a fine spring morning. Tye was looking forward to some sunshine after a long, gray winter. The bare branches of the alder and big-leaf maple trees were swelling with buds poised to unfurl. He knew in a matter of days the landscape would be transformed into a riot of green, and after months of dreary sameness, every morning he would step out his door to a new landscape.

He turned toward the trail that would take him down the hill and home. Normally he walked through the woods at a slow, stealthy pace. Now he wasn't running, but he didn't care as much about the noise he was making, either.

He wondered if he was overreacting. A car pulling up his driveway shouldn't have been cause for alarm, but over the last several months, he'd been shot at, stabbed, and nearly drowned as he worked to find people missing in the dense wood of the Pacific Northwest.

The trail ended at the T-shaped intersection of his driveway. The driveway led through the trees to the county road at the bottom of the valley. To his left was the house that belonged to his friends Gary and May. His property was to the right.

As he walked down the freshly laid gravel of his new driveway, he recognized the tracks of Kaity's Jeep, then he walked around a corner and saw it parked behind his pickup truck.

She was nowhere to be seen, but from inside his yurt, he heard soft music playing, one of her favorite albums. He relaxed. Apparently, nothing was wrong.

The camper shell on the back of his pickup was unlocked, so he made quick work of stowing the shotgun inside. He didn't want Kaity to see him with it. He felt foolish parading around the property with it.

Just past the new gravel was a freshly cleared flat spot. Electrical conduit and plumbing pipes stuck out of the ground, and stakes and twine marked the outline of where their new tiny home would be delivered a few days from now.

Past that, a narrow footpath led through a patch of alder trees, and his yurt came into view. The little green octagonal shelter blended into the woods. It had been home for a few years.

Kaity was squatting in front of the wood stove, blowing a small flame to life, when he walked in. Here in the dense trees, it would take a while for the sun to warm the yurt.

She shut the doors to the stove and stood. She was almost as tall as him, with a shock of short black hair sticking out from under her fleece cap.

"There you are," she said and hugged him.

"Hey," he said. "What's up?"

"The tiny-house company wanted me to re-check some final measurements. I know you could have done it, but I thought I'd run out here real quick before work and surprise you."

Kaity worked as a librarian in the city of Vancouver, Washington, nearly an hour's drive away. She split her time between staying with Tye here in the yurt and her house in town.

"That's a lot of driving to take some measurements," he said.

"That's not the only reason I came." She kissed him.

Tye pulled her to him, all the other concerns of the day forgotten. He took her right hand in his.

"You don't have to wear the cast anymore?" A few weeks earlier, she'd fractured her hand punching a man in the face. Considering he'd helped kidnap both of them, the guy deserved it.

"The doctor says I'm good to go, as long as I don't punch anybody again." She looked at the time on her phone. "I have forty-five minutes before I have to leave for work. I have some great ideas about how we could spend the time."

Before he could reply, a car door slammed outside. He flinched and turned toward the door.

"Whoa," she said. "You're jumpy. What's wrong?"

Out of reflex, he almost said, "I'm fine," but bit the words off before they came out of his mouth.

"Don't be a typical dude and tell me you're fine," she said. "You've been a little edgy the past few days. What's going on?"

He sighed and felt his shoulders slump.

"I'm sorry. Somebody has been walking around up at the northern edge of the property. I found a track, almost like they meant for me to find it. And they messed with my trail camera."

"There's no hunting season right now. Kids screwing around?" she asked.

"It doesn't feel that way," he said. "I've been feeling off in general, like something is about to happen."

"Do you have the card from the camera?"

He pulled the card out of his pocket and handed it to her. Kaity's backpack was sitting on the bed. She unzipped it and took out her laptop and stuck the card in the slot.

"Let's see," she said as she scrolled through the pictures. "Deer. Deer. Owl. That's cool. Another deer. And somebody flashing a peace sign at the camera. I guess that's better than if they'd just used one finger."

"Maybe I'm making too big a deal about this," he said.

She turned and put a hand on his cheek. "You realize your intuition has kept us from getting killed a couple of times, right? I think we should pay attention to this."

"Thank you." He felt a lump in his throat that surprised him. All his life he'd had visions and feelings about the future but had kept them hidden from most people.

"It might be good to take your mind off it for a while, though." She pulled him to her again. "Forty minutes until I have to leave for work. Tick-tock."

As he bent over to kiss her, he heard footsteps on the gravel.

"Really?" Kaity said.

"It's probably Gary or May. Hopefully, it will be something quick," Tye said.

He didn't bother to wait for a knock, just opened the door and stepped outside.

It was his friend Gary, who lived in the house at the other end of the driveway. He was a tall, sinewy, bearded man, with a long ponytail of dark hair falling down his back. He wore stained work clothes and heavy leather boots.

"Hey, Tye," he said. "Hey, Kaity," he added when she peeked out the door. He looked back and forth between the two of them. "Sorry to interrupt, but you know the neighbors down the hill? Deborah and Vivian?"

"Yeah. Deborah is the one that just had surgery, right? May is helping her out."

"Yes. Them. Deborah thinks she may have shot somebody last night. They were trying to break into the house, and they ran off into the woods."

Tye sighed. "I'll get my stuff."

WARRIOR SOUL CHAPTER 2

Deborah and Vivian lived down the hill on the other side of the county road, next to the river. Tye parked his truck beside Gary's barely running International Scout.

"I was going to give Vivian a ride to work," Gary said as he shut off the Scout. "Their Subaru is in the shop. Something with the transmission."

The river noise was a constant murmur down here. Behind Deborah and Vivian's two-story log home, the river ran in a deep canyon carved by eons of water flowing down out of the mountains to the east.

"This is beautiful," Kaity said as she climbed out of the passenger side of the truck. She turned in a circle, taking in the giant Douglas fir trees that ringed the house. "This place hasn't been logged in the last 50 years like ours has. I guess ours will look like this someday."

Tye stopped for a moment, other concerns forgotten. He and Kaity were buying a tiny home to place next to his yurt, but it was the first time he'd ever heard her use the words "ours." He was struck at that moment by how much he just liked looking at her. She was wearing a fleece cap, a puffy jacket, and stained hiking pants, and he found her attractive because of all that, not despite it.

She caught him looking at her and smiled.

The door of the house swung open and a slender woman in her sixties wearing a pants suit stepped out.

"Thank you for coming," she said. "I didn't know what to do. Deborah doesn't want to call the sheriff." She bit her lip and rubbed her hands together. A little brown dog peered from around her ankles and gave a low growl.

"Hush, Chester." She bent over and the little dog jumped in her arms. "Why don't you all come in? It will be easier to show you than to try to explain."

Vivian and Deborah had moved in only a few weeks earlier. Moving boxes and cans of paint were stacked in the hallway. Vivian led them into a living room with floor-to-ceiling windows that looked out over the river below. A stocky woman with short gray hair was on the couch. Her foot was in a plastic boot and propped up on pillows.

There was a glass-paned door leading out to a wood deck outside. A splintered bullet hole marred the frame just above the doorknob, and the glass door was spiderwebbed.

"Well, I don't see a body," Gary said.

"Not sure I hit him," Deborah said.

"What exactly happened?" Tye asked.

"I haven't been able to sleep since the surgery two days ago." Deborah gestured at her foot. "I've been sleeping out here on the couch so I don't keep Vivian awake. Last night, Chester was super restless, whining and barking at the door."

As if to confirm her story, Chester gave a low growl.

"So I went and got my pistol," Deborah continued. "And I just sat here on the couch. I thought maybe it was a bear, and if I saw it, I'd fire a couple of rounds out the window to scare it off."

That wasn't exactly how Tye would have handled the situation, but at least the steep hill across the river would stop any errant bullets.

"Then somebody started jiggling the handle to the back door. There was no moon, so I only saw an outline, but it was a person, not a bear."

"What did you shoot at them with?" Gary asked. "That's a big hole."

From the couch cushions, Deborah produced a stainless-steel revolver. It had a massive frame but a short, stubby barrel. Tye drew back a little when she whipped it out, but she had it pointed in a safe direction, and her finger was off the trigger.

"It's a .480 Ruger Super Redhawk Alaskan," Deborah said.

"What the hell do you shoot with that?" Gary asked.

"Pretty much anything I want," Deborah answered. "Up in Alaska, I carried it when I worked on the pipeline, in case of bears."

She opened the cylinder and handed the gun to Gary, who ejected six fat cartridges into his palm. Each one was the size of his thumb.

"Looks like you replaced the round you fired."

"No sense walking around with a gun that isn't full-up."

"I reckon." Gary set the gun down on the side table.

Tye walked over to the back door and squatted to look through the bullet hole. Kaity stood beside him and looked out the window.

"I'd expect to see a bunch of blood if she hit anybody," she said.

"Or just a body on the porch, considering the size of that hand cannon." Tye looked over his shoulder at Deborah. "We could walk around and see if there's anything to see."

"I'd appreciate that," Deborah said. "I would have gone outside at first light, but you know..." She gestured at her foot.

"Yep. I get it." Tye opened the back door gingerly, lest all the glass fall out. He stepped back out into the sound of the river, followed by Gary and Kaity. Despite his care, a few shards of glass fell out of the door.

"We ought to tape that up for them," Gary said.

"Yeah, we can do that," Tye said. He surveyed the damage. Where the bullet had exited the door frame, it had blown out big splinters, then traveled through one of the porch supports, nearly cracking the two-by-four in half. From there it had presumably sailed across the river, where hopefully it had buried itself in a tree trunk or the dirt of the hillside.

"If we have occasion to visit them in the night, let's make sure we announce ourselves," Tye said quietly.

Gary and Kaity both nodded.

"There's a drop of blood," Kaity said. She pointed at the deck.

Tye squatted to look. The splotch of blood on the deck board was about the size of a quarter. The center wasn't dry yet.

"Not enough for a bullet wound. Must have gotten hit with a splinter from the door," Gary said.

"Or some glass," Tye said.

"Here's another." Kaity was tracking the droplets down the steep stairway that led to the river below. Tye and Gary followed along. Kaity had been working on her tracking skills, and Tye was content to let her take the lead. They were mindful of the rotten boards on the stairs that hadn't seen any maintenance in a long time.

"It's a shame this house sat empty for so long," Gary said. "It will be a nice place once Deborah and Vivian get it spruced up."

"They have their work cut out for them," Tye said.

"I think he crossed the river," Kaity said from the bottom of the stairs.

Tye joined her at the river's edge. There in the narrow strip of sandy beach between the bottom of the stairs and the water, he saw an indistinct set of prints heading toward the house, and another set heading back.

"Yep. That's a bold move right there," Tye said. "Big guy. Maybe some kind of moccasin on his feet. He definitely crossed the river."

"That seems super dangerous," Kaity said.

"He wouldn't have been able to do it a week ago," Tye said.

The river was only twenty yards across at this point. Right now, it was shallow, a little over knee-high in a few spots. A week ago, during the height of the spring snow melt, it would have been up to Tye's shoulders, and the current would have been raging.

"I think I see a spot on the other side where he climbed out," Kaity said.

"That's an odd damn way to burglarize a house," Gary said. "You wouldn't be able to carry much away across the river. Even though the water is low, I'd hate to try that crossing in the dark."

"It makes me wonder if he had something more nefarious planned," Tye said. "That water is still pretty cold. I don't particularly want to wade across, but I reckon I could drive to the other side there, work my way down the bank, and try to pick up the trail from there."

Kaity pulled her phone from her pocket. "I should have left for work five minutes ago."

"I can go by myself," Tye said.

"You mean, you want to go alone through the woods, trailing a potentially violent criminal?" Kaity asked. "Because that's worked out so well the other times you've done it."

Gary sighed. "I'm supposed to dig some trench for the new house's sewer line, but it could wait a few hours. I could back you up."

"So, we're getting involved in this?" Kaity asked.

"They're neighbors," Gary said.

"Yep," Tye said. "They're neighbors."

WARRIOR SOUL CHAPTER 3

"Did Kaity drive out here before work just so she could see you?" Gary asked as they drove across the Dole Valley Road bridge over the river.

"She did," Tye said.

"You better not screw this one up," Gary said. "She's a pretty good catch."

"I agree," Tye said. He slowed the truck to let a doe and two fawns walk across the road in front of him. The houses out here were spread far apart on five- and ten-acre parcels, separated by dense stands of Douglas fir trees where no one had logged in decades and even denser stands of red alder where folks had sold their timber.

They passed a dilapidated house on the left side of the road. Tye slowed automatically to look the place over, as it belonged to some friends. It needed a coat of paint, but it didn't look like anyone had caused any mischief in the owner's absence.

"How are Miss Natalie and her mom, anyway?" Gary asked.

The previous summer, Tye, Kaity, Gary, and May, Gary's wife, had rescued a young girl named Natalie from a kidnapper.

"They're still staying with George and Brian," Tye said. "I guess Natalie still has nightmares if they try to stay in their house."

"I can't blame her, seeing as how she was snatched right out of the backyard," Gary said.

"I think it's easier for Marsha not to drink if she's not the only adult in the house, too," Tye said. Marsha, Natalie's mother, had been battling a drinking problem when they met her. "I think she and Brian are hitting it off pretty well, and old George is happy to have some company out on that property of his."

"Sounds like a happy ending for everybody," Gary said.

"I met Kaity because of it."

"When you two are old and gray, you can tell people how you met because you found her in the middle of a forest trying to rescue a little girl. It's a much better story than 'We met in a bar.'"

Tye laughed. He slowed the truck down to turn east into the Yacolt Burn State Forest. The roads here were gravel but well-maintained, so he was able to keep some speed.

The forest was actively managed for timber production. The large stretches that had been recently clear-cut looked like moonscapes, with muddy ground and big piles of branches and other debris. Interspersed with the cuts were big stands of mature timber. Tye had learned not to get too emotionally attached to them because it was only a matter of time before they fell before the saw.

He drove through the intricate network of gravel roads without stopping to consult a map. Over the winter, he'd spent a lot of time on these roads, sometimes with Gary, sometimes with Kaity, often alone. Part of it was a desire to know the surrounding landscape. Part of it was a practical need to scout the area for the fall hunting seasons. Tye tried not to eat any meat aside from deer and elk he killed himself.

The other reason was he'd needed time to think. The last six months had been a roller coaster. He'd been involved in helping solve Natalie's kidnapping, which had led to Tye and Kaity establishing a search-and-rescue consulting business. After that, they'd been involved in solving two murders in rapid succession: one on an island in Puget Sound and another in a wilderness area up in the mountains.

On top of all that, his relationship with Kaity, which had started as a slow burn, was now proceeding at a breakneck pace. Sometimes he found it hard to believe they were building a home together.

Finally, he stopped a hundred yards away from an old metal gate across the road. Tye parked the truck in between two trees so it wasn't blocking the road and shut off the engine.

He and Gary both stepped out of the truck and quietly eased the doors shut rather than slamming them. Then they stood quietly for several minutes, moving as little as possible, saying nothing.

Before he started a track, Tye liked to establish a baseline of animal behavior for the land he was walking on. The animals here were used to occasional vehicle traffic, but still, the simple act of driving the truck down the road had created a disturbance. The longer they stood there, the more birdsong Tye heard in the immediate area. A Douglas squirrel stuck its head out of a bush, studied them intently for a few seconds, then decided they weren't worth raising an alarm and skittered up a tree trunk.

A gentle breeze brushed his cheek. The sun was warming the air in the river valley below, so as they descended, their scent would be blowing uphill. They would be less likely to spook animals like deer and elk.

Satisfied that things had settled down, Tye opened the camper shell as quietly as he could so he and Gary could fetch their gear.

"I was thinking of taking the gauge," Gary said quietly.

Tye nodded and unlocked the storage compartment under the bunk. Gary withdrew the old Mossberg shotgun, fed five rounds of buckshot into the magazine, and put a pouch containing some extra ammunition in the thigh pocket of his cargo pants.

Tye settled a sixteen-liter Hill People Gear backpack on his shoulders and eased the back of the camper closed. If something went wrong, he had a decent chance of surviving a wilderness emergency with the Buck knife on his belt and the lighter in his pocket, but the little backpack carried enough gear to give him several extra layers of security.

Tye took a knee and examined a mud puddle on the dirt road. Recently, two other vehicles had passed the spot where Tye had parked the truck. One had been a motorcycle, with knobby off-road tires. The other had most likely been a truck, judging from the width of the tread.

"If I'm reading this mud puddle correctly, it looks like a truck and motorcycle drove in, but only the truck came back," Gary said.

"That's the way I see it," Tye agreed. "There's a chance the motorcycle tracks were fouled by the truck on the way out, but I don't think so."

Tye walked up to the gate and soon found the spot where the truck had been parked, and not far away, the impression of the motorcycle's kickstand in the dirt.

"Three people total," Tye said, pointing at the tracks. "Two were in the truck. One on the motorcycle. All three walked around the gate."

"But only two came back," Gary said from where he was kneeling by the gate. There was a narrow opening between the gate post and an alder tree, just wide enough for a person to squeeze through.

Tye craned his neck and walked bent over from where the motorcycle had been parked, to the truck tire tracks. "I'm pretty sure the two that came back loaded the motorcycle into the back of the pickup."

"But the motorcycle rider didn't come back up the hill," Gary said.

"Nope. Those riding boots he was wearing leave a pretty distinctive track."

"Well, this is damn curious," Gary said.

"It is," Tye agreed.

"I need to go get that ditch dug, but now my curiosity is piqued."

"Mine too. Let's see where the trail takes us."

They walked around the gate and set off down an abandoned road that was overgrown with weeds and small saplings. This stretch of forest belonged to a local conservation land trust. The hundred-acre parcel had been slated for development for a housing development, until the deal fell through and the land trust bought it. Tye was grateful every morning when he woke up and saw a stand of alder trees across the river instead of a bunch of houses.

The land was open to the public but was rarely visited because it was tucked away on the far side of the state forest through a maze of roads. As they walked down the old road, Tye saw plenty of deer and elk tracks, but no trash, broken glass, or empty shell casings that were all too frequent signs of human passage around here.

The only human sign was the trail of the three people that had walked in and two that had walked out. Discerning the age of a track was more of an art than a science. Most of the tracks were mere impressions in the weeds, but occasionally, Tye would find a partial impression of a boot print in a muddy spot. The vegetation was just starting to spring back up, and the marks in the mud were crisp, with plenty of detail. That suggested to Tye the tracks were hours old, and not days.

Tye and Gary fell into a rhythm born of long practice. Tye looked a few feet ahead, watching for the next set of tracks. Gary followed a few feet behind, shotgun cradled in his arms, looking out in the distance for threats. During their search-and-rescue days, they had mostly looked for people who wanted to be found, but not all cases were what they seemed at first glance. Some people went into the woods because they wanted to cover up a crime and didn't take too kindly to being followed.

The trail was consistent the whole time. Three men walked in. Two walked out. It led in the exact direction Tye had intended to go. The old road switchbacked down the slope until it came to a flat area overlooking the river. Soon, they were directly across the river from Deborah and Vivian's house.

There was a fourth set of tracks leading up from the beach. Tye pointed at them and squatted to take a closer look. Gary stayed standing, looking around them in all directions.

The new tracks were big. When Tye put his size-ten boot down in comparison, it was dwarfed in size. Just like the tracks at Deborah and Vivian's house, the tracks lacked any crisp features. Now Tye was even more sure whoever had made them was wearing moccasins or something similar.

Tye stood shoulder to shoulder with Gary but facing in the opposite direction. This way they could talk in low tones and see all around them.

"Those are the same as back at the house," Tye said. "I don't see any more blood, so he must have not been hurt very bad."

"Interesting. Keep going?"

"We've come this far."

Gary nodded, and they resumed tracking. As they moved east, they left the thick stands of alder trees behind and moved into a grove of stately old cedar trees that had escaped the chainsaw. Under the alders, the understory had been a thick riot of low-growing plants, but here, the ground was too shaded for most plants to grow, and it was much more open.

There was a well-defined game trail here, so broad and clear it could have easily been mistaken for a human-made hiking trail. Judging from the dozens of old and new tracks, Tye figured a herd of a dozen elk used this trail at least weekly.

Something shiny caught Tye's eye. He bent to find a shell casing, still shiny and clean. It was odd-looking. Most handgun cartridges were short, often less than an inch, and were cylindrical. Most rifle cartridges were over an inch and a half and had a bottle-necked shape, wider at the base than the neck.

This one was only a little longer than a pistol cartridge but had the bottleneck shape of a rifle case. Tye found a twig, stuck it in the neck of the casing, and lifted it to his nose. The smell of burnt gunpowder was strong. The head stamp on the base of the cartridge read ".300 BLK."

"Recognize this one?" Tye asked.

Gary looked away from scanning the surrounding woods. "I think that's one of those new cartridges the guys who like to play commando are shooting. Wonder what they were shooting at."

Tye put the case back where he found it. He jerked his chin down the trail. "We keep heading this way, we'll likely find out."

The hair on the back of Tye's neck was standing up, for a reason he couldn't quite put his finger on. As they'd moved east down this trail, the birds had gotten more quiet. Now no birds were singing immediately around them. He could hear a lone robin in the distance behind them, but that was it.

He tapped his ear and looked at Gary, who nodded. He'd noticed it too. They moved a little slower, taking more care to scan up ahead with each step.

The shadows were deep here. The sun hadn't quite climbed high enough in the sky to illuminate the river canyon. Tye couldn't make out the dark shape on the ground beside the trail up ahead, but in his gut, he knew what it was.

In a few more steps, they were close enough to tell that it was the body of a man wearing motorcycle boots. He was still and lifeless. The morning breeze ruffled his hair, but there was no other movement.

Gary sighed. "I guess I'm not gonna get to dig that ditch today after all."

ABOUT THE AUTHOR

David Barbur lives in the foothills of the Cascade Mountains. He can often be found wandering the forest with a longbow in his hand, tracking animals and trying to figure out what happens next in his latest story.

Follow David on social media:

Printed in the USA
CPSIA information can be obtained
at www.ICGtesting.com
LVHW091959081223
765941LV00008B/294